EVERGREEN

J. KEVIN TUMLINSON

KNOVELTON

ALSO BY J. KEVIN TUMLINSON

Dan Kotler

The Coelho Medallion

The Atlantis Riddle

The Devil's Interval

The Girl in the Mayan Tomb

The Antarctic Forgery

The Stepping Maze

The God Extinction

The Spanish Papers

The Hidden Persuaders

The Sleeper's War

The God Resurrection

The Demon Core

Dan Kotler Short Fiction

The Brass Hall - A Dan Kotler Story

The Jani Sigil - FREE short story from BookHip.com/DBXDHP

Dan Kotler Box Sets

The Book of Lost Things: Dan Kotler, Books 1-3

The Book of Betrayals: Dan Kotler, Books 4-6

The Book of Gods and Kings: Dan Kotler, Books 7-9

Quake Runner: Alex Kayne

Shaken

Triggered

Compromised

Aftershock

Historic Crimes Crossovers

The Man Below

The Outsiders Gambit

Evergreen

Evergreen: Book 1

Evergreen: Trace Contact

Citadel

Citadel: First Colony

Citadel: Paths in Darkness

Citadel: Children of Light

Citadel: The Value of War

Colony Girl: A Citadel Universe Story

Sawyer Jackson

Sawyer Jackson and the Long Land

Sawyer Jackson and the Shadow Strait

Sawyer Jackson and the White Room

Think Tank

Karner Blue

Zero Tolerance

Nomad

The Lucid — Co-authored with Nick Thacker

Episode 1

Episode 2

Episode 3

Shorts & Novellas

Getting Gone

Teresa's Monster

The Three Reasons to Avoid Being Punched in the Face

Tin Man

Two Blocks East

Edge

Zero

God Mode

Collections & Anthologies

Citadel: Omnibus

Uncanny Divide — With Nick Thacker & Will Flora

Light Years — The Complete Science Fiction Library

Dead of Winter: A Christmas Anthology — With Nick Thacker,

Jim Heskett, David Berens, M.P. MacDougall, R.A. McGee, Dusty Sharp & Steven Moore

YA & Middle Grade

Secret of the Diamond Sword — An Alex Kotler Mystery

Wordslinger (Non-Fiction)

30-Day Author: Develop a Daily Writing Habit and Write Your Book In 30 Days (Or Less)

Watch for more at kevintumlinson.com/books

CHAPTER ONE

"You're sure you've got the pattern?"

It was getting close to the thirty-minute mark, which meant I wouldn't have the pattern much longer. These things weren't like pass codes. They were intentionally complex, so that even if someone watched over your shoulder, there'd be very little chance of them remembering what you did. As a security measure, the abstract pattern was a pretty good one. It was nearly unhackable. Nearly.

It took most people days or even weeks to master their patterns. I did it in less than a second. Which was handy, but it didn't mean this would be easy, and it didn't mean I could just relax. If I couldn't draw the entire pattern within the next 30 seconds, I'd lose it, and we'd be in deep trouble.

Or my client, Jerry, would be in deep trouble. I'd probably be dead.

"I... have it..." I made a few quick swipes, a sort of finishing move for the pattern that the mark had thrown in for grins. Just as I finished the second swipe, my memory blanked. Every trace of the mark was gone, and it was just me again. Me and my shadows.

There was an unlock sound from the computer, and Jerry laughed. "You did it. Man, I'll never understand how you do this stuff. I've never met a hacker who could break an abstract." He slapped me on the back, hard, and then shoved me out of the way so he could start pilfering the computer's contents.

I watched him fly through screen after screen, data mining, finding all the important bits that he could use for... well, whatever he'd use them for. I tried not to know that part. It was a job, and that was all. I didn't want to be involved any more than I was.

I could never explain to Jerry that I wasn't a hacker. In fact, unless I shook his hand or something, I probably couldn't do even half of what he was doing at the moment. I rely on that touch.

That's the way it works. One touch. Thirty minutes. Then back to zero. This one had been close, thanks to the streets being busy, and traffic being heavy. I'd spent most of the thirty minutes running on foot, crossing block after block, trying to make it to the safe house before the clock ran down. It was close. Way too close.

I left Jerry to do his work. He had pre-paid—a requirement I had before I'd even take a job. This usually worked fine for repeat business, but whenever I had new clients, there was always that moment when they wanted to balk. That was fine by me. These things could get risky, and they were almost always illegal. Which meant they were being commissioned by thieves. You can't trust thieves, as a rule. So if they won't pay upfront, there's a good chance they won't pay at all. Better not to work with them.

I moved quickly away from the safe house, with my hoodie pulled over my head and my hands in my pockets. I was wearing gloves and a long-sleeved shirt—necessities for my work and my life, especially in the city. You could never be too careful, though. Accidental touches were a pain. Thirty minutes of some random stranger in your head, nagging you about what happened, where they were, accusing you of kidnapping them—it could get ugly.

The walk home was a lot less frantic than the run in, and I had time to think and reflect. Almost by habit, I started "Zen walking." It's a thing, I swear. Mostly it's about finding a breathing rhythm while you walk, keeping your thoughts on your breath so that your head clears and you reach a calm, peaceful state. It helps after a job—gives me a chance to clear my head.

Though, really, when the mark's engram is gone, there's not much left to clear. Usually.

When your business is absorbing the memories and skills of someone else, though, keeping your head clear becomes a survival skill.

THE BEST TERM I've found for what I can do is *osmosis*.

In biology and chemistry, osmosis is when molecules in a solvent are transferred from a lower concentration to a higher concentration, until both are equal.

Because science.

That probably didn't help. Doesn't matter. I'm talking about a different kind of osmosis, anyway. Something a little weirder.

There's this idea that information might be transferable by a sort of osmosis, under certain conditions. Most of those conditions are kind of woo-woo—psychic phenomenon, magic, planetary alignments, that sort of thing.

But not all woo-woo is created equal. Some woo-woo is true-true.

In my case, I have the ability to spontaneously and involuntarily transfer information from another person into my own brain.

All it takes is a touch, and I know everything you know.

When I touch someone skin-to-skin, I get all of their memories and skills, all of their thoughts and ideas, even their fantasies and secrets. Anything mental. They have no idea this is happening—the transfer is one-way. I make contact, and the mark has no idea that whatever was in their head is now in mine. They keep their own memories. I get a copy. A perfect copy.

It can come in handy, especially when you make your living doing the sort of things I do—skip tracing, finding people who are on the run, uncovering passwords, digging up hidden details, or acquiring a skill so you can do a job that someone else either won't do or can't be trusted to do. It isn't glamorous work. The people I end up being in contact with are not usually good people.

My ability makes this kind of work easy, though. You can accomplish all sorts of things when you can know everything your mark knows.

There are a few catches, though.

First, the information I gather from a touch can only last for 30 minutes. After that, it's gone.

Sometimes I can cheat that. I might record video or audio of myself, describing something I need access to later. Or I might draw or write what I need to remember. In the case of some information, like the abstract code I just delivered to Jerry, I really don't have a choice but to perform a task myself. It's too complex and too nuanced to write down, and seeing it on video isn't much help. It would take weeks for me or someone else to learn the pattern for an abstract security protocol, and the abstract might change during that time.

You almost blew that gig. Who sets up a safe house across town from the mark?

Another side effect is hitchhikers.

"I didn't have anything to do with the planning. I just did what I was hired to do."

And what if you hadn't made it? We'd all be dead.

That voice was Henry, my old... well, mentor, I guess. He was the one who taught me how to focus what I do. He taught me how to just relax my own will and let the memories and skills of someone else do their thing. To practice, we had used him as a test subject, and I had absorbed his memories over and over for months.

That was how we found out that prolonged exposure can create a "permanent engrammatic duplication." That's Henry-speak for "I absorbed their memories permanently, and now I have a copy of their personality in my head."

When this first started happening, it was a big surprise for both me and Henry. We spent a month out of physical contact with each other, to see if maybe the copy of his engram would fade. In that time, I actually stayed away from every human being on the planet. I didn't want to risk permanently absorbing a second personality.

Henry, scientist and nerd that he was, spent that time trying to figure out what had happened. He would have conversations with me, so that he could consult with his duplicate in my head. He was pretty excited to discover that *Inside Henry* was just as smart as *Outside Henry*. Two brainiacs for the price of one. And together they were able to figure out what happened.

Repeat contact would eventually lead to a permanent

copy of someone in my head. Kind of like practicing something over and over until you have it down. Henry explained it as, basically, my brain formed neural pathways in the shape of Henry, over and over, until they became permanent.

The tricky part is that the amount of contact isn't a constant. The exposure has to be pretty high, that much we knew. We just couldn't figure out for certain just how much contact was too much.

Through some accidental trial and error, I figured out that after about 30 touches I'm in the red zone, and there's a good chance that someone's engram is going to take up permanent residence.

It's not as bad as it sounds. Or it's exactly as bad as it sounds. Someone taught me once that it's all a matter of perspective. She was good at finding the more positive side of things. I never really was.

The voices pop up from time to time, usually when I'm really tired, or right after a particularly stressful job. But they fade eventually, going back to wherever they hang out in my subconscious, doing whatever they do all day. I don't ask. I want some mental privacy, and I figure it's only fair to give it in return. Besides, there are five permanent voices in my head, and every one of them has his or her own list of "things Jaylin Rowlin doesn't want to know."

Henry is my least favorite.

We had a parting of ways after I found out that he was planning to pimp me out to the criminal underworld. I didn't want that life. I still don't.

I sort of fell into it anyway, though.

D'oh.

In my defense, my "gift" sometimes makes it tough to have what you might call a "normal life." If I accidentally absorb more than one person's memories at a time, things can get a little muddy in my head. So I tend to avoid crowds, unless I'm covered head to toe. I wear a hoodie with long sleeves, and I'm always wearing gloves to minimize contact. People think that's weird. People who are in my life long enough to get to know me, anyway.

So not a lot of people.

Relationships...

I've had a few. They usually don't end well. Turns out, girls really don't like it when boys know all their secrets. And... well, to be honest, there are some things a guy just shouldn't know about the girl he's into. Scary things.

But there was one girl...

I don't think about her, if I can help it. It's too dangerous. It's like touching the eye of a stove, not knowing if it will be hot or not.

Sooner or later, it will be.

It took most of an hour to get home. Actually, "home" is stretching things a little. I don't really have what most people would call a home. I tend to move around a lot. It's sort of a necessity. A survival strategy. Thanks to my abilities, and my line of work, I can be "in demand." And not in a good way.

It hadn't taken long for word to get out about me, once Henry started quietly advertising my services. When it comes to getting your hands on secure information—the kind of data that sometimes only resides in someone's head —there aren't many people out there who can deliver my kind of results. And none who can do it the way I do—no blood, no torture, no violence, and no trace. I get the intel so fast, and so unobtrusively, there's no way to know it was me. Which means there's no way to trace it back to my clients.

I get results, fast and safe.

That tends to give a guy a reputation. One I bank on, to be sure. But also one that makes it hard for me to be anything less than paranoid to an obsessive degree.

There are a lot of people who would like to get their hands on me, to find out how I do what I do. Not all of them are criminals.

But just among the criminal set, there's a weird sort of neutral zone when it comes to me.

At any given time, I'm turning away offers to work for all sorts of organizations. Sometimes those offers are of the variety that I "cannot refuse." Having me on a crew would give some of the families—as in *the* families—a significant advantage.

Ironically, it's that unwanted popularity and universal usefulness that keeps me from being forcefully inducted into service.

It's a sort of unspoken cease-fire. If any one family were to nab me and press me into service, the others would declare war. They'd take me out at all costs, no doubt. But they'd have to go through a lot of people to get to me.

Thank God.

Better to leave me as a free agent—a neutral third party who is available to the benefit of all. Sort of a community resource for a really dangerous and screwed up community. Like a firehouse in a demilitarized zone.

Scary, actually.

And then there are the "alphabet agencies."

CIA, FBI, NSA, DHS—at one point or another they've all looked into me. Which is why I sleep in a different place every night and keep a low profile whenever I'm out. I'm not sure whether they know what I can really do, but at the very least they know that I'm good at getting impossible intel. They know enough about me to be dangerous. To me.

Maybe you should consider a change of occupation. Or at least a change of location. New York hasn't been good for you.

A female voice this time. The most familiar female voice in my life. Not the scariest or meanest voice. Not the most annoying voice. But the one that I try not to bring to the surface. The one that can hurt me the most.

There are only a couple of female voices rolling around in my head, neither of whom I'm particularly eager to talk to. Both scare me, though for different reasons. One can take out a room full of people using a shrimp fork, when she's not balls crazy. The other one is my ex-girlfriend.

Kristen.

"I know how you feel about this," I said aloud.

I don't have to speak out loud to talk to the others in my head. I can respond mentally if I want. They hear me, if I let them. But sometimes I get confused about who is thinking what.

Besides, Kristen's smarter than I am. Thinking at her is basically playing on her turf. She'd be sure to get the upper hand.

Jaylin, you could be so much more than this. You should leave. Start over somewhere else. Learn who you really are and use your gifts to make the world better.

"And where should I go, exactly? How long would I last, going straight? What kind of help could I be, really? The NSA would probably grab me, and I'd be on an operating table having my brain scooped out with an ice-cream scoop."

Don't be silly. Clearly a melon-baller is a better tool for brain scooping.

Now that she was awake, I would be too. For hours. Because as much as I pretended to hate this back and forth,

I couldn't turn away from it. Now that she was here, now that she was talking to me, all I could do was talk back to her all night. It was always this way.

Because she was the one I missed.

At least Henry and the others were keeping quiet. It was just me and Kristen right now. Just the two of us, as I made my way through Manhattan and to the place I planned to spend the night, alone.

Whatever "alone" means.

CHAPTER TWO

It was late in the morning when I woke up and rolled off of the sofa.

I had intended to sleep on the bed, laying on top of the comforter with a spare blanket pulled over me, so I could quickly smooth things out and leave no trace of being there when I left. I miss beds, sometimes.

But the conversation with Kristen had gone on most of the night and had only ended when my body involuntarily betrayed me and fell asleep. When that happens, whoever I'm talking to gets a kind of "busy signal." I'm checked out, mentally. They go back to their own them-shaped engrammatic spot in my brain.

I usually feel kind of bad about it, but so far it's mostly only happened with Kristen. And she hasn't yelled at me about it yet.

The place where I had crashed for the night belonged to a couple who were on vacation in San Diego. I had "lifted" their alarm code and other useful info when I saw the husband loading a suit case into the trunk of a cab. A casual bump, an apology, and an offer to help load his suitcase led to an instant of skin-to-skin contact from my ungloved hand brushing his.

An instant is all it takes.

I'd learned their apartment number and where the spare key was hidden, the alarm code, the fact that no one would check in on the place for two weeks, and that there was cable and Wi-Fi. Plus, "Leaving on a Jet Plane" got stuck in my head for 30 minutes.

Dammit.

This place was nicer than most of the spots where I usually crashed. A lot of times I would just duck into a hotel and sneak into an empty room. I'd absorb the computer access codes for the in-house booking system, usually by brushing hands with the manager or someone on duty, and then I'd wait for an opening so I could book myself into something nice for the evening.

Relax... I always pay.

I make a good living, doing what I do. True, what I do is technically *stealing*. But a fella has to draw a line somewhere. Mine is "steal only when you're being paid to do it." I won't pretend there's much of a moral distinction, but I do have principles.

I use pre-paid credit cards to pay for my rooms, and I leave before checkout the next day. I never stay in the same hotel for more than a night, if I can avoid it. I don't want any of the hotel staff to start recognizing me.

It's better when I can find a place like this apartment.

For starters, there's usually food. I pay for this too, leaving some cash somewhere for the owners to find. I pay well, and usually for a lot of junk food and garbage—the kind of stuff people are comfortable leaving behind when they travel for a week or two, and don't want to come home to spoiled groceries.

But fair is fair. I eat it, I pay for it.

I also leave the place like I found it. Sometimes even better. I like things to be neat and organized. Try living with a bunch of extra personalities in your head, and you start to see the importance of order and organization.

After tidying up the sofa a bit, I shuffled into the kitchen and made myself some coffee and a peanut butter sandwich for breakfast. The couple must have planned to be out of town for a while, because there was nothing perishable in the fridge. No eggs. No milk. Just a lot of salad dressing and a block of American cheese slices. I put a couple of these on my peanut butter sandwich, just for the heck of it.

Don't judge me.

I washed the sandwich down with the coffee, then washed and dried the cup and put it back in the cupboard. I crumpled up a twenty and dropped it on the floor in the bedroom, trying to make it look like something that might have fallen out of a pocket or a purse. Then I re-activated the alarm, locked the door behind me, and hid the key back in its spot on my way out.

This was a good place, and it would be available for the next fourteen days. But unless I was in a pinch, I wouldn't set foot in here ever again. Tonight I'd sleep somewhere else, in a different part of town, selected randomly.

That was the way. If I didn't know where I was going to be for the evening, the alphabet agencies and mafia types couldn't know it either.

At some point, later in the afternoon, I'd throw a dart or flip a coin and let fate decide what part of town would be home for the evening.

This morning, though, I had an appointment.

I walked into a busy coffee shop about six blocks from

where I'd slept the night before, ordered something from the bar, paid with a pre-paid credit card, and sat with a triple-shot Americano as I waited for Vic to walk in.

I had absorbed someone's email username and password as I brushed through the line in the coffee shop, and I used my prepaid smartphone to email Vic with instructions. The phone would be wiped, its call history cleared, and then tossed or left behind on my way out. I'd buy a new one at a pharmacy or a bodega or something, before leaving this part of town. If I was lucky, someone would pick up my discarded phone and use it until the prepaid minutes were gone, helping to muddy my trail even more.

Sometimes you have to let human nature work for you.

I go through a lot of burner phones. Occupational hazard. I don't always throw them away after one use, but I almost always do when I've arranged to physically meet someone using that phone. If anyone happens to be following me or whoever I'm meeting, I don't want them using that phone to track me. Meet ups mean one and done.

Vic arrived late, which wasn't unusual. Since I never tell him where we're meeting until I get there, he almost always has to hoof it across town from wherever he was at the time. He doesn't mind. I pay him very well and often gave him other little bonuses.

He ordered coffee, and then sat down near me, but not *with* me, thumbing through an iPhone app as he waited.

I "accidentally" dropped my phone near him, and when I picked it up, I put a hand on his bare arm.

The rush of information that follows a grab is always a little disorienting. There's a brief instant of confusion as my brain reorients and integrates the new engram. A second ago, I was "Vic," looking in one direction, sitting and pretending not to notice me. I was also Jaylin, trying to look casual as I put a hand on his arm. The two sets of memories collided, the cognitive dissonance resolved itself, and soon I was me again, with Vic's memories and personality along for the ride.

I recovered from dropping my phone, straightening and walking out of the coffee shop, Americano in hand. As I passed through the door, I dropped the pre-paid phone in the trash, camouflaged by the Americano cup. I had what I needed.

Vic was "clean." He wasn't setting me up. He hadn't been contacted or co-opted by any federal or criminal agents. And we would meet at a different location, one I would text to him from another burner phone, in thirty minutes.

The timing was important. Thirty minutes. Long enough for me to get him out of my head.

We'd done this routine before. Lots of times. Vic knew that there was always a pre-meeting before the meeting. He didn't know why, or how I could determine that things were on the up and up, but he knew that if he passed inspection at meeting one, I'd arrange for meeting two. If he didn't, he'd find himself sitting alone for 30 minutes, no text from me, and any contact with me would be over for good. Those were the rules. And I knew—because for the next thirty minutes I *literally* knew Vic as well as he knew himself— that he understood the rules, and would stick to them.

I only had a few more goes with Vic before I'd have to find someone else to be my go-to guy. We were getting close to the thirty-touch mark, and I couldn't risk taking on another permanent hitchhiker.

And that was too bad, because Vic was one of the good ones. He was sharp, but he didn't ask questions that were too tough to answer. He followed through on everything he said he'd do. Another rare quality. And If I were being honest about it, I just kind of liked the guy. He was honest and kind. He had his suspicions about me, but since I had never asked him to do anything illegal, he was willing to play along. Plus, the money was very good, and very easy.

Thirty minutes later, I texted Vic with the new location. Ten minutes after that he walked into the restaurant where he'd been thinking he'd like to have lunch that day anyway.

I was already sitting at one of the booths in the back, near the exit.

I purposefully have him show up more than 30 minutes later, so his engram will have faded by the time he gets there. Nothing is more confusing than having two different conversations with the same person, inside and outside of your head. I can do it, but it can get on my nerves.

"I don't get how you always do that," Vic said as he dropped into the booth across from me. "Never a word. You just figure it out from a glance. You're like that Sherlock guy on BBC America."

I smiled. Vic didn't know my secret, and never would. He just assumed I had a gift for sifting clues from obscure data. He knew I did skip tracing and some kind of data acquisition for a living, so it seemed logical to him that I was a genius. If he only knew—I make up 90% of what I do as I go along. The other 10% is dumb luck. And 5% is poor math skills.

"Got anything for me?" I asked. I already knew the answer, but it was best to let him tell me.

Vic smiled. "Yeah. Got three bids last night."

"Who won?"

"Some guy calling himself 'matherphracker.' He's offering two hundred."

I nearly spit out my coffee.

"Two *hundred?*"

Vic smiled. "I knew you'd like that."

I thought about it. "It's a lot. Two-hundred K." I shook my head, and said again, "That's a lot. Seems like it might be a trap."

Vic shook his head. "I don't know. You're the Sherlock. I just bring the leads. But that's a big one. My cut would be..." he looked up, calculating.

"Twenty grand," I said.

I was kidding about the "bad at math" thing.

"Yeah. So you can imagine how much I'd like you to take this job."

I nodded. "I get it, Vic. If it checks out, I'm in, and you'll get your cut. You get the finder's fee anyway, of course."

He nodded.

"But that's a lot."

"So what do you do?" Vic asked. "How do you check them out, to make sure they're legit?"

I shook my head and waved for the waitress. I paid in cash and left a generous tip. I also handed Vic his finder's fee, in the form of a pre-paid credit card. "You know I can't tell you that. Trade secret."

Vic nodded. "I know. I also know we're almost up, aren't we? You told we'd only do this thirty times. This is twenty-nine. Next to last." He looked at me, and I could see that he was conflicted.

"That's the deal," I said.

He watched me for a long moment, nodded again, smiling a pained smile. "I'll miss it," he said.

"I know," I told him. "It's just the way it has to be, Vic. I'll pay your bonus, just like I promised."

"Good," he said. "But it's about more than the cash. I... I dunno. I sort of feel like I'm part of something big."

I shook my head. "You can be a part of something better than this, Vic. Go back to school. Get a degree. You have the money now."

Again he nodded. I stood then and walked out of the back exit. Vic would go out the front. We'd meet again in a week or so.

It would be the last time.

VIC LEFT the rendezvous information in a Craigslist ad.

That was the system we worked out from the start. I used it with all my handlers. Post an ad using "touch" as one of the words in the headline. Post under a specific section, depending on the day of the week. Advertise a specific product for sale—one of five products that we would rotate through. Give the address in reverse. Note the time in 24-hour format, as the last four digits of the phone number.

It wouldn't fool a crack code breaker, but I was betting it would never have to. I switched handlers every so often, so if the NSA or anyone else was scanning and looking for me, they'd have to start over with each new handler. And with each handler came a new set of rules for the posts—new items for sale, new keyword, that sort of thing.

Today was Tuesday, and Vic had posted an ad for a sofa for sale. I took note of the address and the time, and made my way to that part of town an hour early.

I would need to find a place to crash tonight. There was a nice hotel in the neighborhood that I had stayed in once before. I don't usually like to repeat visits, but it had been years since I'd stayed in this place. I felt safe enough with it. And I had just enough time to brush the manager's hand and then sneak a pass at the computer, booking myself in as

"Garret Ramsey," the first random name I could pick out of a phone book on the way in.

Accommodations settled, I was now only twenty minutes out from the meeting. I made my way to the spot, and spent some time watching from across the street, making note of everyone in the place.

Seem paranoid?

Yes. Yes, it is.

Paranoia is life. Paranoia is the spice.

When the meeting time came, I saw my guy walk in from the street. I could tell he was the one, because he was acting a lot like I was, though a lot more obvious about it.

He stopped across the street first, about half a block from where I was lingering, and he watched the bar for several minutes, noting things in a small notebook. He slipped the notebook back into his pocket and ducked into the bar. I waited until he took a seat, then followed within a couple of minutes.

"Hi," I said, smiling at the guy as I shadowed him to a back table.

"Uh..."

"I saw your ad for a sofa."

That would be the pass phrase, if Vic had given it to him.

"It's like new," the guy said. The pre-arranged response. So far, so good.

I held out a hand, ready to do a deeper dive and make sure this guy was exactly who he said he was. And then things went wrong.

He took my hand, seemingly on instinct. But he was wearing a glove.

Dammit.

"So you're the famous Evergreen."

I cringed.

The name had been a sort of code name a few years back, when Henry was pimping me out for "covert" jobs that turned out to be a little shady. Or a lot shady.

I had asked him, at the time, why he chose "Evergreen."

"When you absorb the skills and memories of someone else, it causes your brain waves to scan erratically on an EEG. The ink on the ticker tape is green, and with all those jagged peaks it always reminds me of a pine forest. So, Evergreen. It seemed as good a code name as any."

I had objected on the grounds that I would have liked a spin at choosing my *own* codename—something cool like "Ice Man" or "Viper" or "Brain Scan."

Maybe not that last one.

Evergreen stuck.

"And you must be 'matherphracker'" I said. And I wasn't even ironic about it.

"Just a screen name. Not even mine. Is it safe to talk here?"

If it was possible, the guy seemed even more paranoid than me. "As safe as we'll get, for now. But this conversation needs to pick up. I'm starting to get nervous. And I don't stick around for nervous."

He nodded. "There's something I need, and my sources tell me you're the only one who can get it."

"Depends on what it is."

The guy made another quick glance, making it look somewhat casual. He was actually good at this. Which set off a tiny alarm in my head. I was staying put, for now. But I was on the edge of bolting, $200K be damned.

"There is a man I've been in contact with who claims to know something about my past. It's delicate information, and if it got out, it could cause problems for many people. I need to know if he's serious."

I waited, but the guy didn't say anything else. "That's it? Some guy knows one of your secrets, and all you want to know is whether he's lying about it?"

"That's it."

I nodded. "I don't want to shoot myself in the foot here, but so far that doesn't sound like a job worth two-hundred. Which tells me this person is high profile, or is extremely hard to get to."

The man nodded. "Both."

"Politician?"

"President."

I blinked. "Of a corporation?"

"Of the United States," he said.

CHAPTER THREE

MATHERPHRACKER RACED OUT OF THE RESTAURANT and matched pace with me. He was glancing around, making sure no one was paying any particular attention.

"Is it the money? I could pay more. Half a million!"

"I told you, I'm not interested."

I was scanning as well, looking for any signs that someone was watching. I hadn't touched this guy. I had no idea who he might be connected with, or whether he was just a lunatic who had somehow cracked the code Vic and I were using.

I picked up the pace.

Matherphracker suddenly grabbed my arm and spun me, slamming me into the wall. A couple of people passing by glanced our way, a bit of panic in their eyes. They kept walking, pretending not to notice any assault. Thank you, kind citizens.

I felt *her* stir in my head. The other female engram. The one I was afraid of for a lot of other reasons. She wasn't fully active yet, which was good. I could take care of myself. She'd make things messy.

"I'm afraid I can't accept that as an answer," Mather-phracker said, his voice a hard edge.

Use your training, Jaylin, Henry's voice said. *That's what it's for.*

I gritted my teeth. Stress always brought Henry out of the vault. Or sometimes it was *her.* In times like these, when I was in physical danger, it was a bit of a crap shoot. I had more than one personality in my head who could dismantle this guy, but there were dangers and complications associated with that. Part of my training with Henry had included being able to access the skills of some of my hitchhikers, if I needed them.

Particularly hand-to-hand combat.

I grabbed Matherphracker's hand, putting pressure on his thumb and using a quick, explosive twist to turn his arm behind him and spin him so that he face-planted into the wall.

He grunted, and even *growled,* and I could feel him shifting his weight. I poured on the pressure, forcing him to stay in place.

I glanced around, making sure no one was running this way with guns drawn. This guy had some sort of agenda, but I had no idea what it was or how I figured into it. Until I did, I'd have to treat him like he was a serious threat to my life.

Again I put pressure on him and pushed him against the wall. Then, with a somewhat awkward one-handed maneuver, I removed his glove and made skin-to-skin contact.

Things got clear in an instant.

His name—his *real* name—was Andrew "Drew" McClellan. He wasn't from here, originally. Meaning, not only was he an import to the city, he was also an illegal immigrant. And therein lay the problem.

Mr. McClellan held a high-level role in Shallister Hoffman—a company that relied on numerous government contracts to keep its half-million employees in monthly salaries, among other things.

The company was high profile. Billions were at stake. Plus the jobs and homes of a few million people worldwide.

To make matters far worse—McClellan was the son of a former terrorist. His father ran a cell of the IRA in Ireland, and he had been directly responsible for several bombings that resulted in the death of hundreds of people.

If it came to light that one of Shallister Hoffman's top executives had been lying and covering up his true identity, all these years—that he had ties to a wanted terrorist—things could go very, very wrong. Public confidence in the company would disappear overnight. The FTC would plow through the business with a bulldozer, and they'd find plenty more to keep them busy. The FBI and the NSA would both burn the place to the ground and rake the coals. And a few million people would pay the price for it while executives from Shallister Hoffman skated, annual bonuses intact.

"What does the President know about you?" I asked. But I already knew the answer.

"I don't know," McClellan said.

I needed more. I needed him to start opening up to me, so I could explain the "intuitive leaps" I was going to make. Because now that I had "shaken hands with the client," as it were, I had discovered something very, very scary.

This was bigger than just some guy trying to keep his job. This went deep. If Shallister Hoffman went down, it could take a large chunk of the economy with it. Not just in the US, but worldwide.

The lives of billions of people around the world would be impacted by this.

"Ok," I said. "I'm going to reveal something to you. And when I do, you're going to come clean on anything I ask you. Got it?" I put more pressure on his arm, to emphasize the question.

"Yes!" he said, gritting his teeth from the pain.

"Your name is Drew McClellan. Your father was the leader of an IRA cell, responsible for numerous bombings. A lot of people died in his cause. You left Ireland and faked your work visa, and worked a series of crap jobs until you eventually landed your position at Shallister Hoffman, using a fake ID and a bogus resume. Do I have your attention?"

There was a long pause before McClellan quietly answered. "Yes."

"You're wondering how I know that. Don't. My business is knowing things I shouldn't. And as you can imagine, I get *very nervous* when there's something I *don't* know. And right now, I'm nervous, Drew. Now I'm going to let you go, and I'm going to walk away. And you are going to have to find some other way to un-screw yourself and the rest of the world."

I let him go and started to walk away. As expected, he rushed to catch up.

"One million," he said, panting.

I almost stopped walking. I knew he had access to that sort of money, but he hadn't intended to go that high.

Having access to someone's memories doesn't necessarily clue me in to how they will react to something. There are a billion little nuances that can shape the direction someone chooses. From the instant I break contact with someone, the memories I have become sort of static. The quantum computer of the person's brain keeps spinning and calculating and processing, though. So I can know what they *knew*, but I can never exactly know what they're *thinking*.

"One million is a lot," I agreed. "Two million is more."

"*Two*! You're trying to talk me up from two-hundred-thousand to two *million*?"

"Actually, I'm trying to tell you that I'm not doing the job. You're the one who started raising the number."

He paced beside me, considering, shaking his head, cursing. "I *need* this information."

He did. He really did. And, as a sick dread started worming its way through me, I knew that it was about more than just his job. The company he worked for had tendrils in just about everything. If they lost these government contracts, people would suffer. Lots of people. Jobs would be lost, homes would be foreclosed, and hundreds of support businesses would go under. It would be a very big upset to the economy, and to the lives of millions.

Drew McClellan, despite being a high-level liar, wasn't actually a bad guy. In fact, he saw himself as carrying on some of his father's mission, in a less dangerous and destructive way. The company McClellan worked for—Shallister Hoffman—was a consulting agency with input into everything from defense and national security to technology that could impact the major exchanges and crush the world economy. They were in the top 25 list of US contractors, and were also contracted by the UK, Australia, and China, to name just a short client roster.

These guys played in an ocean that was wide and deep, and contained a lot of sharks, and yet most people on the planet had never heard of them. Most people, in fact, had no idea that their day-to-day existence was tied to decisions made by guys like Drew McClellan. Guys who had secrets big enough that the President of the United States would try to shake him down.

That's why I was getting a sick feeling in my gut. This wouldn't end well.

"Two million," Drew agreed, and I felt my stomach drop. "It's yours. Please," he said. "I need this information."

We stopped at a street corner, waiting for the light to change. I wanted to throw up. I wanted to run from this and never look back.

This is your chance, Kristen's voice said in my head. *This is your time to do something good for the world!*

And I knew it was over.

"Two million," I said. "I'll get you the information."

BRAVE WORDS. *Confidently spoken. Now… how do you plan to pull this off?*

Kristen's voice was gone now, replaced by Henry, who was far less concerned with me making a positive impact on the world than he was with keeping me (and thus *him*) alive and free to continue breathing and roaming about in it.

"I don't know yet," I said. "But I don't have time to argue. I have to document everything before it fades."

I had gotten some follow-up details from McClellan, including a drop point where I could have Vic (or maybe his successor) deliver or pick up as needed. I gave McClellan instructions on paying me, at which point he had balked.

"You want it *all* up front?"

"Those are the rules."

"What's stopping you from taking the money and running?"

"My reputation," I said. "I'd have a hard time getting work if it got out that I don't follow through."

"You're not going to need any work, after this job," McClellan said with contempt.

"Don't be so sure," I replied. "The level of risk alone on this job would justify asking for it all up front. It's up to you, of course. If you think you can get this information without me, I can have a new client by the end of the day."

A slight exaggeration, but not by much.

He reluctantly accepted, looking a little green, and told me the money would be in my offshore account by the end of the day.

Which was only partially true. It would be in *someone's* offshore account by the end of the day, though that person wasn't really aware they had an extra account out there. Neither were the fifteen other account holders I used as cover. The money moved around so quickly, and so often, there wasn't much chance of it being discovered.

Granted, this was a much larger amount of money than I was used to. I would have to shake some hands in the financial district soon, get some insight into where I could quickly move and then access two million.

With the money issues settled, though, I shook hands with McClellan one more time, to give me another 30-minute window. Even with that, I'd be cutting things close. I raced for the safe house, with Henry's voice dogging me all the way.

I tend to avoid having an "HQ." Having a centralized place, where someone might be able to track me down, works counter to my survival strategy. But it's exhausting to try to keep moving constantly. Sometimes you just need a familiar place to call home, even if it's just for the odd night every few months.

I have a handful of places across the city that fit the bill. Or close enough. They're a collection of places I maintain personally. I rotate which one I'll duck into at any given time and try to space things out enough so that no one should be able to see a pattern. These places are paid for in cash, usually—mailed to the landlords from various drop boxes around the city.

The cash comes from various bank accounts under the names of people or businesses that have no direct connection to each other. If someone started looking, they might eventually trace their way through all of it. But it would take them a while. And I wouldn't be on the other side.

No single account was in my name, or used any information associated with me. Every account was opened using cloned identities, temporarily acquired using my "gift." Some accounts actually belonged to a couple of my permanent guests.

Getting the picture on my paranoia?

Once you've been inside the heads of a few hundred people, you really get a sense for how dangerous people can get. It makes one a little "cautious."

This particular safe house used to belong to Henry, back when he and I were training. When he... *left*... the lease on the place lapsed. I used the first bit of money I ever made from my "job" to lease it again, under Henry's name.

I made a special request for the landlord to lease it as-is. Some of the equipment was beyond me, without Henry to guide me. Luckily, I had my own copy of him, in my head. Sometimes he even helped.

This would be one of those times.

Self preservation was something Henry could get on board with, and if I was going to take on this gig, I'd need all the backup I could get. Henry had no desire to live in a cage or be strapped to a table for vivisection. And since my body was currently where he lived, he would do whatever he could to keep it safe.

I ducked into the safe house after watching the street for a minute or so, looking for anything unusual. I didn't have much time—the 30-minute clock was ticking down and soon everything I knew from McClellan would be gone. There was information I needed to have on record.

Henry's memories gave me the access code for the doors, and I practically slammed them closed behind me, dropping the security bar in place before I rushed to a couple of tarp-draped objects in the middle of the room. I yanked these off, reaching quickly to steady the HD video camera as the tripod tilted forward. I turned the camera on and sat down at the small table with the laptop. I started typing as the camera recorded my voice.

"Andrew 'Drew' McClellan, with Shallister Hoffman. Employee identification number…" I recited the info, along with every personal and professional detail I could get. I didn't often bother with this sort of dossier on a client, but this was a special case. Very special.

As I talked, I typed, creating a file with all the information I could dredge up about McClellan's past, his father, the meeting he had with the President, and every other spare detail.

One of the benefits of my "talent" is the ability to compartmentalize and multi-task better than any average Joe. Henry explained it as using "frameworks."

"When you absorb someone's memories, you create a headspace for them. It's a self-contained memory node, but it's still part of your brain, accessed by your mind. It can be completely separate from your consciousness, but still accessible by your sub-conscious."

Meaning that I could use the extra bandwidth of someone else's memories and skills to help me do multiple tasks at the same time. That old adage about not being able to do two things well? I could do four or five. Maybe more, if I pushed myself.

Right now, I not only had McClellan's headspace, I also had Henry's, and Kristen's, and a couple of others who thankfully preferred to stay quiet most of the time. One brain, but multiple thinkers. It was exhausting, but it gave me huge advantages.

As the clock ticked down on my 30 minutes with McClellan, I scrambled to get all the important details recorded. I'd have to review this all later, to refresh my memory and make all of this my own internalized info, not just McClellan's. It wouldn't be as crystal clear as it was now, but I would at least have access to the info, if I needed it.

Time's up, Henry said.

And just like that, everything I knew about the man I'd just met was gone.

I spent the next hour watching the video back and reading through the file I'd written, getting myself familiar with everything I would need to know. I used the memory techniques Henry taught me to internalize all the information.

Part of me always wanted to revolt at anything I learned from Henry, but despite the way things had turned out with him, he actually *was* a good teacher. I had learned a lot from him—a lot about myself—even if I didn't want to admit it.

There wasn't much in this info that would help me get closer to the President. Drew McClellan hadn't even met him in person. Their conversation had taken place over the phone. Two men, dressed in dark suits and carrying government-issue weapons, had escorted McClellan to a hotel room, where he received the call. They had stood over him the whole time, emphasizing the threat.

That was interesting, but it didn't tell me anything that I could use to get close to the most powerful man on the planet.

I had no leads. There were any number of politicians who had access to the President, but I might touch all of them and never come any closer to reaching the man. My chances of pulling this off without being shot or arrested were pretty slim.

I needed a plan.

I used the laptop, routing through a VPN on the West Coast to a secure server with a masked IP address, which then rerouted to another masked server somewhere in the middle of nowhere. Bouncing around like this wouldn't keep the NSA or the Secret Service from tracking me, if I caused too much stir and spent too much time poking around where I didn't belong. But it would keep me anonymous enough for a strict data search. Google was a safe enough start.

What I needed was something that would let me have just a few seconds of skin-to-skin contact with the President. Just one handshake, and I could find out what he had on McClellan, and report it back. Job done. And enough money to keep me nice and hidden indefinitely.

I might not have to take any more of these jobs. I might be able to hide out for the rest of my life.

You could never stay in hiding, Henry said. *You like this life. Admit it.*

Sometimes I slip and let things I'm thinking bleed over to any engrams that are active. I hated it, when it happened, and I immediately clamped down, using the very techniques Henry had taught me to shut him out of my private thoughts.

I didn't bother answering. Because, in part, it was true. I *did* like this life. I was as free as anyone could be, sleeping in a different place every night, moving around the city with no worries about things like rent or credit card bills or any of that nonsense. Doing work that was maybe a little dangerous, but all the more interesting because of it.

And then there were the downsides.

I was alone. I couldn't know someone for too long without that relationship becoming a risk, for me and for them. I couldn't remain connected to anyone because there would inevitably come that day when we've shaken hands once too often, where there was just one more accidental contact than I had intended, where I suddenly *knew* them, and had them in my head, with the others. Permanently.

I couldn't risk that.

And so, free as I was, I was more a prisoner than even the extra engrams in my head.

I focused on the Google search, keeping my mind from wandering in dark places.

"This is promising," I said aloud. Henry didn't respond, which wasn't unusual. Henry was one of the voices that came and went as he pleased. I had no idea what these errant personalities did in my subconscious, while I was busy paying attention to something else. But there were times when it seemed like they had their own virtual lives running, somewhere in my skull. And, I suspected, they might have more friends than I did.

On the screen in front of me was a news story that had been aggregated by Google. It had today's date.

PRESIDENT TO GREET CHESS CHAMPIONS AT NATIONAL TOURNAMENT IN MANHATTAN

IT WAS PERFECT.

The event was low key, and open to the public, and the President was scheduled to do a meet-and-greet with some of the players.

All it would take for me to earn my two million was a quick handshake. A few seconds, and I was in.

There would be tons of Secret Service there, obviously. Getting into the place was going to be a challenge. I'd have to dip into my stash of fake IDs—the really good ones. I'd have to run a tight and risky game.

And I might have to learn to play chess.

CHAPTER FOUR

———————————

THE TOURNAMENT WAS IN A LARGE CONVENTION center, with one glass entrance facing the street. I'd been there a few times with... *her*.

I hesitate to think her name these days. Sometimes that's all it takes to bring one of my hitchhikers forward. Unfortunately, telling yourself "don't say her name" is a little like saying "don't think of pink elephants."

You rang? she said.

Pink elephants.

"Hi Kristen."

I'm actually very excited for you. This is a great chance to make some friends.

On the surface, this sounds like a nudge from someone who cares about me, encouraging me to be more social. But the truth was, Kristen knew exactly why I couldn't make "friends." And as sweet and kind a person as she was, I knew that she was holding on to some resentment about how things ended with us, and how she had become a permanent part of me. So this may have *sounded* like encouragement, but it was really a little jab to remind me that I could never get too close to anyone.

At least, that's how I felt it.

The truth is, Kristen probably meant it exactly as it sounded, and I was probably just too miserable a human being to accept it at face value. She may not have wanted to punish me for copying her into my head, but I did.

I had used Uber to catch a ride, and I got out about a block from the convention center. I walked the rest of the way, after stopping briefly to get a cup of coffee at a nearby Starbucks. The coffee was cover, in case Secret Service was watching the surrounding area. I needed an excuse for approaching on foot, rather than arriving right at the door.

I didn't want to arrive directly at the convention center, anyway, because I didn't yet know how I was getting in. I needed time to look the place over, to find an opening.

I found that opening as a van filled with chess players arrived.

They were enthusiastic, and all wearing "team" T-shirts, which seemed odd at first. Then I realized that this was the chess team from a local high school. They were here to play in some of the smaller tournaments, and to watch the "celebrities" play in the main attraction. They were all very enthusiastic about being here, and about meeting some of their chess idols. I got the impression that meeting the President of the United was just sort of a bonus.

I moved in among the group, careful not to make skin-to-skin contact with anyone. The place was crowded, and that made me nervous. One casual bump and I'd have a chattering teenager in my head for the next half hour, delaying my plans and maybe putting the nix to the whole thing.

But with some deft moves, a few quick turns, and the

protection of my ever-present hoodie, I managed to move along without incident.

As I suspected, there were a number of Secret Service agents standing among the regular convention screeners. Some were directing people through security, while others simply watched the crowd, reporting details to each other via wireless microphones in their sleeves. It was like every movie I'd ever seen. Only I was "the threat," which made me extremely nervous.

As the chess team and I entered the building, we were funneled through metal detectors and body scanners, none of which were a worry for me. Some of us, however, were randomly selected for a pat-down.

Guess who?

"You can't bring that in here," one of the convention screeners said. He nodded at my coffee.

"Really? I'm sorry. Do I need to take it outside and toss it?"

He looked around and indicated a garbage can a few feet from the metal detectors. "Just throw it in there."

I nodded and went to the trash. Just as I was about to toss the cup in, though, I was stopped by the most obvious and cliché secret service agent I've ever seen.

He wore the standard dark suit and dark glasses, and even had a skin-tone ear bud in his left ear. I didn't check, but I was positive that if I looked I'd see the bulge of a service weapon under his coat. Though it may have been hard to detect, hidden among the bulge of muscles threatening to tear their way out of his sleeves.

"Sir," the ultimate Secret Service agent said. He motioned with one hand, indicating a spot nearby. "Step over here, please. Bring the coffee cup."

I did as I was told.

The agent took the cup from me and used what looked like a popsicle stick to swirl the contents. He held the stick up, looking at it over the top of his sunglasses. Apparently it passed inspection, because he took the cup and the stick and tossed both into a different trash container.

"I'm gong to pat you down, sir. Please stand with your legs apart and your arms out to your sides."

I did as I was told.

By habit, I wear long-sleeved shirts and gloves. Most of the time I'm also wearing a hoodie, and sometimes jacket or coat on top of that. You can't have too many layers between you and the world, when you're me.

Apparently my gloves were something of a concern to the agent.

"Remove your gloves, please."

I felt my heart thump. "Uh, well, I have this condition. It's sort of a phobia, actually. I don't like to touch things with my skin. Especially people."

"Remove the gloves," the agent said again. His voice had a hard edge, and I knew that I had no choice. I removed my gloves.

The agent took them and placed them on a small metal table behind him. He opened a paper package and pulled out some sort of swab, running it over the gloves and looking at it for a reaction. There wouldn't be one, of course. But somehow it still made me nervous. Just being under this amount of scrutiny was nerve-wracking.

He turned to me, my arms out to my sides, and knelt, starting to pat me down from the ankles up.

"Should I take off my shoes?" I asked.

"Remain standing," he said, and roughly patted my legs up to my waist.

If you're wondering about the more "sensitive" bits, the answer is yes.

He continued patting my waist, and then my chest, taking my phone and notepad out and placing them on the table. Probably to be swabbed. Finally he started on my arms.

"You're sweating," he said, suddenly pausing.

"I don't like being touched," I said. "I'm sorry."

He stared for a moment, then continued, unmoved by my apparent emotional trauma.

He was edging ever closer to my hands.

He wasn't wearing gloves, which I found strange. I've been to airports. The guys always wear rubber gloves when they pat you down. I wasn't sure why this would be. different, but I was becoming increasingly nervous about how it would end.

When I make skin-to-skin contact, nothing really happens to the person I'm touching. I have a reaction, but it's usually pretty small. A momentary "brain fart," mostly, as I integrate the memories of the other person. But they don't feel a thing.

It wouldn't hurt anything for me to absorb this guy's memories—it might even help me with navigating security. But for thirty minutes after contact, I'd have this guy in my head. Which meant I'd be limited on how many people I could safely touch if I needed to. One of those people had to be the President. Duh. But my plan also involved a couple of well-placed and well-timed handshakes.

I can have more than one framework in my head at a time, but if I get too many, too close together, things get a little confusing. I get a bit addled, and it's harder for me to think straight. I tend to randomly blurt things that make no sense, as bits of thought collide and I lose track of who I am and who's thinking what.

I can usually keep it under control with two or three new personalities. After that, it can get a little loud in my head.

The agent was moving closer to the bare skin of my hand. Another inch and I'd know everything he knew. I inhaled slowly, using some of Kristen's Zen techniques to keep myself steady.

He stopped, just at the cuff of my sleeve.

I fought the urge to let out a loud exhale of relief.

He moved to the other sleeve, and again I held my breath as he got closer to my skin. But again, he stopped.

"You can put your arms down and relax, sir," he said. "I apologize for the inconvenience. I did my best to respect your condition."

I nodded, relieved. "Yes, thank you," I was winded as I talked. "I really appreciate that."

He turned and swabbed my phone and notebook. Then, satisfied that there was nothing dangerous there, he said that I could pick everything up and move along.

I pulled on my gloves first and then put the phone and notebook back in my pocket. I nodded at the agent, smiling as best I could, and he pointed me in the direction of the conference hall.

THE HALL WASN'T EXACTLY JAMMED with people, but it was a little more crowded than I had hoped.

Crowds always make me nervous, even though I live in the most crowded city on the planet. Call it irony.

There were hundreds of tables, arranged in what

seemed like an unconscious nod to the chessboard grid. Each table had its own board, already set up and waiting, and a chess clock to one side.

The tables were all wood-topped, which stood out to me. It had to be expensive, to have so many wooden tables in here. I had expected to see hundreds of those white plastic tables you can buy by the gross at Costco. Someone must have wanted a better aesthetic for the President's visit.

I shuffled among the people who were standing and chatting about past matches and moves they'd seen. The range of ages was astounding. From young children to octogenarians, I was pretty sure every possible age was represented. And here they were, talking each other up like they were old friends.

Common interests, Kristen said. *You should try spending time with people more often, Jaylin.*

It was always weird to hear my name.

No one calls me that. Most people have no idea what my real name is, actually. Even Kristen, when we had been together, had never known me by that name. Not for a long while. Not until near the end.

Hearing her say it now, in my head, was like getting dunked in ice water.

I shook it off and concentrated on the plan. Which had the unfortunate side effect of bringing Henry to the surface.

You need to blend in. The game you're playing is more complex than chess.

He was right. I had to make it look like I had a legitimate reason to be here, but I also had to keep myself low enough on the radar that I'd remain unremarkable.

My plan was to actually play in the tournament, holding my own and even winning a few games until the

President arrived and I could position myself close enough to him to get a handshake.

I had done a bit of research before coming here. The tournament itself was more or less a free-for-all, with anyone being able to enter and play. But the main event was a separate, more elite tournament, played out by a handful of national champions. Access was restricted.

But there was a loophole.

You could win your way into that tournament, on the main floor, if you could beat one of the current top-spot players. And that was exactly what I intended to do. But first I had to shake someone's hand.

Quentin Wehunt was currently a top-ranking player and chess champion. He had devastated his competition for the past few years in grueling back-to-back sessions. He had, according to numerous interviews, worked and trained day and night, seven days a week, perfecting his skills and making himself into a chess god.

I was going to do it in three seconds.

"Mr. Wehunt? I'm so excited to meet you! You're an inspiration for me!"

Wehunt gave me a pitying look, but reflexively reached out and shook my proffered hand.

"Thank you," he said, before snootily turning back to his companions, whom I now knew to be his coach and two assistants. Oddly I didn't know the names of the assistants, even though they'd been with Wehunt for most of a year. Which meant Wehunt had never bothered to learn their names.

When I absorb someone, their personality usually becomes dormant. The knowledge, memories and skills are there for me to access, but the personality itself usually gets shut away.

But with some people, such as champion chess players who have spent years honing their concentration, I get a voice almost immediately.

What's happening? Where am I? What did you do to me?!?

Relax, Quentin, I thought. *You're fine. See? Over there? That's you. The real you. I'm just borrowing some of your skills for a bit. I promise, you'll be fine.*

Quentin disagreed. Loudly and constantly. He babbled about kidnappings and alien abductions and any number of things until I could finally get him siloed—wrangling and stowing him in my subconscious. He'd be back, eventually. When I access someone's memories and skills, I'm getting in sync with their engram, so it's a bit like calling them to the front. Strong wills or highly trained minds can emerge and start making noise, if that's their thing.

I'd deal with that, if it came to it. For now, I had a little less than thirty minutes to play my way into the big-boy tournament.

It wouldn't be enough, I knew. The timing of a game could run into hours, depending on how much time the other player took between moves. But I did have one shot.

"Victor Ramis?"

Victor turned at the mention of his name. He was one of the "lesser giants" of the main event tournament. And, by the tournament's rules, if someone beat him, they could knock him out of that position and take his place.

The trick was beating him in the time I had left.

"I think I could take you in a game of speed chess," I said, belligerently. "If you've got the stones for it."

Victor's nostrils flared and his face went a bit red. He wasn't really much of a hothead, from what I could determine. But his ego had been severely bruised lately, after numerous losses to some others in the tournament. According to one interview, this was his "comeback" shot. He was already keen for a fight.

We sat at one of the tables, and an official gave us the spiel. Time was ticking down for me, and I said, "I'm good. We know the rules. Let's do this. Have to beat him in," I checked the large tournament clock, "23 minutes."

Victor had a few choice words about that, essentially equating to a much more vulgar version of "We'll see about that."

We started playing in earnest, with Victor on white, opening the match.

"The Sicilian," I said. "How original."

Victor snorted, offended, but said nothing. I was planning to prod him like this the whole game, but I was shushed by the official.

That was fine. According to Quentin's memories, Victor was playing a hack game.

This was confirmed by Quentin himself, who popped up as I started accessing his skills. Finding himself immersed in a game, he suddenly dropped his panic and became a critical observer.

He's so slow!

We're playing very quickly, I said.

But he is thinking so slowly.

I could feel Quentin's pleasure, but it was tempered with a sort of boredom. Victor would never stand a chance against Quentin Wehunt. He just didn't have the skill, or the focus. Quentin, for all his snobbishness, really was a champion. He had earned it. He'd worked hard for it, overcoming some pretty awful things in his life. His coach...

I shuddered away from the memories.

I tried hard not to get into too many personal details

from the minds of the people I absorbed. This was partly out of a sort of respect—my ironic way of trying to give them some privacy and dignity—but mostly I just wanted to protect myself. I had enough drama in my life. I didn't need to borrow from someone else.

Victor and I played at a brisk pace, slapping the clock with each turn and staring each other down, *daring* the other to take time to think things through.

This is wonderful! Quentin suddenly said. *I must remember to play speed chess more often. It's a refreshing change!*

I didn't bother breaking the news to him, that he wouldn't remember to try this. In a few minutes he'd be gone, and the real Quentin Wehunt would have no memory of this game.

Time was ticking down, though. If I couldn't wrap this up quickly, there was a chance I'd lose, and my whole plan would be shot.

But I had some advantages over Victor. Besides having a champion chess player in my head, I also had several mental frameworks at my disposal, allowing me to do what Henry calls "multi-dimensional analysis."

I could essentially put multiple minds to work on thinking ahead, seeing the moves and making decisions.

Poor Victor wasn't playing one guy. He was playing multiple people at one time. And all our mental processing was being filtered through the knowledge and skills of a grand master.

I made my final move. "Check mate," I said quietly, and hit the clock.

Victor had reached forward, was about to make a strike of his own, and froze.

"No," he said.

I waited.

"No!" he shouted. "How... that isn't possible!"

"Game goes to the challenger!" the official announced, and a crowd of people—where had *they* come from?—applauded in quiet golf claps as Victor pushed angrily away from the table and stormed off.

Well that was a fun diversion, Quentin said.

I looked up at the clock. *Yeah. And now it's over.*

Quentin may or may not have tried to respond at that point, but I never heard it. The clock ticked off the last second of my thirty minutes with him, and he was gone.

CHAPTER FIVE

Ok, you're in. Now what?

Henry would already know the whole plan, of course. As compartmentalized as we were, he knew me too well—how I thought and how I would react to things. But he was constantly trying to get me to think through what I was doing, to slow down and act, not *react*.

Now I have to play my way high enough into this tournament to earn a spot on the podium, I thought.

There are six people in this division. These games tend to go on for a lot longer than 30 minutes. You're not going to be able to blitz-chess your way to the top.

He was right. I was playing against a serious limitation, in that my knowledge and skill in the game would fade before most matches were even half over. But I had a plan.

For the next few hours I would play until my limit was coming up and then get a quick refresh by "accidentally" making contact with my opponent. In an instant I would know his entire strategy, including its weaknesses, and I could play him under the table using his own skills.

As the tournament wound on, this was becoming easier to do. We were starting to gather a crowd as I used some of my unfair advantages to devastate the lower-position players. Having the ability to mentally process multiple options simultaneously was coming in very handy with chess.

You're getting too much attention, Henry said.

I glanced up from my current devastating attack. He was right. I hadn't intended to be such a "rising star" in the tournament. But I was finding it difficult to rein it in.

You're having fun, Kristen said.

He's putting us in danger, Henry replied.

Great. A two-fer. These were fun. Accessing the various head spaces in my brain all at once sometimes brings a few dominant personalities to the top. I usually ended up with a migraine.

But they were both right. I *was* having fun. And it *was* putting us in danger. I had to get a grip.

But not before I beat the pants off of the guy sweating and cursing under his breath in front of me.

"Checkmate," I said, sweeping in with a play he'd known was coming for 12 moves now. He'd done a very admirable job of trying to work out of it, but unfortunately for him I could think way, way ahead.

He let out a grunt of disgust and stood quickly. I thought at first that he was going to sweep the pieces from the board and storm off. Instead he huffed, then smiled a bit, and held out a hand.

"Outstanding game, mate," he said. He had a heavy Australian accent that I hadn't paid much attention to before.

I glanced at his hand and hesitated.

He must have read it as disdain, because his expression changed to one of disgust. "I see. All handshakes before the game, but too good for it when you win." He turned and walked away, and I felt like a complete asshat.

That could have gone better, Kristen said.

It could have. But I couldn't risk shaking his hand. The clock was still ticking down on my last contact with him, and I didn't want a refresh jeopardizing a winning strategy.

For now, I needed to keep things clean.

It might not matter much longer, Henry said.

Why? I asked.

But I really didn't need to ask. Henry had just registered something I was seeing before I clicked to it.

The attention in the room had suddenly shifted away from me and my record winning streak to a gaggle of Secret Service agents who were clearing and securing a path. And, after a moment, as my chess skills counted down to zero, the President of the United States entered the room.

There was no announcement. Just an explosion of applause as the Commander-in-Chief entered, a security detail surrounding him as he waved and smiled at everyone gathered.

He took his position in the roped off area where I'd been handing out beat-downs on chess boards for the past few hours. The vast majority of the people gathered were herded to positions behind the velvet ropes, where they pressed together to watch the President.

I was standing with five other souls, all lined up.

"Ladies and gentlemen," the President said into the now quieting room. "I apologize that I will not be able to stay as long as planned. I've been called away. But I had a few minutes, and after watching some of the games from the skybox, I wanted to meet some of the fine minds gathered here."

The other top-tier players and I were nudged into a progression.

Well, that's lucky, Henry said.

We'll see, I replied. My spidey-sense was tingling. There was something about this that I didn't like, and some instinct was telling me that I was in trouble.

Still, this was the objective. Get here. Shake the man's hand. Find out what he knew about McClellan. And then get out as quick as I could.

The guy in front of me shook the President's hand and chatted for a moment about the tournament and chess in general. The President smiled and gripped his hand and forearm in a strong handshake.

My turn, I thought.

I was nervous. This was the highest profile job I'd ever taken, and it was likely one of the most dangerous. If anyone here knew about me, or even suspected, I would be cooked. Best-case scenario I'd be pressed into service against my will. Worst case, I could be strapped to a table and dissected.

Suddenly I realized, without quite thinking it through, I had put myself in a stupid, dangerous position.

Why had I agreed to this?

Two million dollars was a lot of money, but was it really worth this risk?

Don't forget all those people, Kristen said quietly, firmly.

She couldn't know what I was thinking, but she knew *me.* She'd know how and what I was feeling right now. She was reminding me that this job went beyond money. There were millions of people who would be impacted if Shallister Hoffman went down.

I couldn't help them much if my brain was in a jar, though.

"Mr. President," I said, my voice warbling slightly. I reached out my hand.

The President looked at me for an instant and put one hand on my elbow. I tried not to jerk away like I was touching hot coals.

"You're putting on quite a show," the President said. "I have loved chess since I was a boy. I've never seen anyone who could adapt his play style as often and as quickly as you."

I swallowed. "It's... I just... I love the game," I said.

He looked at me and smiled. "One of my agents tells me you have a phobia about touching."

My stomach twisted. I wanted to vomit on him. Which, aside from making me a nationally recognized idiot, would utterly block me from making contact and completing the mission. "I... I do," I said.

Say exactly what I tell you to say, Henry said, and in an instant his words were coming out of my mouth.

"I only shake hands with people I deeply respect," I said. And, as if to punctuate that statement, I held my hand out, firm.

It shook a little, which wasn't entirely intentional, but it did help with the show.

The President looked down, then back up to meet my gaze. He chuckled and gripped my hand.

And suddenly I was flooded with information that a few million people would have paid far more than two million dollars for.

In the right hands, some of what I now knew could create more wealth than I could imagine, or could create a new world power. I had details I never would have expected, about a range of things I never even knew existed.

There was just one problem.

The President had never heard of Andrew "Drew" McClellan.

"Well, the respect is mutual, son. Keep playing. You're a remarkable talent."

With that, I was ushered forward so that the rest of the group could have their turn at bat.

I stepped past the President and was guided out of the roped off area by Secret Service agents. As the room continued to focus on the POTUS, I drifted back, letting the press of the crowd swarm around me. I pulled on my gloves—no sense getting any accidental exposures. I might not have the information I came for, but I didn't want to muddy my thinking any more than it already was.

I ducked through the crowd and then made my way to the street. There was still a high level of scrutiny, as Secret Service agents kept the entrance secure, watching both the street and the hall itself.

I was noticed leaving, for certain. I stepped out onto the sidewalk and stopped, rolling my head as if I were working out tension from the tournament. I took a few deep breaths and did a couple of squats in place. I was trying to affect an air of a "serious chess champion out for a breather." So when I started walking away, my hope was that anyone watching would assume I was out to clear my head.

A few blocks away I ducked into a diner, ordered a cup of coffee, and then sat at a booth in the back while I dictated everything I could manage into my smartphone.

CAPTURING DETAILS FROM A MARK, before they faded, was a long-standing habit. And usually a good one. This time? I wasn't so sure.

A lot of what I was recording was information of a very sensitive nature. State secrets that could be dangerous in the wrong hands. Just having them on my phone made me into something I never would have expected: It made me a traitor to my country.

But I needed leverage.

There was something very bizarre and very dangerous going on here, and I had fallen into it face first like an idiot. McClellan had somehow set me up. The President knew nothing about him, and there was no information in his head that McClellan should worry about. Not personally.

You're committing an act of treason, son.

Oh holy crap on a cracker. It was *him*.

"Yes, I know Mr. President," I said, in a low whisper.

You do realize what will happen, when it's discovered that you exist?

"I can guess. Actually, I can remember. You've encountered people like me before," I said.

The memory wasn't pleasant. And it opened a floodgate of related memories.

Not with your specific gift, no, the President said. *But people with enhanced abilities? There are files on millions of you, some pre-dating the United States.*

I took this in, then accessed everything the President knew about those "enhanced" humans, dictating everything I could into the phone. In particular I made sure to include details about a defunct facility known as "the Pit," tucked away deep in the hills, and miles underground, in Los Lunas, New Mexico.

I can tell you're not a bad man, the President said.

"I try not to be, Mr. President."

Then do yourself a favor. Go back to that tournament. Find Agent Dixon. You know our security protocols. Use today's key phrase. He'll get you an audience with me. If you talk to me directly about your abilities, I'll be able to help you.

I laughed. "Mr. President, please don't forget that I know everything you know. The second I approach Agent Dixon, I'll have zip ties around my wrists and ankles and a bag over my head. I'll never see you. I'll be in a cell, doped to the backs of my eyeballs. And I'll spend the rest of my life either working for the government or being kept in a deep, dark hole."

There was a pause.

You're right. Of course. But you're currently a danger to national security, and you need to be dealt with.

"I'd prefer to deal with myself," I said. "You know I'm not a real threat."

The information you've recorded represents a very clear and present danger.

He had me there. He was right. The stuff I'd just dictated into my phone could never get into anyone else's hands. My smartest play was to delete it and destroy the phone before tossing it in the river.

But again, I needed leverage.

"Mr. President, it was an honor meeting you today. I've never absorbed anyone like you."

The clock was ticking down. Time was almost up. I accessed what the President knew about his security detail, and discovered that I was still well within the zone of Secret Service scrutiny, and would be for another hour, as they moved the President out and withdrew from the tournament. My best bet was to stay put, for now, and duck out after they'd cleared the area.

I saved my recordings in a folder on the cloud,

encrypting them and locking the folder with passwords. And then I wiped the phone clean.

I snagged one of the heavy-handled butter knives from my table and slipped with it into the bathroom where I locked the door and then proceeded to perform surgery on the phone. I smashed the glass with the butt of the knife, and used the blade to pry the shards out a piece at a time, throwing them in the trash. I then starting tearing through to the guts of the phone, finding the memory card. I leveraged the card out using the edge of the knife, ripping the soldered joints and mangling the card badly in the process. I finished the job by smashing it until it was just bits of silicon. I threw the shattered phone into the trash, and then wrapped the shattered memory chip in toilet paper, which I then flushed down the toilet. I flushed several times over the next few minutes making sure the pipes would be cleared. Once I was done, I stepped out of the bathroom and walked through the diner and out into the street.

The security window was closing now. The Secret Service would be pulling back. The President's knowledge was gone from my head by this point, so I had no idea about positions or tactics. But I knew enough to keep a low profile, to blend into crowds, and to take a few turns to get me out of the neighborhood.

Several blocks later I went into a cafe I've used from time to time and walked straight through to the back door which led me into an alley across from one of my safe houses.

I was gambling now. Hoping the Secret Service had no reason to be tracking me. If I could get into the safe house quickly, they might assume I had continued down the alley and out into one of the streets at either end.

"Evergreen," a man's voice said as I hurried my way to the door on the other side of the alley.

I froze, then looked back to see a man stepping out of the back door of the cafe. He had a gun aimed at me, concealed partially, holding it close to his side.

I didn't know who he was, but I was reasonably sure he wasn't Secret Service.

I looked at him for a moment, then leapt and sprinted down the alley, headed for the street closest to me.

He didn't yell, and he didn't shoot. He didn't even give chase.

He didn't have to.

Two more men stepped out before I could get out of the alley. They also had guns and were a little less discreet with them.

I skidded to a stop, looking from the guys in front of me to the guy behind me. There was nowhere to go. I was trapped.

I turned to face the guy behind me, who, at least, had actually spoken to me. In my mind, that put him in charge.

"You did a good job, getting to the President," the man said. "I lost a bet because of you. I never would have thought of getting to him through that geek fest."

"Who are you?" I asked.

"I'm your new client."

"Sorry," I said. "I already have more clients than I want."

He chuckled. "McClellan? You don't have to worry about him."

That sounded ominous. "What do you want?" I asked.

The man stepped closer and then put away his gun. He nodded to the men behind me, who also tucked away their weapons. "Well, now, that's a very good question. I've wanted a lot of things in my life. And I haven't always gotten them. My employer, though, he gets everything he wants. And what he wants right now is you."

The two men behind me grabbed my arms and forced me out of the alley and into a car.

"So what if I'd run the other way? To the other end of the alley?"

The man smiled as he settled in beside me. The two goons who had grabbed me climbed into the front seat. "I have another car and another couple of friends waiting on the other side. We've been following you since you left the diner. We found the phone, by the way. Very wasteful."

"It was a lousy phone. Kept dropping calls. It had it coming."

The man chuckled again. "Yeah," he said. "That's funny."

The car pulled out into the street and joined traffic. For the next hour we navigated through the city. Eventually we came to a stop outside of a hotel I had stayed in a couple of times. We entered via the elevator in the garage and rode to the top suite.

When the doors opened, I was forced out, and then left in a lounge area where I waited with the two goons watching me.

About forty minutes later there was a ding from the elevator, and as the doors slid open, I felt my breakfast start to fight for an exit. I was breathing heavy, fighting back the sick. I could feel sweat beading and running down my side.

"That isn't possible," I said.

The man stepping off the elevator had a limp, which was understandable. His right leg was a prosthetic. I felt a stab of guilt when I saw it.

"Hello Jaylin," the man said in a voice I knew all too well.

Well, Henry's voice said in my head. *This just got very, very interesting.*

"Hello Henry," I said aloud. "How in the hell did you get out of prison?"

CHAPTER SIX

"It's a long story," Henry smiled. "And one I'm not likely to share for a while." He limped into the room, relying on a highly polished cane that had a silver knob on top.

"What are you involved in, Henry? This isn't your style."

Henry took a seat in one of the large, plush chairs, and used his cane to indicate that I do the same, pointing at the chair across from him.

I glanced at the two big bruisers who were watching me and quietly took my seat. I leaned back, crossing my right leg over my left, glancing down at it and then back up at Henry.

Well played, Henry said in my head.

"Well played," real-world Henry said.

Great, I thought. *Two of you.*

Oh, this is going to be great fun! inner Henry said.

"I imagine you're having a nice little dialogue with my mental doppelgänger," Henry said. "How is he?"

"Annoying," I said.

"But useful, I'll bet."

I kept silent.

"It took quite a bit of effort to get you to this place and time," Henry said. "It took a great deal of planning."

"You could have just emailed me," I said.

Henry laughed. "Right. I'm sure you would have put something on your calendar. You've actually been difficult to track. Your paranoia is profound. I taught you well."

Not that well, inner Henry said. *You still managed to get yourself caught.*

Do you have any idea how he could have gotten out of prison? I asked.

If it were me, I would use what I knew to make as many connections as possible, until I could be in a position to buy my way out.

"I found that you were using one of my old labs as a safe house. That was foolish."

"It was handy. I'll burn it once I'm out of this."

Henry smiled, almost coyly. "Oh, Jaylin. You'll never be out of this. Because of who you are, you'll *always* be tangled in this." He looked toward the window for a second, gripping the cane with his left hand while running his right hand over the silver knob on top. He was looking at me with a steady, studying expression.

"Maybe you kept my lab out of a sense of nostalgia," he continued. "You miss our time together. You decided to honor me, in some small way."

"Honor? Why would I honor you?"

He looked back, and his expression was dark.

You never had any respect, inner Henry said. *But I actually did love you like a son, you know.*

You loved what I could do, and you wanted to find a way to replicate it for personal gain.

Doesn't mean I didn't love you.

It occurred to me that Henry—both Henrys—could be playing at a longer game here. I kept that quiet, inside and out.

"You wouldn't," outer Henry finally replied. He shifted the cane so that it stood rigid, gripping the shaft with his left hand in a firm fist. "Well, who needs honor anyway? I'll have something better, soon."

"Trained attack bears?"

Henry smiled. "Power, of course. Not to mention the means to gain more of it."

"I destroyed everything I got from the President," I said.

Henry nodded. "My men tell me you smashed your phone and flushed the memory chip."

"So there you go," I said. "Nothing. The chances of me getting that close the President again..."

"But you wouldn't have bothered smashing your phone if you hadn't recorded the information electronically. And you forget, I'm the one who trained you. And part of that training was to replicate the data as quickly as possible. Which is exactly what you did."

Oooh, inner Henry said. *I'm good.*

"Don't bet on it," I said aloud, as much to my inner Henry as to the outer one.

"Oh, I have, actually. I've bet quite a lot. And I'll win that bet, Jaylin. You can count on that. My men have already been through your safe house—my old lab. They've already confiscated the equipment there. We can pull the information we need off of that."

"Good luck," I said. "I wiped everything. The accounts are locked. The only person who knows how to get in is me. You'd need another me to get that info."

Henry nodded. "True," he said. And then he held up

the cane, aiming the silver knob in my direction. "Good thing I brought one."

I STRUGGLED AGAINST THEIR GRIP, but it wasn't much use. Henry had hired guys who could bench-press Smart Cars, if not Buicks. I was in pretty decent shape, from all the running I had to do. But my endurance and lean body mass wasn't going to cut it with this bunch.

They forced me into a chair that looked like one of those massage chairs you buy in SkyMall. It had the requisite horror movie straps for my arms and legs, and the two bruisers seemed more than happy to make them tight and secure.

At least it was a plush and comfortable chair.

By this point I had stopped resisting, instead focusing on trying to make skin contact, if I could. If I could get some inside info, I might be able to think of a way out of this.

The problem was that they were wearing button-down shirts and gloves, covered from neck to toe. And their death grips on my arms prevented me from making a quick slap or scratch to the face. I couldn't even manage a head-butt.

Maybe you should let them do their work, Henry suggested.

Maybe you should bite me, I said.

Don't blame me, I'm not the one calling the shots here.

Except we both knew that he was. The other he. Inner Henry might not be the one giving orders, but he was an exact copy of the man who was. Granted, there were several years of parallel development missing between the two of them. But the engrammatic apple didn't fall far from the tree.

One of the guys reached down and picked up a controller that was wired to the chair. He used this to tilt me backward until I was lying nearly flat.

"Can you put that on full-body vibrate?" I asked. "My sciatica has been flaring up lately."

The two man-handlers stepped away.

"Comfy?" Henry asked.

"Kind of an odd choice for a torture chair," I said.

Henry chuckled. "It would be, yes. But I don't need to torture you," he said.

I felt a sick twist in my stomach.

So I finally did it, inner Henry said.

Did what? I asked. But I was afraid I already knew the answer.

"No one on the planet has studied you more than I have," outer Henry said. "All those years we spent together, mastering your gift—did you think I was doing it just because I liked you?"

"I thought you were doing it because you wanted me to be your little mental sneak thief."

"Well, that was a nice bonus. Selling your services meant having the money to fund my research. You have a unique gift, Jaylin. Since we worked together, I've discovered there are more people like you, out in the world. Perhaps not with the same ability. But there are people who have additional gifts. Abilities that can be astounding in their implications. There's every indication that the instances of people like you are increasing. Which means the human genome may be shifting and changing—moving toward the next step in evolution."

"This is getting boring, Henry," I said.

You're stalling. He's going to know that. Just relax. This is going to be fun.

"You have had unique access to my mind for a very long time, Jaylin. You did from the start. And yet you never seemed to know what it was I was planning for you. Why do you suppose that is?"

I didn't know. I had thought about that for years. When I touch someone, I have access to everything they know. Every thought that was in their head at the point of contact. Every memory. Every skill. I had asked myself a million times why I never saw outer Henry's play coming. And inner Henry had never volunteered an answer. I hadn't even bothered asking, really. The betrayal ran too deep. And when you have to live with the person who betrayed you—carry them in your head every minute of every day— you'll take any escape from them that you can get. Even if the only option is ignoring them.

"I knew after only a few sessions that there was a chance you could absorb a personality permanently. I know a lot about your potential, actually. You can do so much more. But without me to guide you, to help you... you're destined to remain just a homeless thief for hire."

"That's what you made me into," I said. "I'm just following the program."

Henry laughed. "That was never the endgame, Jaylin. That was just a means to an end. That was creative funding," he smiled. "And practice." He shook his head. "You're capable of so much more. You just have no idea."

He turned and walked to a small table across the room. He picked something up and hobbled back to me, his cane making heavy thumps on the solid wood floor. He stood beside me and held up a small, round piece of metal. It was torus shaped—a small, round ring of metal. In its center was a pulsing blue light.

"I was nearly done with this when you betrayed me."

I laughed, loud. "*I* betrayed *you?*"

Henry shook his head. "Perspective, Jaylin. Remember? Everything is about perspective. But why quibble? When we parted ways, I was nearly done with building this device."

"And what is it? A high-tech jelly donut?"

"It's you. Or, well, to be accurate, it's a prototype of a device that can replicate your abilities, to a degree."

The sick twist came back.

I can't believe I finished it, inner Henry said, a little awed.

Finished what? I asked. *Henry, what is that thing?*

As if hearing my question, outer Henry said, "I'm calling it an engrammatic replication device. ERD for short. I first started work on the prototype when you absorbed that girlfriend of yours."

Kristen. I didn't want to think about her. Not out of any fear of mental or emotional pain, but because I didn't want to call her forward by accident. I wasn't sure what was about to happen, but I didn't want her to be a part of it. I'd caused her—the *real* her—enough pain. I didn't want her mental counterpart to suffer any more because of me.

"Your little stunt, sending me to prison—that cost me a lot of time, Jaylin. I could have had this technology perfected by now. Instead, I have this. A device that works..."

He paused, looked at me, shook his head. "...but only on you."

I laughed, loud and hard.

"Yes, yes. I know," Henry said, his expression perturbed. "Irony is funny. But there's something else I couldn't perfect. It's hypothetical, but the data leans pretty heavy toward the result."

"It's going to make me fat?" I asked.

"It's going to hurt like hell," Henry replied. He wasn't smiling about it, to his credit.

You never believe me, Jaylin, but I actually do care about you.

I said nothing. Just waited.

Henry looked at me, a strange emotion in his eyes. And then he sighed and sent me to hell.

CHAPTER SEVEN

IT'S NOT THAT I'VE NEVER BEEN IN PAIN BEFORE. I'VE just never *been* pain before.

And that's what this felt like—as if my body had been replaced by a swirling, roiling mass of pure pain that was falling and burning, getting brighter and hotter until I would eventually explode as a last, abrupt ember hitting the ground.

Worse than the pain, though, was the screaming.

At first I thought it was me. And I'm certain I *was* screaming, on the outside. But inside, in the landscape of my mind, I could hear *other* screams. Henry, for starters. He was loud and close.

And the others—the luckless bastards and whispers from the back of my mind. They tended to stay hidden, locked in their own headspace. Now, though, they were out, raw, writhing with the rest of us.

And Kristen.

I would have done anything to stop what was happening, for her sake alone, but I couldn't so much as beg in the state I was in.

As the pain and fire burned through every part of who I was, I could feel a pulling, as if someone had turned on a vacuum and was sucking what little was left of me outward. For an instant, short and sweet, the pain disappeared, replaced by...

Nothing.

I was surrounded by nothing.

I was *made* of nothing.

I was in a darkness so complete it was retroactive–cascading backwards through my life and my sense of self, replacing any light or hope. It was as if I'd never known what "seeing" was. As if darkness was all I'd ever known, ever *could* know.

And then I started to drift back, like the broken end of a piece of taffy, a curling string falling back into the main mass, slowly and not quite in the shape I'd been in before.

As I settled back into reality, I was relieved to see light again. But it was different from before. I was seeing... something new. Something outside of myself. Outside of everything.

I saw thin tendrils of light, twisting and looping, forming strange patterns of knotwork that permeated everything. The pattern became tighter and tighter as I pulled away, or fell back into place, until the landscape was smooth and the pattern disappeared into the details of the mundane world. For a second there, it was like I could see the very fabric of reality—so real I could have reached out and grabbed it. And then, an instant later, my perspective shifted. The pattern disappeared. The window closed.

I was back.

I was staring upward at Henry—outer Henry—who was looking down at me with an expression that might have been concern. If I hadn't known better, I might have believed he was worried about me. Maybe in the shape I was in, at the moment, I just *wanted* someone to be worried about me.

"He's alive," Henry said. "Get that IV in his arm, but do *not* let him touch your skin, got it?"

"Got it," a man's voice said.

I felt a minor stab of pain in my arm, which almost made me laugh. Compared to what I'd just gone through, that little prick of pain was a lollipop.

"We lost you for a second there," Henry said, and I thought I could detect a note of relief in his voice. "Welcome back."

"What... happened?" I croaked.

Henry looked at me, then shook his head. "Nothing. Nothing happened, Jaylin. The transfer started, and then you went into a seizure. I removed the ERD, and you snapped out of it.

I looked at the IV in my arm.

"Nothing toxic, don't worry. Just something to keep you hydrated."

"No sedative?" I whispered.

Henry smiled, and there was no caring, only malice, in that smile. "That would work counter to our plans, Jaylin."

I noted he had said "our."

Are you ok? Kristen's voice asked.

Are you? I replied.

I felt like I was being ripped apart, she said.

Me too, I said.

Me too, by the way, Henry said.

So did I, said Caleb. One of the "others." The "youth."

And me, said Jacob. The "old man."

All present and accounted for.

All except one. If you could call her "one."

Julia. As I thought of her, though, I could sense her on the edges, watching. Of all of us, she was the one most likely to endure torture without shattering. I hoped that meant she was content to lurk at the edges and not step forward.

I felt sick. My thinking was a little scrambled. They'd never all come at once before. Usually Caleb and Jacob stayed in whatever corner of my mind they occupied, and kept quiet. The link I had to them was weaker, somehow. I could draw on them, if I needed to. I could talk to them, any time. But they didn't tend to make spontaneous appearances.

Julia...

It was best not to think about Julia. But thank God she didn't emerge very often.

Henry had a theory—that my detachment from the others had something to do with the level of emotional bond I shared with each personality. That bond determined how "in touch" they were. I had a strong connection with Kristen and Henry. Not so much with Caleb and Jacob. None whatsoever with Julia. So, Kristen and Henry got a lot of "upfront" time, asserting themselves sometime without me even wanting them there. Caleb and Jacob would some-times come out in moments of extreme stress, but otherwise I'd have to call them forward. Which I rarely did.

Julia was something else entirely. I actively tried to keep her from emerging, if I could. It was complicated. There was so much going on there. It felt threatening to have her front and center. Hearing her voice came with risks.

Outer Henry hobbled to a table where a laptop streamed data. He placed the ERD on a small device connected by a USB cable to the computer. The data on the screen shifted and changed, and an alert box popped up. I couldn't read it from my angle.

Outer Henry slammed the end of his cane against the floor in a loud thud. The equivalent of stomping his foot, I thought. Frustration.

I fought the urge to smile.

He turned to me. "How did you resist it?" he asked.

I had no idea. In fact, as far as I could tell, I hadn't resisted at all. For a moment there, I was pretty sure I wasn't even in my own body anymore.

"I've already field-tested the primary technology in this," he said. "Back before you betrayed me. I was able to replicate basic patterns of thought from you. I know it works. I could get a reading on your engrammatic pattern. The refinements I've made are merely a translation of that. So, that means you were able to resist. Which means..." he stopped, hesitating, looking stricken. "Why? Why are you betraying me?"

"You're nuts," I said. "I'm not the one strapping an 'old friend' to a table and torturing him with a cyber-donut."

Henry scowled and waved, stepping forward and leaning on his cane. His face was close to mine now, and he was looking into my eyes the way someone might peer through a peephole, trying to see someone on the other side.

He was looking right in my eyes, but he wasn't looking at me.

"Not you, idiot," he said, his voice a low grumble. "You I can handle. I'm talking to the one person in that head of yours who is an actual match for me."

I blinked.

That would be me, Henry said. *And he's right. I'm totally betraying him.*

"WHY?" outer Henry asked.

Good question, I said to inner Henry. *Why? Your plan is working. You have me where you want me. Why?*

Inner Henry replied, *Really? It's not exactly in my best interest to let outer Henry suck your brain out through a tube. This may not be the house I grew up in, but it's where I live now.*

That made sense. Henry was a self preservationist at heart. And if the ERD posed any danger to the Henry in my head, he'd do anything he could to put a stop to it.

"What is he saying!" outer Henry shouted.

Inner Henry was whispering some things in my ear. I laughed. "He's telling me about the time you got drunk and tried to pick up a girl in a bar only to find out 'she' was pre-op."

Outer Henry's face went bright red. "It was an honest mistake!" He staggered back a bit, shook his head, gripped the cane and stood straighter. "I never would have expected betrayal. From either of you." He shook his head and turned back to the data. "I'll just have to try again. And again. Won't that be fun?"

"I'm looking forward to it," I said, though inside it was all I could do to keep from throwing up.

Henry hobbled out of the room, followed by the two guys who had helped strap me down. I was as alone in the room as I could be, considering who I was.

I don't think I can go through that again, Kristen said.

I know, I replied. *I'm going to find a way out of here.*

And how do you propose to do that? Henry asked.

It was a good question. And I had no answer for it.

The room was a small office or study, off of the main lounge of the suite. It didn't contain much. A couple of tables, a bookcase filled mostly with decorative items, and a few odds and ends that had been brought in to help rip my brain apart. The chair, too, of course.

I looked at my arms, strapped with long, padded straps to the arms of the chair. My legs were bound the same way on the foot rest. Everything was wrapped tight enough that I couldn't get the leverage to pull free.

The IV needle in my arm was held in place with medical tape. A tube ran from that to a drip bag on a rolling stand, which was near my elbow. That wasn't much use, unless I could get free and use it as a weapon.

In other words, there was no way out of this chair, as far as I could determine. I was good and stuck.

I slept, off and on. The ERD had taken a toll on me, and I needed the rest. Henry and his two goons hadn't come back into the room in a couple of hours, from what I could tell. The voices in my head had quieted, too.

I was feeling better, but still trapped. I couldn't think of a way out. But maybe that was the problem.

Maybe I was doing too much of the thinking.

Henry, Kristen, Jacob, Caleb—wake up. I had almost called out for Julia as well, but decided against it. She might actually have been useful in this case, considering her past. But she was too unstable. Too many marbles rolling loose in her bag. It made her unpredictable, and right now unpredictable was dangerous.

They all roused. That's the only way I can describe it. I didn't call the voices forward very often, especially not all together, so it was an odd feeling to sense them coming to the surface at my call. It was like being in a room when someone next door has turned on an old television set. There's a sort of whine and hum, and sort of odd pressure that lets you know that something is there, even before you're fully aware of it.

I need to think of a way out of this, and I'm not up to the task. But together, maybe we can be. There's more brain power here than Henry—outer Henry—can match. So start thinking and making suggestions. How do we get out of here?

For the next few minutes, I didn't so much hear their voices as get impressions from them, ideas and thoughts that bled through as they worked hard to figure a way out.

One brain, but five headspaces. The engrams were running through everything they could think of, parallel processing, coming up with every conceivable idea.

Eventually a plan was formed.

It wasn't perfect. It could even get me killed. But it was all I had. And, more importantly, everyone in my head was onboard with it.

"Help!" I shouted. "Help!"

One of the goons must have been just outside the door because he stepped in before I'd finished my second "help."

"Shut up," he said, his voice low and on the edge of a growl.

"Listen, man, *I have to pee*. Like, *seriously* have to pee."

The man smiled and shrugged. "Don't let me stop you."

"C'mon, man! I know things are all kid-nappy and torture, but I don't think Henry wants me lying here in my own piss! Didn't he give you orders to take care of me?"

And there it was—a quick flash in the guy's expression. Annoyance. Resentment. We thought it might show up, but it was a gamble. The expression on the goon's face told the whole story.

These two guys didn't work for Henry.

There was someone else. The *real* big boss. Someone even Henry had to answer to.

"C'mon," I said, quieter, pleading. "You can keep my hands bound. Just let me slip into the bathroom. You can take everything out of there before I go in. No problem. You can even watch, if that's your thing."

He was already moving toward me. "Don't make me break your arms," he said.

Which didn't sound so much like a threat as it sounded like he was fighting a compulsion.

I didn't push it.

He was wearing gloves and long sleeves, so he was prepared for my abilities. He was holding my arm in a death grip as he practically yanked me from the chair after ripping away the last strap. I stumbled a bit as my feet touched the floor, but he held me up and practically dragged me out of the room to the guest bath.

We were alone in the apartment, I noted.

He shoved me inside the bathroom, and I realized that it had already been swept clean of anything I might use as a weapon. There wasn't so much as a bar of soap or even a hand towel in there. The shower curtain and all of its rings had been pulled and removed, too.

I looked up, and the guy smiled. "Thought you'd find a little something in here, huh?" he said. He made a slight flourish with one hand, as if offering me the kingdom, and made a great show of closing the door to give me "privacy."

I had to act fast.

It was clear that the guys working with Henry were well trained. Whoever he had managed to hook up with was powerful and connected, and preferred his or her goons to be ex-military. That was Jacob's observation, anyway. Took one to know one.

It helped that I actually did have to pee. I made some noise, flipping the toilet seat up, and started a stream, trying to keep it steady but slow, to help buy time.

Normally, I'm a paragon of urinary aim. But this time I

was going to have to freestyle it while my hands remained free to work.

I carefully removed the lid of the toilet, struggling to keep from making any noise as I lifted it away.

Jacob had been right. No one thinks about the toilet lid. If that had been removed, we had a backup plan to use the lid of the toilet seat, but it would have been trickier.

I was able to hold the heavy ceramic lid with one hand, allowing me to redo my pants and then flush.

I turned quickly, raising the toilet lid high and stepping into the space that would be behind the door, not quite between the door and the wall. There was enough gap beside the toilet that I could stand there without being wedged in.

As predicted the guy opened the door as soon as he heard the flush.

I kicked outward, slamming the door against him, but he was ready for that, anticipating that I would try something.

The door stopped short against the outer edge of his booted foot, and I heard him chuckle as he gave it a forceful shove, presumably in an attempt to knock me back against the wall. I gave no resistance, even stepping aside so the door could swing freely.

As it slammed open, he involuntarily followed it in, head first. I caught just a glimmer of surprise on his face before I swung the toilet lid down hard, with as much force as I could manage. It connected with his forehead with a pretty impressive impact.

The guy went staggering back, and I pressed my advantage, rushing him and raising the toilet lid again, bringing it down fast on his head. He groaned, and part of me grudgingly had to admire him for still being conscious.

I knelt on top of him, one knee on his sternum, and

raised the toilet lid again, bringing it down hard enough that I could feel bone crunch. Blood splattered outward, at that point. I felt gorge rise in the back of my throat, but fought the urge to vomit.

I had never killed anyone before.

I have, Jacob said. And there was a grim tone that went deep. I could feel it as much as hear it.

I quickly searched the guy, and found keys, a pocket knife, and his wallet, which contained identification and some credit cards, as well as the hotel key card.

Get his thoughts, Henry said.

I hesitated.

The guy was dead.

That wasn't entirely a barrier, though.

Henry and I had discovered that after someone dies, there's a brief window—about 15 minutes—in which I can still absorb their knowledge and skills. But there's a heavy cost. This guy would become one of those permanent voices in my head.

We weren't sure why this happened. Henry had theories. I did, too. It seemed to me like some part of the person I touched might be desperately looking for a life line—some way to cheat death. And I was it. So they followed and took up permanent residence.

There was also the side effect of having to see the murder I just committed from the other side, which I did not look forward to.

He has information we're going to need, Henry said. *We have to know what he knows, to get out of here alive.*

He was right.

I took a deep breath and then reached out. At first I was going to touch the only exposed skin I could find, which was on the guy's ruined face. I couldn't bear that, though. For starters, his face was a bloody mess. But also, touching someone on the cheek is a bit... intimate. I couldn't do it.

I yanked off one of his gloves and gripped his hand, as if giving him a firm handshake.

I felt that momentary disorientation that comes with contact, and then I was filled with all the emotions that Carter, the man I'd just killed, had felt.

I will kill you! He shouted in my head.

I ignored that. A momentary burst of strong will. I could think around it. I'd done it before.

He did what had to be done, Jacob said.

I got the impression that, somehow, the conversation went on from there. Shouting, mostly, at least from Carter. But I didn't have time to puzzle over it. Right now I had work to do.

Carter knew every inch of this hotel. He had contingency plans for getting out, and he had an escape car stashed.

He also had a gun, which I grabbed. I knew how to use it. I could field strip it blind folded. Carter was a bad ass.

Before I slipped out, I ran for the room where Henry had used the ERD on me. It was still there, on the USB reader. I yanked the plug out of the laptop and shoved the ERD and its reader in my pocket. I also grabbed the laptop itself, slamming the lid shut and tucking it under my arm as I raced out of the suite.

I didn't bother with the elevator. Too public. Too much of an opportunity to be spotted. Instead, I raced down the stairs, feeling the burn in my legs but not daring to stop.

I made good time, and once I hit the ground floor I ducked out through the back of the building, found Carter's getaway car, and got the hell out of there.

CHAPTER EIGHT

ANOTHER SAFE HOUSE. THIS ONE IN A SPOT I RARELY visited. The safest of safe houses. I kept it completely out of my rotation, checking in on it only once a year just to make sure it was still secure. It was expensive, but worth it.

I called it "The Last Resort."

Carter's knowledge had helped keep me off the radar on my way out of the hotel and helped me map a route that his people wouldn't be able to track. I knew the gaps in their network. That's useful.

What wasn't such a big help was the fact that I felt like an egg scrambled in its shell. I was still feeling the effects of the ERD, and it was slowing me down. But slow isn't a stop, and I managed to push through despite spending most of the trip feeling like I wanted to throw up until I was inside out.

Just like any other contact, the knowledge and skills I gained from Carter faded after 30 minutes. Because of our more *permanent* connection, however, I'd always have a bit of access if I needed it. It wouldn't be as clear and surface-level as it was now—as if I'd been through all of Carter's experiences first-hand—but I could call it up in a pinch. Like straining to remember a phone number you haven't used in a while. Once you remembered, it snapped back into place like it had never left.

Carter's memories might have faded into the background noise of my brain, but Carter himself wasn't going anywhere. He was a permanent resident now. And eventually, I was going to have to find a way to deal with him.

That was a "later" problem, though. I had plenty of "now" problems to deal with.

As I ducked into the safe house, and Carter's memories started to fade, I still had the lingering feeling of being *murdered*. The rage was still there. So was the fear. Carter didn't want to die, of course. He was shocked by the whole thing. Which, thankfully, was helping keep him quiet for the moment. As he adjusted and acclimated to his new reality, I could concentrate on everything that had just changed in mine.

Henry—outer Henry—was out of prison.

How? And who had funded him on building the ERD?

The question of funding was going to nag me the most.

It meant that someone other than our little circle was now not only aware of me and my ability, but they were also intent on using me for some high-level plan. Something big enough to justify kidnapping, torture, and who knew what else.

How did Drew McClellan factor into this?

More importantly, how had they fooled him enough to fool *me*, when I absorbed his memories?

I'm very hard to lie to. A perk of being able to know literally everything a mark knows.

In the safe house, I dropped bars over the top and bottom of the thick, steel-lined door at the front entrance.

The windows were all bricked in, with iron bars over the outside for good measure—leftovers from before I had the place remodeled. Here on the ground floor there was no way to access this space. Even if someone came in from the second floor, above, they'd have to get past a steel vault door over the stairwell.

The second floor was just a distraction. I had it decorated with things that would make it look like the safe house that it was, with the implication that I would bunk out there if things went wrong. Smoke and mirrors.

In reality, I had never set foot in that second floor. I'd hired people to make it ready, gave them access that didn't involve seeing the first floor, and had them send me photos via email, to approve everything. My cover story was that I was in LA, and that I'd be using the space whenever I was in Manhattan.

The vault door, over the stairwell, was added by a security firm that specialized in panic rooms. It was welded from the outside, and reinforced with two thick, steel crossbeams. The only way it could be opened was if someone did so from the stairwell. Which had never happened, and likely *would* never happen.

The point is, I never went up those stairs. A cleaning crew came once a month to dust and make sure everything was in order, but as far as I knew the whole apartment was filled with cats and Ikea furniture.

My domain wasn't upstairs. It was downstairs.

The ground floor of the safe house was warehouse-like. There were supplies here—food, clothes, a stash of cash. Everything a growing paranoid boy needs to get by. I could make a quick stop here, in a pinch, and then keep moving. I could even shower and sleep here, watch some TV, eat a meal. It had everything I needed.

But for real hit-the-fan days, like today, there was the grate.

Actually, it wasn't a grate anymore. It had started life as a ground-floor access to a utility space beneath the building. But I'd made a few alterations.

I had put a counter top over it, with pipes running down through a plywood bottom, supplying water and drainage for a sink. It was a working sink. There was even a dishwasher in the cabinet.

But the plywood bottom could be popped out, using a pocket knife or screwdriver, and removed.

I did this now, using Carter's pocket knife to wedge into the gap where the edge met the side panels of the cabinet. I pried the floor upward, grasping it with one hand, and looked down the steel ladder that led to the maintenance tunnel of the building.

I climbed down the ladder, reaching up to close the cabinet door behind me, then letting the plywood bottom of the cabinet fall back into place as I went. If anyone happened to look—if they'd somehow manage to get into the safe house despite all the steel and other precautions—all they'd find was an empty cabinet, with pipes cutting through the floor. If they bothered to open the cabinet at all.

At the bottom of the ladder, a chamber opened up to about 1,900 square feet. Plenty of room for a maintenance crew to do their work. Plenty of space for a guy to hide out.

And all the amenities were present and accounted for. There was a small electric range and a microwave, for cooking meals, a small refrigerator and freezer, well stocked with frozen dinners and some non-perishables, and another working sink for washing up and supplying drinking water, if the bottled water ran out. I even installed a shower and toilet.

I could hide out down here for months.

Power was supplied courtesy of a half dozen extension cords routed to various buildings in the neighborhood. I had them cleverly hidden, usually tapping into outlets behind large, industrial equipment that wasn't going to move any time soon. Technically, I was stealing power. But probably less in a year than most people steal from Starbucks on any given day.

There were also the laptops.

I had a dozen or so computers stashed down here—high-powered and fast machines, but small and "disposable" if I needed to ditch them. I liked to keep my internet search history random and untraceable.

I still had the laptop I'd nicked from Henry. I set it up next to the stack of others, all charging quietly in a corner, and opened it up to look at the data Henry had been gathering on me.

I took the ERD and its reader out of my pocket and set these down on the table beside the laptop. I reconnected everything and opened the computer to see what was happening.

The data streaming across the screen didn't make any sense to me. But inner Henry recognized it.

Fascinating, he said.

"What does it mean? What do you have on me?"

Not me, Jaylin. I saved you back there.

"You saved *you* back there, Henry. Saving me was a side effect. So what is this?"

Engrammatic data, Henry said. *Brain scans. Yours, specifically. But there is some sort of cancellation wave built into the overall waveform. Or an attempt at one.*

"Cancellation wave?"

Think acoustics. If you want to dampen sound, you can

broadcast a frequency that is exactly opposite in waveform to the sound you're trying to cancel. It's the same way a white noise filter works. Two opposing waves cancel each other out. Annihilation waves.

"You were trying to cancel out my brainwaves?"

If I could sigh and roll my eyes, I would, Henry said, sounding exasperated nonetheless. *I'm not outer Henry. I didn't do this.*

"But he's building off of the information you both share. Your knowledge of me and my abilities. You were working on something like this, the whole time."

Henry said nothing. I didn't expect him to. Because after all this time, the game was finally being revealed, and he literally had nowhere to hide from me.

Well, technically he'd managed to hide right inside my own brain for the past couple of years. So there was that.

I already knew I couldn't trust Henry. But I'd gotten complacent.

"Henry, I'm in a tough spot here. Because you're the key to understanding what's going on and helping me figure out how to get out of this. But I have a feeling that trusting you is going to lead to me being erased and you getting a brand new body."

Is that what you think? After all these years? I would just wipe you out and take over?

"There have been attempts before."

Another pause. What could he say? It was true.

Just after Henry's engram had become permanent in my head, he had attempted a coup. He had been training himself the whole time we worked together, using what he knew about me and my ability to guide him. He was the one who had figured out that prolonged contact would lead to a permanent engram. He'd calculated exactly when it would happen and then lied to me about it. And he had used a series of psychological tricks and triggers and conditioning to try to make his engram dominant.

His hijacking attempt had failed—mostly because of Kristen. She'd taken up a spot in my brain long before Henry had taken his shot, and she'd been in a better position to push back, to keep him off balance while I reasserted my own control.

She'd saved me.

And since then, I had been wary of Henry and his motives, and had learned a few tricks of my own. No one was going to take over now. Not unless I wanted them to. Which, honestly, was just about the most unlikely thing I could imagine.

Jaylin, I promise, I am not trying to become the dominant engram. I've acclimated to this life. I like it. There are multiple benefits to keeping our arrangement just as it is.

I dropped into a large, plush chair, sagging and feeling the weariness build. This day had not turned out the way I had expected. It went further than even my paranoia could have compensated for.

Jacob's voice arose then. *You can't sleep yet. I know you're tired. But you're in danger. Carter is planning something.*

This made me perk up. I sat up straight, and then stood, rolling my neck and stomping my feet, getting the blood moving. I went to the electric kettle on the counter by the stove, filled it and got it boiling, and then prepped a double-strong serving of coffee in the French press.

It was time to have a talk with Carter.

"What's he doing?" I asked Jacob.

I'm not sure. I just know he's up to something. He's too quiet.

I thought about this. "Henry, would outer Henry have taught Carter some of the tricks you used, to try to become dominant?"

Inner Henry replied without hesitation, *Yes. Absolutely. I would have taught that, plus anything else I had learned, to anyone who might come in contact with you. A safeguard.*

"Safeguard," I said, shaking my head.

So the fight wasn't over yet.

"What do I do?"

Before I got an answer, though, the siege got started.

IT WASN'T PAINFUL. It wasn't even what you might expect from an attack. It was more like a persistent fever dream, or a really bad case of "song stuck in my head." It was a rhythm that kept repeating, and kept getting louder, more persistent.

There were a lot of the old triggers. Keywords, repeated over and over, attempting to engage the old conditioning that Henry had installed. But laid over this was a persistent attack using some of my own memories against me.

First, I was back in the chair, with straps around my arms and legs. This kept repeating and restarting, a loop of me being bound and helpless.

It's the freshest memory of fear you have, said Henry. *Remember, you escaped that. Don't give in to that fear!*

I heard him, even as I was struggling to calm myself. I started the Zen techniques that Kristen had taught me, controlling my breathing, focusing on a calming thought.

The memory shifted slightly.

I was still in the chair, but now the chair was in the woods, next to the stream where Kristen and I used to camp in the Spring. There was the sound of water flowing over rocks, of birds chirping in the early morning light. Sounds of nature filled my head.

It calmed me. It helped. But not enough.

Carter was adding to the imagery, folding in things that *could* have happened—a series of horrific events that kept getting worse, bloodier, more violent and frightening.

I saw images of my arms and legs being severed, of my helpless trunk laying strapped to a table, of a faceless assailant trimming me away, piece by piece.

I screamed.

Kristen's voice came then. *It's ok! Jaylin, you're ok! Breathe! I'm going to help.*

Suddenly the images changed.

I was no longer strapped to the chair, or in the woods by the stream. Instead I found myself on the subway.

The train was rocking gently, and the screech of brakes on metal took the place of screams in my mind.

Kristen was sitting next to me.

We were bundled against the cold, and I was feeling a little too warm. But I didn't move, I didn't even want to— because we were holding hands. Moving to take off my coat meant letting go. And since this date was the first date, and since that touch was the first time I'd really *known* Kristen, I didn't want to let go. Not ever.

"Our first date," Kristen said from beside me, looking into my eyes, smiling.

The figure of Kristen was moving and smiling, but it was the engram of Kristen that was talking.

"I remember," I said, quiet.

"This was before I knew," she said.

"Yes," I said. "I'm sorry."

"I've learned to live with it."

Suddenly I felt a sharp pain in my side, and I looked to see Carter sitting next to me on the train.

"You're not supposed to be here," I said.

"I'm everywhere you are now," Carter grinned. His hand was on the hilt of a knife, the blade plunged into my side, through my coat, past my ribs. He turned it, and I screamed.

And I was in bed.

Kristen was next to me again, only this time there was *nothing* between us.

I could feel the smoothness of her skin, the curve of her back under my palm. I could smell her—like cherry blossoms and wine. We'd had too much to drink, but this wasn't a drunken flurry of sex. This was something we had waited for. Hoped for.

I had stopped touching her, for weeks. She'd noticed. And when I told her what I could do, we got drunk and decided touching was something we could both live with.

The door burst open, and Carter was there. Splinters of wood were settling to the floor even as he raised the gun, aiming it at me from across the room. He pulled the trigger, and I could see the bullet move in slow motion toward me. I just couldn't move out of its path.

The world blurred. Shifted. Moved sideways.

Now we were in the park.

Kristen was on top of a large rock, taking a photo of me in front of the water and the bridge and the Manhattan skyline.

"I should be taking photos of you," I said.

"You have my memories in your head. This is the closest I can get to that. I want to see you everywhere."

I smiled.

This was the real conversation. The things we'd said on this day, while we were together in the park. Memories.

Behind Kristen, Carter walked up the slope of the rock.

I tried to shout but couldn't. I could only smile, the way I had smiled in the photo. I could only watch.

Carter had a long blade. He was moving toward Kristen, the blade extended.

I tried to scream.

Kristen shot my photo, and looked up, smiling. "Watch," she said.

And Carter passed through her, moving toward me.

And that's when I finally got it.

Carter couldn't see Kristen.

He could only see me.

Kristen could hide from him.

Which meant *I* could hide from him. Or...

It was like lucid dreaming—waking up inside the dream, suddenly realizing that you don't have to let the dream have control.

You have the control.

I knew exactly what to do.

I pictured it. I imagined it. And then, it became reality. As close to reality as you get, when everything you see is part of your mental landscape.

We were in a cell. It was the first time I'd been arrested, and I was scared. I didn't come here often, in memory. But it was easier to build from a memory, instead of trying to imagine a place from scratch.

This memory had always frightened me. I tried not to think of it.

But now I could use it.

Carter was there with me. The blade was gone. He was

staring at me. The anger in his eyes—the hate—was almost physical. I could *feel* it, like a hand around my throat.

"I will kill you," Carter said.

"You won't," I said. "You can't. You're here now. You're in this with me. You *are* me, now. Killing me will kill you, too. Get it? It's you and me, now. Us. You're home now."

Carter's face remained hard for a moment, his eyes glaring. And then his features started to relax. He started to grow smaller, softer. He was a child now, looking around at the cell, tears in his eyes.

"I don't want to be here," the boy Carter said. "I don't want to be dead."

I felt the wave of emotion radiating off of him. Anger had been a sharp, pulsing feeling. It had been huge, like an immense wave, a tsunami washing over me. But this was smaller. Softer. Somehow more painful.

This was fear, but something else.

Anguish. Loss. An existential suffering like nothing I'd ever felt before.

I'd never experienced anything like it. I wasn't prepared for it. But I had to deal with the fact that it could be some kind of trick.

"You won't be here for long," I said, trying to let the fear pass over me. "This is temporary. This cell isn't real. Nothing you see is real. There's nothing to be afraid of here."

"Not here," Carter said, and his voice was a hard, grown-up voice, coming from his small, soft child body. "I don't want to be *in your head*. I don't want to be in your collection of dead people. I want to be *me* again."

"I'm sorry," I said. "I'm so sorry. But that can't be helped. This is it, now."

I was on the other side of the bars now, looking in.

Carter—full grown Carter—was in the cell, looking out. His eyes looked hollow, like there was something missing behind them. Like I was just seeing the shell of the man named Carter. Like he was hollow inside.

"You'll stay here until you've accepted it," I said.

Carter stared at me, his hate and anger replaced by something else. Something empty.

The loss of hope.

I turned away—to stop seeing him, more than anything. When I turned away, however, I was suddenly in a different place. It took a moment for the fact of it to register.

I was standing in the below-ground chamber of my safe house.

The real world.

Whatever that meant.

The electric kettle was whistling, demanding that I pay attention. I took hold of the handle, lifting it from its base. I stared at it for a long moment, before finally shaking off the image of Carter's half-empty stare.

I poured hot water over the coffee grounds in the French Press and set a timer to four minutes.

As I placed the kettle back on its base, I stared at the polished surface, seeing a distorted version of my own face there. My own eyes.

I sobbed once, then turned away.

CHAPTER NINE

—————————

First, we should find Mr. McClellan, Henry said.

"You don't think that's the first thing they'll expect me to do? Besides, I'm pretty sure McClellan is dead by now."

I don't mean that we should go to him. I mean we should look for his obituary.

That made sense. Chances were we wouldn't find the truth about how he died, but there was a lot we could learn from the cover story.

I logged on to the Wi-Fi from one of the local businesses. I had used the skills of multiple hackers to help me crack router passwords and set up relays to funnel a signal down to the basement. For a further layer of protection I used a VPN to access Google through a remote server on the other side of the planet. It was a bit slower than a direct link, but it would keep anyone watching for this particular search from pinpointing my location immediately.

I found the obit right away:

. . .

"ANDREW MCCLELLAN, *age 42, was found dead in his apartment on Wednesday. Police have pronounced his death a suicide, citing that his bloodstream contained high levels of alcohol and sleeping pills. McClellan was an executive with Shallister Hoffman, a consulting agency and think tank with ties to the national defense department. Representatives for Shallister Hoffman have stated they were not aware of McClellan's mental and emotional state, and his death is felt as a great loss within the organization."*

BOOZE AND SLEEPING PILLS. At least they'd given him a peaceful exit. And it meant that they wanted this to stay low profile. Murdering him in some bloody or grue-some way would have meant a police investigation. Suicides didn't get quite as much scrutiny.

The story didn't offer much in the way of clues. I still had nothing to explain McClellan's involvement in all of this.

He was an executive with a consulting agency and think tank that had ties to the department of defense, and his father was a terrorist working for the IRA, Henry said. *They were building a believable story.*

"What about the President? How'd they pull that off? McClellan *believed* he'd met with the President."

I'm sure he did, Henry said. *Which meant you believed it, too. Outer Henry played you. He knew you'd only trust your first-hand experience, and even that only so far. You're tough to fool, especially if you get a chance to brush a hand against some exposed skin. But fooling someone is easy, if you meet their expectations. People make a lot of assump-tions, and they fill the gaps in their experience with those assumptions.*

I thought about this for a moment. "You're saying that outer Henry, and whoever he's working for, set up a meeting that made McClellan *assume* he was talking to the President."

Your notes said that the President had no knowledge of McClellan. So he couldn't have been the one talking to him. Do we know how this meeting with the President took place?

I shook my head. "No. Those memories are long gone. And there's nothing in my notes about the meeting itself. That wasn't the information I needed to record."

Outer Henry would have counted on that, inner Henry said.

He was right.

"He knows how I think. He knows exactly how to manipulate me." I slumped back, feeling miserable. "He played me, and Andrew McClellan was killed for it."

Don't start feeling sorry for yourself, Jaylin, inner Henry said. *We have work to do.*

I felt resentful at that. I wasn't feeling sorry for *me*. I was feeling guilty for having been the reason McClellan was killed.

But after a moment, I let it pass. Because Henry was right about one thing, at least. I couldn't stay hidden here indefinitely. Sooner or later I would have to get back out on the streets. I would have to find out who was after me, so I could make a plan to avoid them.

Maybe it's time you leave the city, Kristen's voice said.

"Maybe," I said.

Henry spoke up, *Running isn't going to solve this. Whoever outer Henry has affiliated himself with, they have resources. Money and power. Operatives. They want you, Jaylin. They won't stop until they have you.*

I settled back in the chair, staring at the laptop in front

of me. To the side was the laptop from Henry's makeshift torture chamber-slash-lab. The ERD was sitting on the table next to it.

I picked it up and studied it, feeling the weight of it in my palm.

"Henry said this could do what I do. It could record engrams. Why does it only work on me?"

I wouldn't call that working *exactly.*

"You interfered. You did something. What did you do?"

I fed it the wrong frequency, Henry said, and I could sense his shrug. *The suppression wave it uses is tuned to your engram, specifically. It was meant to shut your engram down, cancel it out with a counter wave, and then replicate and record it. Outer Henry was after the knowledge he'd need to get to your notes. He wants the information you stole from the President.*

"His employer wants it," I corrected. "I think Henry just wants to try out his new toy. Maybe find a way to give himself my abilities."

Likely, Henry said. *It's what I would do.*

"But you stopped him by getting in the way," I said. "Self preservation."

That's me. Only out to save myself.

I thought about this. "Crap," I said.

Henry said nothing, but Kristen piped up. *What is it? What have you realized?*

"I should have known better," I said. "Henry, you're a son of a bitch."

What is it? Kristen asked again.

I shook my head. "Henry—inner Henry—wasn't trying to save me. He was trying to escape."

Again, silence.

Is that true? Kristen asked, and I knew she was directing the question to Henry.

There was a brief hesitation.

Only partially, Henry admitted. *I thought I could hitch a ride back, while also blocking outer Henry from gaining access to the President's data.*

"Sure," I said. "I believe you, no question."

It's true, Jaylin. I swear it.

"Why?" I asked. I didn't believe him, but getting his answer might give me some clue as to his real motives.

Outer Henry would get what he was really after, while whoever he's working for would be denied a chance to do whatever damage he or she is trying to do.

"Wait, what is Henry after, if not this information?" I asked.

Knowledge. He wants to know how you do what you do, and how it really works. I could give him inside information. He'd know, from personal experience, exactly how your abilities work. That would help in perfecting his technology.

I hated to admit it—I still wasn't sure I even believed it—but it made sense. Inner Henry was definitely out to save himself, more than anything. I could count on that. But that didn't necessarily mean he was lying. In fact, he had no reason to lie about this, particularly. He'd come right out and given me his motive. Probably because he had nothing to lose, but might gain my trust.

Fat chance of that.

Honesty didn't change the fact that Henry's plan for self-preservation was maybe the most dangerous outcome I could think of.

Inner Henry knew pretty much all of my secrets. If that knowledge got out, all my precautions and safeties would be compromised. I'd be good and screwed. Forget leaving the city, I could leave the *planet* and I still wouldn't be safe.

I'm not really out to get you, Jaylin, Henry said. *I promise.*

"So being strapped down to a table and tortured was just a way for us to bond?" I asked.

I can't control what outer me does. You know that. But if I could get back in his head, I could possibly figure out a way to fix this.

"Or turn me over and use the President's data as a bargaining chip," I said.

Honestly, Jaylin. I never realized you had such a low opinion of me.

"Then you haven't really been paying attention, Henry."

Kristen's voice piped up. *Jaylin, please. Don't be cruel. Henry has helped you, when he could. We're all here, together.*

Except that Kristen, too, would leave if she could. There were times—many times—when I felt her bitterness and anger at being trapped in my mind. Those were the hard times, the moments that made me regret everything. Was it worth it, the time I spent with Kristen? Just to have her hate me in the end?

I don't, she said. *Not really. Not ever. I just felt betrayed.*

I cursed myself. I'd let my guard down, dropped the compartmentalization, and my own thoughts must have bled through. It happened sometimes—when I was tired, when I was dealing with something that I thought might overwhelm me.

Who else in my head might have heard this conversation? Carter? Jacob? Caleb? What about...

I didn't think about it. I would just have to keep my

guard up from now on. Keep my thoughts siloed. Apparently, with outer Henry out there making brain zapping jelly donuts, it was more important than ever to keep secrets, even from my own inner voices.

Especially from inner Henry.

What's next? Kristen asked, obviously wanting to change the subject. And I was grateful for that small mercy.

"I honestly don't know," I said. "I think we could be safe here, for a while. But I don't really know what to do next."

Can I make a suggestion? Jacob asked.

His was a voice I didn't hear often. He kept quiet, content with living in the background. So when he spoke, all of us listened.

Take a look at the President's data and see if you can figure out what Henry and his employer are after. That might give you clues as to who you're dealing with. Until you know who's after you, there's no way to plan.

Henry said, "*If you know the enemy better than you know yourself, the outcome of the battle has already been decided.*" Sun Tzu, The Art of War. *Very good, Jacob. You're right. We need to know our enemy before we make a move.*

"We?" I asked.

Of course, Jaylin. No matter what else may have happened, I'm literally in this with you.

"Until you find a way to escape and get back into outer Henry's head?

There was a brief pause, *Yes, until then.*

At least he was finally being honest.

THE INFORMATION WAS NOT AS thorough as usual. I was limited to the capabilities of the phone, at the time.

My ability to hyper-multi-task didn't really come into play when all I had to work with was a smartphone keyboard. But I did manage to capture a great deal of useable data.

There is some truly scary stuff here, Jacob said.

Kristen replied, *But which part of it is the information outer Henry was after?*

I shook my head. "Could be anything."

Could be everything, Henry said. *We have no real point of reference. No way to narrow things down.*

Oh, Jacob said, *we do, actually.*

I blinked, thinking. "Carter," I finally said. Though just saying his name gave me a sickening twist in my guts.

He'd gone quiet since we'd locked him away. I had a feeling he was just waiting for an opening. But I also felt like he needed the time. He'd been a tough guy, in life. But this situation—there wasn't really a way to prepare for something like this. That would be hard on anyone. It was reason enough to leave him alone.

But leaving him alone was a luxury none of us could afford.

I sat up in my chair, rolling my neck to relax the tension there, and did some deep breathing exercises that Kristen had taught me. "I can go in. Use the jail setting. He's still pretty new, so he may not have acclimated yet. He may still be thinking in terms of the outer world. We might be able to fool him into thinking he can get out, if he cooperates. Cut him a deal."

Are we really going to trust anything this guy says? Henry asked.

Actually, Jacob replied, *I think he needs to see a familiar face. Someone he trusts. At least to a degree.*

I thought about this for a second. "Henry? You want to send Henry in?"

He knows outer Henry, Jacob said. *If he's still a little confused, he might fall for it.*

I see no reason why this couldn't work, Henry said.

"Great. Just the assurance I needed. The guy who wants to turn me over to be tortured feels confident in our plan."

It's the best plan we have, Jaylin, Kristen said. *And right now, this is Henry's best chance to protect himself.*

"So once again, we're depending on Henry's sense of self preservation to keep us all safe."

You know, I'm right here, Henry said, sounding a bit hurt. *And I'm not really a bad guy.*

Save it, Jacob said. *If this has any chance of working, we need to act now.*

I agreed and again started to relax myself.

There are no actual "places" in my mind. But there is a sort of mind map there, filled with all sorts of virtual environments. One of the perks of my ability is being able to visualize in amazing detail. Having the combined mental acuity of several people in your head does have its advantages.

Any place I can visualize or remember can be constructed, right down to the finer details such as smell, texture, even taste—if, for example, you wanted to lick the walls of your jail cell for some reason. Or eat a burger. That counts, too.

When we locked Carter into his cell, I essentially created a tiny bubble of reality for him, and locked him inside. Basically, I created a memory—a symbolic version of the cell, with his engram attached to it. Over time, he would be able to escape that bubble, unless I made a conscious effort to keep reinforcing it. That's how I sometimes kept another troublesome personality at bay, anyway.

I visualized the cell and added to that the memories I had of one of the interrogation rooms. I moved Carter to the interrogation room, rousing him from a sort of hypnotic state in which I kept feeding him suggestions, like telling him that guards had come and moved him to the room.

It was flimsy stuff. If he concentrated too hard, he'd see through it. But he had no reason to question it, given that he'd been in a cell and now was in an interrogation room. Logically, somehow, he had to have been moved there.

Our minds will accept any string of facts, even if they're illogical, if we have no other explanation to fall back on.

Carter was still acclimating to being part of my merry band of mental projections, so the hope was that he would be disoriented enough to believe he was out, in the real world, in a real police station. I layered as much physical detail as I could think of, to keep that feeling of "realness" strong. Smells, textures, the sound of people in other rooms, the chill of the air conditioning. Even a cup of coffee, a little too hot and a little too burnt to enjoy.

There was a two-way mirror in the interrogation room. Honestly, I couldn't remember if one appeared in the *real* interrogation room, so I used memories of cop shows and movies to fill in the details.

I stood on the outer side of that glass, watching Carter as he sat, handcuffed to a table. Beside me, vague but recognizable if I focused, were the engrams of Kristen, Jacob, and Henry.

Henry went into the room and took a seat.

As he entered, suddenly he went from vague to distinct. My imagination had plenty of material to work from, regarding Henry. But it was my most recent memories of him that needed to feed this scenario.

At the last second, before Henry took his seat, I remembered the cane, and the prosthetic leg. I created them, working them in smoothly. From Carter's vantage point, he would have "just noticed." The cane and the leg were details that he could latch on to, making this vision more real to him.

In theory. It wasn't like we'd done this before.

"Carter," Henry said, taking his seat.

"Doc. I... my head's a little fuzzy." Carter looked around. "I... think I died."

Henry chuckled. "Don't be ridiculous, Carter. You were drugged. It will pass. But I need to know you weren't compromised. I've managed to bribe the officers to turn off the cameras and to keep the observation room clear. So we're safe to chat. You'll have to verify a few facts for me. Understood?"

Carter nodded. "Where are we?"

"A precinct interrogation room. Things went wrong. The subject escaped."

"He... he did? Wait... he used a toilet tank lid..."

Henry interrupted, getting Carter's memory off track. "Verify for me what our mission was with the subject. What were we after?"

Carter looked up, his expression a mixture of confusion and anger. "What?"

"We had the subject strapped down, and my attempt to use the ERD had failed. I left, and the subject escaped, with you in pursuit. You're confused right now, Carter. But I need you to verify these details, or I can't help you to get out of here."

"Get out? I can get out?"

"If you help me," Henry said. "Tell me, what were we after?"

Carter looked away, glancing at the mirror first, and

then down at the table. "I don't know the particulars," he said. "I know we were after something he learned from the President."

"I need more than that," Henry said. "Who is our employer?"

"What? You know that."

"I need you to verify," Henry said.

Carter nodded. "Emil Lyon," he said.

The name meant nothing to me, but Henry apparently recognized it. I saw him glance at the mirror. "Very good," he said. "Now, is Mr. Lyon in the city at this time?"

"Yes."

"At his usual apartment?"

"Yes," Carter said.

"How long has he been in town?" Henry asked.

"Only a week."

"And how long have I worked for him?"

"Since he got you out of prison. About a month."

Henry nodded. "This all checks out," he said. "Just one more question, Carter. When is Emil Lyon going to China?"

This threw me. How did Henry know that Lyon would go to China? Who was this guy?

Carter replied, "He leaves in two days."

Henry nodded, then stood, leaning on the cane. "I'll start making arrangements for your release," he said, and then hobbled out.

"Wait!" Carter said, standing. The handcuffs pulled him up short, forcing him to stoop. "Wait... am I... did I die? Am I dead? I remember something. The training. You trained me to deal with the guy. Evergreen. I remember..."

"Just wait here, Carter," Henry said. "A guard will take

you back to your cell in a moment." And with that, Henry stepped out of the room.

I implanted another hypnotic suggestion, and transitioned Carter back to the cell, then I dismantled the vision, leaving only the bubble.

I opened my eyes to a room that wasn't much different from the cell Carter occupied.

"Who is Emil Lyon?" I asked.

Someone very dangerous, Henry replied. *Someone I never thought I'd end up working with.*

CHAPTER TEN

Emil Lyon is the majority shareholder of Shallister Hoffman, Henry said.

"Wait... the same Shallister Hoffman where Drew McClellan was an executive?"

The same, Henry replied.

"And you know him?" I asked.

We've had occasion to do business together, in the past, Henry said.

Let me get this straight, Kristen said. *You've had a connection to this the whole time, but decided not to mention it?*

I wouldn't call it a connection, Henry replied. *I had no reason to think that Lyon was in any way a part of this. I recognized the company name—Shallister Hoffman. But that's as far as it went. As far as I knew it was just a coincidence.*

"Some coincidence," I said. "I get kidnapped and tortured—by *you* I might add—and turns out it's in the name of one of your old buddies."

Emil Lyon is most certainly not *an "old buddy." The last*

time I had dealings with him, I lost my tenure and my facil-
ity, and ended up having to scrounge a living on the streets.

I thought about this for a moment. "This is the guy who booted you? He's the one who closed your lab?"

Yes, Henry said.

Jacob piped up. *Seems like you two have made up,* he said. *I wonder what would have brought you kids back together?*

Henry said nothing, which said volumes.

"He wanted something. You refused. And when went to prison, suddenly you realized you had a bargaining chip. It's been a few years since you went in, so I'm guessing that Lyon wanted you good and softened up."

Could we stop referring to outer Henry as "me?" I didn't do any of the things you're accusing me of.

But a version of you did, Jacob said.

And now he wants Jaylin, Kristen said. *For what?*

I promise you, I have no idea, Henry replied.

"Now that's a lie," I said. "Because as soon as Carter mentioned Emil Lyon, you went off script. You asked about China."

Henry said nothing for a moment.

"What's the story, Henry? What did you realize?"

Go back to the President's Data, Henry said.

I opened the file we had compiled while reviewing the recordings and audio transcripts. The notes were well organized now, broken down into bullets by topic.

Search for "China."

I searched. Three entries contained the word China. The first was about a recent visit that was largely a goodwill tour, a meet-and-greet with some of China's officials. The second was about the President's concerns over China blocking or restricting internet traffic. And the third was a mention of China's plans to place a base on the moon within ten years.

"Is it the moon thing?" I asked. "Is Lyon planning to do something with China's space program? Launch missiles or something?"

I don't see faces for my mental passengers, most of the time. Instead, I sort of *feel* their expressions. At that moment, I felt Henry roll his non-existent eyes.

Why would Emil Lyon want to launch missiles? He's not a terrorist. He's a business man.

So what is he after? Kristen asked, and I could tell she was getting impatient with Henry. So was I.

The key is that internet blockage, Henry said.

I looked closer at that note. "There isn't much here," I said. "Some websites that will be blocked or restricted. Something called Paradigm."

Paradigm is the name of a company working on advanced data compression. The Chinese acquired the company and moved it inside their borders. I was part of the project, back before I lost my tenure and my job. Emil Lyon tried to use me as an inside man with the project. A sort of corporate espionage play. I was caught and got the boot.

"So what's his play now? What does the President know that will help him?"

Second sub-bullet. Third sentence.

I looked and read. "Paradigm ER compression confirmed."

I shook my head. "I don't get it."

I should have, right away. I knew this was what Emil was after. I knew the US government was interested, too. The Chinese are restricting access. Meaning they've got it working.

"Got what working?" I asked.

ER. Engrammatic Replication.

I blinked. "Like the ERD? The donut that outer Henry used on me?"

Except theirs can compress the engram of a person enough to put it on the internet.

Lyon wants to put people's brains on the internet? Jacob asked.

Henry chuckled, which as an odd sensation from within.

Not exactly, he said. *Emil Lyon is trying to create an immortality machine.*

IT HADN'T BEEN a full 24 hours since I'd managed to escape—oh, and since I'd *murdered* someone.

I played it as cautious as I could, but it still felt wrong to be out in the open. I wasn't sure just how powerful this Emil Lyon guy was, but from what Henry had told me, and based on recent experience, he at least had the means and resources to track me down.

Everyone I passed, every security camera I saw or didn't see—I didn't like being so vulnerable.

We only have two days, Henry said, his voice startling me. I was moving cautiously, trying to keep a lower profile than even I usually kept. *Once Emil is out of the country, our window is gone.*

"I still don't see how walking into the literal Lyon's den is a good plan," I whispered. It was easier to keep things straight if I could speak aloud, but talking to myself did tend to attract attention in public. Thank God for Bluetooth earbuds. Perfect camouflage. I had the brightest, whitest set

I could find in my ears, to give anyone watching or listening an easy excuse to ignore me.

"Wouldn't it be better to wait this out and let Emil go to China empty handed?"

We need to know what he already knows, Henry said. *If he's leaving in two days, it means he has something. The information you were hired to retrieve from the President was a confirmation, not a data grab.*

That seemed right. "So why bother grabbing me? Seems like Lyon has the means to get that information without having me steal it from the President."

I think the President was just a bonus, Henry said. *What he's really after is you. Or, rather, your abilities. Having you go after such a high-profile target played right into his plans, putting you out in the open, at a time and place he could predict. But more than that, Lyon wants Henry to perfect the ERD. That technology is going to be his biggest bargaining chip with the Chinese. Henry needs you in order to pull that off.*

"But the ERD is locked up, back at the safe house."

Do you really think that's the only prototype? Outer Henry would have multiple units ready, and the plans to build more besides. That's why we have to risk this. We have to know how much trouble outer Henry is in. How much we're all in.

I knew he was right. Despite my gut screaming that we should wait things out, to hide until this all blew over, I knew that if Henry had built a bunch of ERDs, using what he had learned from studying me, it could only lead to bad things.

We took the subway, which is something I normally avoid, for multiple reasons. For a start, as crowded as it is, the chances of me making skin-to-skin contact with a bunch of random strangers are pretty high.

Maybe you should reconsider living in a city with eight million people, Kristen said.

That was my conundrum. New York City was both my curse and my bounty.

Living here meant being at risk of contact, all the time. The streets were nearly always full of people. Going anyplace was an exercise in dodging and weaving, all while trying to make it look natural and not at all attention-grabbing weird. Luckily, New York has more than its fair share of eccentric types. A guy with a phobia about touching other people is just your average day here. Still, living in New York meant living under the constant threat that my abilities might get the better of me.

Not living here, though, meant being exposed. Living anywhere but in the city–to my mind, at least–meant living out in the open with fewer places to hide. In the city I can blend in, hide. Out of the city, I'd stand out. I'd read as peculiar. I'd get noticed.

Or maybe that was just my excuse.

New York was home, after all. I grew up here. I knew this place, possibly better than anyone else alive. I'd seen it inside and out, up and down, even through the eyes of other people—literally.

Leaving would mean starting over at zero.

Leaving would mean being completely on my own—no resources, no safe houses, nothing I was used to or depended on.

I was already alone in the world. As alone as you can be when you have five other people's memories and personalities in your head. The idea of leaving New York felt a little like dying.

Whatever. I didn't have the bandwidth to think about it at the moment. I had an insane mission to complete.

The subway arrived at my stop and I exited into a crowd. Pushing through, pulling my hood tight and avoiding picking up any spare engrams, I made my way to the surface streets and walked the three remaining blocks to the Shallister Hoffman offices.

The building was the usual tower of glass, steel, and concrete that you'd expect. The lobby had a series of rotating glass doors that funneled you directly to a front desk, manned by guards who looked less than thrilled to be there at this time of night.

"It's late," I said, checking the burner phone to get the time. "Nearly 11 p.m. Are you sure Lyon will be here?"

There are executive apartments on the top floors. Emil's penthouse is at the very top.

"You've been there?"

When you're making a deal with the devil, you sometimes find yourself standing before him on his own turf.

"Great," I said. "So at least you know the layout. Do you happen to know the way up?"

There are elevators in the lobby. Possibly a service elevator or two in the back, with the loading docks.

I groaned. "This will only end with me being shot at," I said.

I think we can avoid that, Henry replied. *It may require you to do a multiple.*

I cringed.

"Do a multiple" was shorthand for "absorb multiple engrams." It's something I try to avoid, most of the time. All the time, actually. Because having more than one "fresh" engram in my head makes things very confusing. My thinking gets muddled. Two or more separate, disoriented personalities, trying to figure out where they are and how they got there, and trying to assert control at the same time —it's a little noisy. And exhausting.

"What's the plan?"

Touch one of the guards to get the elevator code for the penthouse, Henry said. *And to get the lay of the place, to help us find a way in.*

"Ok, that's one engram. What's the other?"

Touch Lyon's assistant, Sol Rydell. He's going to be pretty suspicious of you, so you'll have to have a cover story. But we need his knowledge of the penthouse and its own access code.

"Cover story..." I said. "What possible cover story could I come up with that's going to explain why I'm in that building at 11 p.m.?"

Caleb—the "kid" who rarely spoke up—was the one who had the answer.

Look to your left.

I looked left.

One block over was the shining beacon of late night hope and bounty recognized and coveted most by university students everywhere. The one thing that never, ever shut down in New York City. The single, unquestioned reason for anyone to be anywhere, ever.

The sign glowed into the night, and into my heart.

"Pizza?" I asked, smiling. "Isn't that a little cliché?"

Aren't clichés those things that people use because they work? Caleb asked.

I smiled. "Caleb, you don't talk much. But when you do..."

Henry interrupted, *I don't see how this will work. Emil Lyon is not the type of man who eats pizza.*

Jacob said, *No one lives on caviar and goose livers alone.*

Wait... is Lyon a vegetarian? Because that would be hilarious.

Not to my knowledge, Henry said. There was a pause as he considered. *Very well. In lieu of any other plans, pizza it is.*

I went into the pizza parlor and ordered. A short time later I was carrying a box with the pie through the rotating doors of the Shallister Hoffman building. Quite a feat in itself, navigating a cylinder of glass with a square pizza box. But I somehow managed to pull it off without dropping the thing.

The guards watched me as I fumbled my way through. At least one guard was off to the side, his hand on the butt of a pistol. I made my way to the desk where two guards sat, looking a lot less bored and a lot more alert than they were a few seconds ago.

"Delivery for Rory Pond," I said, affecting my best Bronx accent.

What's with the accent? Henry asked.

I'm trying to get into character, I replied.

Stop it. Stop it now.

"Nobody by that name here," one of the guards said. "You got the wrong address, pal."

I looked down at the slip of paper stuck to the top of the pizza box. It did, indeed, say "Rory Pond" on it, just in case anyone looked. I'd scribbled it there myself, along with this address. "Nobody here ordered the Centurion?"

"I don't even know what that is," said the guard. "Now, leave before we *escort* you to the street."

I didn't like the sound of that "escort."

"My mistake, pal. I'll move along. No trouble, ok? No hard feelings?" I stuck out my hand.

On reflex the guard took my hand, giving it a weak and dismissive shake.

Engram acquired. And it was a somewhat quiet one, thank God. Only one quick question—*What'd you just do to me?*—and I had him siloed and cut off.

We were back out on the street after once more awkwardly making my way out of the rotating doors. I walked a bit to get out of view, and to avoid the two cameras hidden in domed mounts on the corners of the building. I knew where they were now. I knew the layout of the whole building.

Now what? Kristen asked.

"Now we use one of those service elevators in the back. But we have to watch for a bit, to see if the two guards on duty back there have started talking about baseball yet."

Jacob said, *It's good when they bring their own distraction.*

I came at the building from an angle, exploiting what Jim—our newly acquired engram—thought of as "the smoking hole." This was the spot where he and other building employees would sneak to for a cigarette, which was against building policy and city codes. Too close to one of the doors. But when ya gotta smoke...

That door was my way in.

There was a keypad on the outside—metal, the numbers still readable but covered in years of grime and dirt. I pulled one of my gloves back on before punching in the code and listening for the click of the door's lock.

Still carrying the pizza, I moved quickly through the hall, which would lead me to the loading docks in the back of the building. There would be one spot where I'd have to move quickly to get out of range of the camera before someone spotted me. The risk of being seen was low, but still higher than I liked. All it would take was one guard looking at the wrong monitor at the wrong time, and I'd be cooked.

I glanced at the camera just before passing under it, then moved at a brisk but constant pace, hoping that if someone *did* spot me, they'd just assume I worked there. I held the pizza box in front of me, close, so that it would be obscured on the camera.

I could feel sweat dripping from my armpits as the stress started to get to me. I used some of Kristen's Zen breathing to try to calm myself, even as I hurried down the corridor to the metal door at the end. It sort of worked. Xanax might have been better.

A quick glance through the window in the door showed that no one was on the other side. I punched in the security code, opened the door, and made my way through while managing to keep myself from glancing back at the camera. If they were watching, hopefully the fact that I obviously knew the door code would be enough to put them at ease.

Once through the door, I found I was in a large bay, like a giant garage. There were roll-up doors on one side, and two of the doors were down, but one was up. A truck was backed onto the concrete ramp that led to the unloading zone. Two guys were moving boxes from the truck using hand trucks, stacking the boxes against a set of metal shelves. They weren't paying attention, and so I managed to walk past them by hugging the wall opposite the bay doors.

I came to the edge of a large, clear glass window, though, and stopped.

The window led into a small office, where the two guards were sitting and talking. They were animated in their discussion, which Jim's engram recognized as "baseball talk."

Great, Henry said. *They're distracted. But they're looking our way. What now?*

I looked around, trying to see a path through that wouldn't get us nabbed. Jim's engram was drawing a blank on routes that might take me around.

It was either walk past this window, or go back the way we came. Back, down that long hallway, with the video camera aimed directly at my face the whole time.

Might as well walk right to a jail cell.

There was only one way through, and it was past this window.

Could we crawl past? Caleb asked.

I don't think so, Jacob responded. *It would look a little suspicious if those guys at the loading bay see a pizza guy crawling past a window.*

So what do we do? Kristen asked.

I thought for a moment, looking around, my thoughts getting desperate.

Wait, I thought. *What if we don't go around? What if we go through?*

Without waiting for anyone to respond, I stepped out from the edge and knocked on the window, waving and smiling as the guards abruptly stopped their conversation and stood up.

I walked past the window and stopped at the door on the side of the office. One of the guards—Paul, from Jim's memory—opened the door. "Can I help you?"

"Emil Lyon sent this down. He said it was for Paul and Tony. You know where I can find those guys?"

"That's us," Tony said, peering over Paul's shoulder at the box of pizza. I opened it so they could get a look. "Large with everything, guys. Compliments of the boss."

"Ain't that somethin'," Paul said, grinning. "Ten years I been here, and never even met Mr. Lyon."

"Well don't get too sentimental," I said. "It ain't the only pie I've delivered here tonight. I just dropped one off for Jim and Clarence, and I have to take two up for Sol and Mr. Lyon himself. Mr. Lyon is watching the game, up in his luxury penthouse. Must be nice."

The two guards smiled and nodded. "Must be, right? Still, at least he made a gesture."

The guys took the pie and had it on the desk in front of them. I waved at them one last time and walked through the door opposite of the one I had used to get in here. Neither guard seemed to notice or care that I didn't have two more pizzas in my hands.

The door I used was a large, swinging door that led to the service elevators. According to Jim's memories, camera coverage was a little light in this spot. Maybe because there were two guards watching it the whole time.

I stood in the grungy elevator bay until a large freight elevator came down from three floors up, and I stepped on, hitting the top-most button I could. It would only take me to the fifth floor, but from there I could get onto one of the secure inner elevators, using the code.

So far, so good. No one came rushing toward me. No alarms sounded.

Pizza, once again, saved the day.

That was incredibly risky, Henry said.

He didn't have to say it. We could all feel my heart pounding, and the tightness in my chest, making it tougher to breathe. Sweat was cutting streams from my armpits to my waistline. And my head was pounding.

It really had been risky. But it had worked. We were in.

Here we go, Jacob said.

"Here we go," I replied.

CHAPTER ELEVEN

WITHOUT THE PIZZA, MY BUILT-IN COVER STORY WAS gone. I'd have to come up with something else on the fly.

I had an idea.

On the fifteenth floor I moved past the secure elevator and into the janitorial room, next to the electrical service door. Jim's memory of the building's layout stopped outside the door, so I had no idea what I would find inside. But I did know it was camera free. A good place to stop and regroup for a second.

The janitorial staff was long gone by this time of night. They'd be back early in the morning to do some cleanup before the building was teeming with people again. Jim knew all the routines and schedules of the janitors who worked here. But maybe Sol Rydell didn't.

There was no smock or apron or anything in the closet that I could use to change how I looked. But there was a rolling cart filled with cleaning supplies and a large waste bag hanging from the front of it. A broom and dustpan stuck out from the handle.

It wasn't a perfect cover, but it might do.

I took off my hoodie, emptying its pockets and wadding it up to put it in the trash bag at the front of the cart. I slid the burner phone into the front pocket of my jeans and rolled up my sleeves. I replaced my leather gloves with rubber ones.

As disguises went, it wasn't the best. In fact, I felt pretty vulnerable, with the skin of my forearms exposed. But it was all I could manage with what I had.

"I hope this is worth it," I said. "We've gone to a lot of trouble to get in here. Which seems a little counterintuitive. This is the guy who had me kidnapped in the first place."

Which is exactly why he won't be expecting a full frontal assault, Jacob said.

"Not much of an assault. What do I do when I get to him? *If* I get to him?"

You do your thing, Jacob said. *Absorb him.*

He's right, Henry said. *We need to know what Emil knows. This is the only way.*

"I can think of other ways," I said. "Running, for example. I could be in a car for LaGuardia in ten minutes."

And you'd be running for the rest of your life, Jacob said.

"I never thought I'd see the day when you and Henry agreed on something," I said.

Allies and enemies—it's a gray line when you're in the soup.

That, I had to admit, was very true.

I pushed the cart out of the closet and made my way to the secure elevator bank. I rolled up to the elevator that would take me straight to the penthouse lobby and punched the code, rolling in as soon as the doors opened.

Time was starting to tick down on Jim's engram. Which was good. It meant I might not have to pull a multiple after all. And from what Jim knew about Sol

Rydell, that might be a good thing. He seemed to be a strong personality.

Another thought occurred to me...

Henry—*outer* Henry—had trained Carter to go on the offensive, if he was absorbed. It had been a battle inside my head, during which I was a bit incapacitated.

Carter had been dead, at the time. Rydell wouldn't be. If I suddenly went catatonic after touching him, he'd have me. I'd be done.

"I think we've made a huge mistake," I said.

What? Henry asked. *Why?*

Which part? Kristen asked. *From where I am, it looks like we've been making huge mistakes all night.*

"If Sol Rydell has the same training that Carter had, we could be screwed if I touch him."

There was a pause.

I see what you mean, Henry said. *But he's the only one who will know the code to get into the penthouse. Without his knowledge, this will fail.*

Can't you silo him? Jacob asked.

"Normally, yes. But Carter was able to put up a pretty good fight, before I had him locked away. His engram is permanent, so maybe it's stronger. But while I'm dealing with Sol's engram, outer Sol will see me go blank. He'll know something's up, and he'll be able to take me down."

So what if I take out inner Sol while you deal with outer Sol? Jacob asked.

That was intriguing. "I'm not sure. We've never tried that. This is all new."

Worth a shot, Jacob said.

Whatever was going to happen, it was going to happen in the next few minutes. The elevator rose to the penthouse, and the doors slid open quietly.

Mistake or not, this was it.

I rolled out of the elevator, cart in front of me, and looked around.

"Well, I definitely wasn't expecting this," a voice said.

I looked to my left and saw Sol Rydell dressed in a dark suit and tie. He was wearing gloves. Aside from his face, there wasn't a speck of skin exposed.

He knows who I am, I thought.

Keep calm, Henry said.

Keep the cart between you and him, Jacob said.

I did both.

"Evergreen," Sol said. "We have men looking for you all over the city, and you roll in here like you're about to give the place a dust and polish. You got balls, kid."

He reached into his jacket and pulled a handgun from a hidden holster. "Don't make me take them off. Mr. Lyon doesn't like things to get messy in his own home."

"I'm just the cleaning crew," I said, ducking a bit behind the cart. "Just here to clean up, that's all!"

Sol laughed. "Seriously? I literally just called you out, kid. You're done. Get on the floor, face down, hands at your sides."

Don't do it, Jacob said.

I'm not seeing that I have any other choice! I replied.

But turns out I had more of a choice than I'd thought.

Suddenly, I felt my adrenaline spike. Actually, it was more than that. I could feel a heat rush up from inside of me. Anger. Rage. But a calm rage. Calculating. Controlled.

Hyper-multitasking is a side effect of my abilities, and sometimes it comes in real handy. This was one of those times. Thanks to multiple engrams, with multiple perspectives and multiple thought processes, I could think very quickly.

Time seemed to freeze, and everything in the room shot into crystal clear focus at once. I was in my own head now, looking at a holographic version of the room, of Sol Rydell, of the gun. The cart was in front of me, filled with cleaning supplies and some odds and ends. There was neatly arranged furniture in the lobby, making it a sort of waiting room. On the small table next to the elevator was a ceramic vase filled with flowers. Across the room was a door with a keypad, leading into the suite. And below my feet was a runner rug.

The permanent engrams I carry around with me are siloed, most of the time. Their knowledge and experience isn't usually available to me directly. Unless, of course, they want it to be.

At this moment, facing immediate danger, everyone in my head wanted to act—either to duck and hide, to run away, or to jump and fight. That might seem like it would cause me to hesitate and maybe make me freeze up with indecision. Instead, it only served to open up everyone's skills, talents, and abilities all at once.

It created a sort of synchronicity between all the engrams, including my own.

All their memories, everything they knew, everything they could *do*, was suddenly under my control, and I could think with the power of seven minds, rapidly processing everything.

I leapt.

As I leapt, I grabbed the broom, swinging it around so the bristled end fanned into Sol's face before the wooden handle came down hard enough to knock the gun away before Sol could even fire.

The handle snapped at the same time, leaving a sharp, jagged point.

I was now carrying a spear.

Martial arts training from two different personalities suddenly kicked in. *Krav Maga*—Julia's specialty—gave me the ability to hit hard using the connecting tissue between my thumb and forefinger as an unbreakable weapon, applied at high speed to Sol's windpipe. Kung Fu—Jacob's hand-to-hand of choice—gave me the ability to snag Sol's arm, one hand on his wrist and the other on his bicep, and twist it backward until it popped out of socket. I heard a gurgled scream from Sol, who was suddenly forced face down into the runner rug.

I planted a knee in his back, keeping him completely incapacitated, and raised the spear above my head.

I could feel it.

I could feel *her*.

Julia.

She'd come out to play with the rest of us. Her Krav Maga skills had dealt the first incapacitating blow. But now the crazy was oozing to the surface. The schizophrenia. The paranoia.

I literally have multiple personalities, all independent of each other and of me. She has some, too. She was an experiment. She was Henry's fascination.

Julia, no, Henry said, calmingly.

And she listened.

It was brief, and it wouldn't last. But it was enough. I had her siloed, pushed back into whatever dark corner she preferred. I could still feel her, ready to come back, ready to pounce. Who was in charge right now, with her? There were so many personalities to choose from. Which one was I dealing with?

It didn't matter.

With Julia back in her silo, the others followed suit. I

felt the adrenalin start to fade, and the fly-like multi-faceted vision in my head went with it. The one became many again.

What do we do now? Kristen asked.

I could tell she was upset. This was not something she would want. This wasn't in her nature. The violence of the moment would have felt like a violation to her, forced on her against her will.

We have to kill him, Jacob said.

We have to know what he knows, first, Henry said.

We kill him, and then Jaylin absorbs him.

No! Kristen said, revulsion radiating from her.

"No," I said. Flat. Final. I did *not* want Sol Rydell in my head forever.

Then what do we do? Caleb asked, sounding scared.

I looked around, hoping to see a lamp cord or something I could use to tie him up. He wasn't even wearing shoe laces.

Neck tie, Jacob suggested.

I reached around, careful to only use the rubber glove and not make skin-to-skin contact. I loosened Sol's tie and whipped it free.

He had groaned when I grabbed the tie, but gave another gargled scream when I twisted his arms behind him and tied his wrists. For good measure I pulled his coat down, wrapping it around the tie, keeping his gloved hands away from the knot.

I could stand up now without worrying that Sol would be able to grab me. Chances were his arm was pretty useless at the moment, but that didn't mean he couldn't do some damage. I avoided his feet and stood to the side.

If I touch him and go catatonic, he might be able to get to his feet and take me out, I said.

Find something to bind his feet, Jacob replied.

I went to the cart, rifled through its contents, and found nothing useful. I did pull my hoodie and leather gloves back on, though, just to be safe. If I had to run, I wanted to make sure I had a bit more protection against casual contact, out on the street.

As I stepped around the cart, I tripped a bit on the runner rug, which had wrinkled somewhat in the scuffle.

Looking at it, I had an idea.

I moved the cart away, then pulled Sol by the shoulders until only his legs were on the rug. He cried out again, and I could hear ragged breathing. I was pretty sure I had crushed his larynx, which could end up killing him if the damage was bad enough, and he went untreated. For now, though, he seemed stable enough.

I rolled the end of the rug up and over his legs, tucking it under him. Then I pulled the other end up and over, pulling it tight. I moved a small but heavy oak end table onto the loose end of the rug.

It wouldn't hold anyone permanently, if they were determined to get out. But it would slow them down for a bit. Especially if they had their hands bound, a shoulder out of socket, and a crushed larynx to deal with.

Feeling a little more confident, I took off one of my gloves and touched the back of Sol's neck.

THE EFFECT WAS IMMEDIATE.

As suspected, Sol had been trained by Henry, and he instantly knew that he was an absorbed engram. Suddenly, the fight we'd had in real life started all over again. Only this time, Sol was pressing every advantage he had.

"I'm going to kill you," Sol said, in an eerie echo of Carter's first words in my head.

"It's been tried before," I said.

This time, facing down Sol, I was better prepared than I had been with Carter. As the memories came, I recognized them for what they were. And without the trauma of a man's death on my hands, I wasn't plagued by guilt or self doubt.

Sol was calling up every bad memory I had, but that was actually working *against* him. Carter had done the same, and recently, so the impact was less this time around. Memories tend to lose their bite when you've dealt with any grief or fear or anxiety that might be behind them.

In fact, my memories were the key to taking Sol down.

All I had to do, in the end, was remember the fight we'd just had. I played it back, blow-by-blow. And, unlike in the real world, this time I had Sol's own memory of the fight to work with. I forced him to feel the pain of every hit, all over again. I forced him to feel the fear that comes with that pain —even for someone trained to deal with it. We never fully lose the fear of pain, we just learn how to tolerate and channel it.

I amplified it. Being able to see it from the inside, I was able to double it, triple it, so that it had a greater impact on Sol than it would have otherwise.

I felt pain myself, too. Every blow to Sol was echoed within me. The pain, the fear, the frustration—I felt all of it.

But it wasn't a direct experience. It was the *memory* of pain—not pain itself. And unlike Sol, at the moment, I had a *physical* body to remind me that I wasn't being punched or kicked or experiencing any actual pain at all. What I felt was more like *empathetic* pain. Like when you see someone get kicked in the... er... *tender bits*, and you can imagine how that felt, without actually *feeling* it.

There was a buffer between us. Sol was getting a double dose of third-degree butt whupping, and I wasn't even breaking a sweat.

The training that outer Henry had given these guys was impressive, but I saw the flaw in it now. Once I'd overcome the memory onslaught with one person, it was easier to deal with when I was hit by another. Sort of like facing your fear of flying can knock it out of you for good. Once I'd faced this kind of mental attack, it really wasn't such a big deal.

After a moment of internal struggle, I blinked in the real world. I had been catatonic as I'd dealt with the attack, just as I'd feared I would be. So that, at least, *did* present a danger when facing someone with this training. But my recovery was quicker than it had been with Carter. That was hopeful. Maybe the more I dealt with it, the less impact it would have. Or maybe I could work up some kind of defense for it, so that I could keep myself from getting waylaid the next time it happened.

I had inner Sol siloed and shelved, tucked away into a mental "holding cell." He was strong, and I could hear him screaming at me, telling me I was going to die. But I could ignore him for thirty minutes. That was all it would take.

Outer Sol, on the other hand, couldn't be ignored.

Kill him, Jacob said. *You have his memories now. Leaving him alive is going to put us in danger.*

I was having a hard time arguing that point. But putting the guy down, while he was tied up and face down, injured even—it felt just about as wrong as anything I'd ever experienced.

I had killed Carter. It was ugly, and it haunted me. I had managed to silo it, like one of my hitchhikers. But like my permanent guests, there was always some small part of it that bled through.

I couldn't add to that. I couldn't stand the idea of it.

"I can't," I said. "I just... I can't. We have to think of something else."

I'm so relieved, Kristen said. *I was so worried you would do it.*

I didn't reply. I had certainly *thought* about it.

So what do we do with him? Caleb asked.

If you can't kill him, Henry said, *we'll have to further incapacitate him.*

I agreed.

I looked around once more. My options were the same, of course. But at least, for the moment, I had more time to piece things together.

I lifted Sol to the small sofa. The rug was still wrapped around his legs, and his hands were still tied behind him. I picked up his gun and tucked it into the waistband of my jeans.

Put that in the back, will ya? Jacob said. *It's bad enough you're putting a loaded gun in your pants, at least have the common sense to aim it away from your junk. And keep your finger away from the trigger.*

I did what he said. Carefully. Extra carefully.

Looking at Sol, I could see his holster. It was a network of straps, connected by small, plastic buckles. I took it off and used the straps to tie his ankles. The rug was wrapped around his legs, and with his ankles and wrists tied I felt confident that he was immobilized. As a final touch, I took one of the cleaning towels from the cart and gagged him with it. He groaned through all of it. With his crushed larynx, the gag may not have been necessary, but it seemed like a good idea. A precaution.

With Sol secure and out of my way, I looked at the secure door on the wall opposite the elevators. Emil Lyon would be on the other side of that door. Had he heard the scuffle out here?

According to Sol's memories, Emil had turned in a couple of hours ago. His bedroom was on the far side of the suite, next to an enormous floor-to-ceiling window, where he could get the best view of the city. It was unlikely that he'd hear anything coming from the waiting room. The walls of his apartment were not only sound proof but bullet proof. Emil was sleeping in a vault, for all intents and purposes.

I stepped up to the keypad and punched in the access code. There was a click from the lock, and I opened the door slowly, peeking inside before opening it wider to give me more light.

The apartment was *immense.*

The space I stepped into, as I slipped through the open door, was just off of the living room, which shared a large, open concept space with the kitchen and a breakfast area. To the left of the front door, a few feet away, was the door to Emil's study, where he preferred to work while in town. Next to that was a small workout room, where he spent two hours each morning after waking up. Sol would bring him orange juice and his iPad, for reading news and catching up on email.

Emil's bedroom was down the hall, past three other bedrooms reserved for rare but occasional guests. I pulled Sol's gun and slowly made my way down the hall.

Safety's on, Jacob said.

I know it's on, I replied. *I don't want to shoot the guy. I'm hoping I can just get in and get out before he even wakes up.*

You're going to die, a voice said.

Sol.

Thanks, Sol. I'll keep that in mind, I replied.

I moved quietly down the hallway and came to Emil's door. I listened for a moment, hoping to hear snoring or some other sign that he was asleep. Either the door was too well insulated for sound, or Emil was a quiet sleeper.

Or he was awake, waiting to shoot me as I entered.

Now what? Kristen asked.

Now we need a better assessment of the room, Jacob replied.

From Sol's memories, I knew that the bedroom had another entrance, from the far side of the study. I had avoided it before, because it actually led through a closet and then an *en suite* master bathroom. The bathroom would be echoey, thanks to the floor tile and all the hard surfaces. It would amplify any noise I made as I moved through. But it did offer the advantage of giving me a line of site to Emil's bed, and I could use the wall of the shower and the bathroom counters as cover, in case of gunfire.

Another possibility occurred to me—what if Emil was calling for help?

How confident are we that Emil slept through our scuffle? I asked. *Sol's memories tell me that the suite is pretty sound proof. But there's a camera. Emil could have watched the whole thing.*

There was a slight pause before Jacob said, *You picked a hell of a time to tell us there was a camera.*

Sorry, it's not like information just presents itself. I have to look for it.

No point arguing about it. We were in the situation we were in. And the fact that I couldn't quite figure out *why* we're here didn't change much.

There's nothing for it but to go on the offensive, Jacob said.

I sighed.

He was right. If we were doing this, we had to just roll with it. Now.

Turn off the safety, Jacob said.

I hesitated. Hitting that switch on the gun made this somehow more *real*. It was like hitting a switch to turn off the lights before walking out into a darkened hallway.

Adrenaline. Fear—irrational or otherwise.

Fight or flight. Though maybe not as hot and immediate as it had been during my fight with Sol.

I could feel the skills of the others returning. That, at least, was an advantage.

I clicked the safety off and held the gun just as Jacob had taught me. Finger off of the trigger. Firm grip. One hand under the butt. Arms bent, barrel to the ceiling until I was ready to aim.

I was still standing in front of the bedroom door. Time to use another trick Jacob had taught me.

I stepped back to give myself a bit of run-up, and then stepped forward, fast, raising my heel to kick directly into the doorknob. The focused force of the kick was enough to shatter the door frame into splinters at the point where the latch met the strike plate.

I rushed inside, using the light from the door to get a visual.

"Down! Down!" I shouted, keeping the gun trained on the most likely spot where Emil would be—in bed.

He was there and awoke with a start. He scrambled away from me, trying to get to the other side of the bed. I grabbed him by the lapels of his pajamas, dragging him forward until he fell to the floor. I held the gun to the top of his head, pressing hard enough that there could be no doubt it was there.

Emil had his hands up. "I am making no resistance," he said. His tone was calm, despite everything that had just happened. "I am complying."

He's attempting to take charge of the situation, Henry said. *His compliance is real, but he's using affirming speech to establish that he's in control.*

What do I do? I asked.

Say this, calmly...

"Your name is Emil Lyon."

There was a pause, and then Emil said, "Yes. That is my name."

"You are the majority shareholder of Shallister Hoffman."

Again a pause, "Yes. I don't see..."

"You are leaving for China in two days, to present data gathered from the ERD."

This time, Emil said nothing, but glanced up at me. I could see it in his eyes. He now knew who I was.

That's it, Henry said. *Three yeses. Or close enough. You have some dominance now. He's listening, instead of trying to take control of the situation.*

"Evergreen," Emil said.

Inwardly I cringed at the codename, but for now it seemed to be a layer of protection I could use.

Sol had also called me Evergreen.

Did that mean that they didn't know my real name?

Did it mean that outer Henry hadn't yet revealed my real identity?

That was something to think about. Later.

"Emil Lyon," I said. "You've been looking for me. And I want to know why."

"You have the means," Emil said. "Go ahead."

Don't, Henry said.

"Wasn't planning on it," I said.

"No? And why not? Are you concerned about what you'll learn? I have no real secrets, you know. I'll tell *you* anything."

"Is that because you know I'd learn it anyway? Or because you don't see me as a threat?"

Emil smiled. "Both."

He's starting to play you again, Henry said.

"I want to know why you did all this. From what I've learned, you already have the ERD technology. You have Henry. You don't need me. And you definitely didn't need the information from the President."

"The gambit with the President was just a test," Emil said.

"And what did it reveal?"

"That you are resourceful. You are capable. The technology—it can replicate your abilities. Eventually. There are still bugs that Henry has yet to work out. I suspect he is holding out on me. But the Chinese are *very* resourceful. They'll have the problems solved, soon enough."

"So you really don't need me," I said.

"Oh, I need you. The Chinese may perfect the technology, but that could be decades away. Until then, I need you to act as an agent on my behalf."

I smiled. "Too bad, then," I said. "Your recruitment methods suck. There isn't enough money in the world to get me to help you."

Emil chuckled. "No, I suppose there isn't. Money, by and large, is poor leverage when dealing with someone who has no real need of it. There are *people*, though."

I thought about that. "Henry? He and I aren't exactly friends these days."

Thanks, inner Henry said.

"No, that's true," Emil agreed. "Henry has his own interests, and they often work counter to the interests and goals of others. Mine. Yours. But he's hardly the only soul you know. There's also Kristen Harrell."

I felt my stomach twist.

Careful, Henry said.

I... she... wouldn't want you to be in danger, Kristen added.

"Are you saying you have her?" I asked.

Emil smiled. "No. She's safe. For now. But my people are watching her. We know where she is at all times. She can continue living her life, far from you and all the grief that comes with you. All you have to do is work for me. And you can start by taking that gun away from my head. Now, please."

"And if I don't? If I pull this trigger? What happens?"

"She dies. So does Henry, if that matters."

I hesitated.

Give in for now, Jacob said.

What? I replied. *Just like that?*

For now. Jacob said.

I hesitated again, but pulled the gun away, slowly, snapping the safety back on. I tucked it into the back of my jeans again. "Ok, Emil. You win. You have me."

Emil smiled as he stood. "I *always* had you. But it's good for you to realize it. It makes the whole business less troublesome."

"So you're going to China in two days."

"I am," Emil said. "But not for the reasons you believe.

The Chinese are working on this technology. I have the key. But I intend to derail their efforts permanently."

I blinked. "What? Why?"

"Eliminate the competition. Oh, it won't be nearly as permanent as all that, in the end. The Chinese are nothing if not resourceful. They'll replicate the technology within days of it being released to the market. But that will take quite a bit longer than they had planned. I don't intend to create a market for this technology right away. Engrammatic replication is far too valuable to be widely available just yet."

"So what *is* the plan?" I asked.

"What is it always? Wealth. Power. Immortality."

I knew it, Henry said.

"But you'll need the Chinese, won't you? You'll need Paradigm."

"I already have Paradigm," Emil said. "The company may be inside Chinese borders, but the compression software has always been under my control."

I shook my head. "I don't get it. Why bother, then? You have the software. You have me. You have Henry. What's the missing piece? What's in China?"

In answer, Emil smiled and then reached out and touched my cheek.

"Oh crap," I said, as Emil's memories gave me more answers than I ever wanted.

CHAPTER TWELVE

I can't believe it, Henry said.

That's just sickening, Kristen replied.

Just the sort of thing I'd expect, Jacob said.

So cool! Caleb added.

"Human cloning," I whispered aloud.

Emil smiled. "They're much more advanced than the rest of the world would believe. The engrammatic replication technology is one of the final pieces for them. They're using artificial intelligence research as a cover, but the reality is that they have a way to cheat death. Or they will, soon."

Handy, in a country where they're already overcrowded by billions, Jacob said, his tone dry and biting.

And advocating the murder of baby girls, Kristen replied, bitterly.

"You have a body there," I said.

"A cancer-*free* body," Emil smiled. "Yes."

The cancer. Pancreatic cancer. I could almost *feel* it, the way Emil could. Painful. Persistent. It was always there, eating away at him like some oily black beast gnawing at his insides.

At the moment, the cancer was being held at bay by more experimental treatments than I could count. They'd been pretty effective at slowing the cancer's progress, at least. Despite this, however, Emil had only months—maybe a year, if he was lucky.

His doctors didn't hold out much hope in luck.

"You're holding up pretty well for someone who's more radioactive than the Hulk," I said.

"The experimental procedures have helped quite a bit," Emil nodded, smiling. Then the smile faded. "Not enough, of course. Never enough."

"So your plan is to retrieve your clone body, sabotage the Chinese, and perfect the technology here in the US so you can cheat death."

"And repeat," he said, smiling once more. "Again and again, as needed. At least until science can create a body that won't deteriorate."

"You're working on that, too," I said.

"Isn't science amazing?" Emil beamed. "It can create wonders of technology and even keep a man from dying before his time."

"Have you ever stopped to consider maybe it *is* your time?" I asked.

"Well that poses an interesting philosophical question, doesn't it?" Emil replied. "Who determines how much time we have? God? That has never sat well with me. Shouldn't it be us? It is *our* life, after all. Or maybe it should be you, *Evergreen*. Don't you have a few formerly living souls in that head of yours? Minds that lived beyond the expiration dates of their bodies?"

"Not exactly the same," I said.

"And yet, not altogether different," Emil smiled. "Each engram you absorb gets to cheat death, in some small way. They live on in a new body that isn't theirs. *My* new body will just happen to be a bit more engineered."

I thought about all of this, trying to wrap my head around what I was learning. He had things well planned, well plotted. Everything he needed was already in place, already in motion. Before I'd even known he was my enemy, he'd already planned multiple ways to beat me.

And yet, he still needed me.

"So you want me to play spy," I said, "and get you the rest of the puzzle pieces. Government and military secrets from all the major players."

"And in return, you and your friends can live without fear."

He meant that, at least. I could see it in his memories. He'd been counting on me being able to see that.

If I helped him, eventually Kristen would be safe. That was a guarantee.

I would never be a free man again, of course. But I would live as comfortable a life as I pleased. I'd have anything I could ever ask for, except freedom to leave. I'd live in luxury, somewhere far from anywhere—or anyone—that mattered.

Thinking about it in that light—was it really so bad?

I had to admit, after everything I'd been through, all the constant running and hiding, trying desperately to keep my abilities a secret and to just keep myself *alive*—the idea didn't actually sound all that bad to me. I might not have freedom, but who could honestly say they were free, anyway? What was freedom, really? If I could have anything I wanted, but had to stay within a square mile for the rest of my life, was I any less free than, say, a rich eccentric? Didn't members of royalty basically live like that?

I was almost ashamed to admit it, but the idea—the offer —it was actually tempting.

And maybe if he hadn't used Kristen as a weapon *against* me, I might have just rolled with it and gone along.

But he had. Which proved that despite everything he knew about me, all the intelligence he'd gathered, he didn't actually *know* me.

But I knew *him*. And he'd made a couple of huge mistakes.

First, his plan to use Kristen as a pawn in this was actually pretty airtight. If I killed him, he couldn't do the video check-in he'd scheduled, confirming that the plan was still on track. That was outlined very clearly in his memory— possibly sitting at the top as he touched me, because it was important to his little game. It was his failsafe.

And it was also his first mistake.

Because just as his failsafe plans were right at the top, and easy for me to access, so were the names and locations of all the operatives he was using, as well as the timing of the calls. He was checking in every 48 hours, and last night was his most recent check-in. If I killed him now, I would have nearly 32 hours to get to Kristen and protect her.

His second and biggest mistake was that he hadn't bothered to silo everything he knew about the Chinese, Paradigm, or his own operations. I could see the entire landscape of his plan just by looking for specifics. I could also see that he was counting on me being too worried about Kristen's safety to do anything with this information.

He'd been sloppy.

And there was something else buried in the muddle of

details in Emil's memories, and in its way it made me happy.

Emil had *manipulated* Henry, forcing him to do a lot of what he'd done through threats and leverage. And Henry had revealed a lot to him, usually under duress. But he hadn't told him *everything*.

"I like the idea of living without fear," I said, smiling.

Emil nodded. "I thought you would."

I quickly reached back and grabbed the gun from my waistband. In one smooth motion I had the safety off and the barrel pressed against Emil's head.

"What! What are you doing? If you kill me, Kristen and Henry are *dead*!"

"I'll take my chances," I said.

"You have my memories! You know what this will mean!"

"I do," I said. And before I could lose my nerve, I pulled the trigger.

The sound was deafening, and it left a ringing in my ears. The gun had bucked against my grip, causing my arm to ache from a strange, muscular vibration. Blood had gone everywhere in a dense cloud, and that, along with the gore of brain material, splattered onto the floor, the bed, the walls.

I felt sick to my stomach. I wanted to vomit. It was all I could do to keep from throwing the gun away from me.

I had killed before. But this was... different. This was close. Personal. Not in self defense, like the other time. Not directly.

This was more like rage. A cold, icy rage.

My God, Kristen said.

I didn't think you had it in you, Jacob said.

What have you done? Henry asked.

"Not the worst," I replied, grimly. "Not yet."

I knelt down beside Emil's body and took off one of my gloves.

Jaylin, wait! Kristen said.

But it was too late.

I touched Emil's skin and felt the engram transfer.

I had already absorbed Emil's memories, but this time it was different. I had never experienced anything like this—absorbing someone's engram twice in a row—especially a *permanent* engram. There was a moment of confusion as identical memories collided, but new memories folded in with them. Memories of only the past few moments.

Memories of death.

What did you do? What did you do!

Emil's voice, now a permanent part of me, screamed in horror and frustration in my mind. I quickly siloed him, locked him in the deepest, darkest hole I could think of. It wouldn't hold him indefinitely. But it was enough. For now.

Now what? Henry asked. His voice was somehow quiet, awed. Henry plays at being nonchalant most of the time, but this had disturbed him.

I understood. It had disturbed *me*.

I wasn't even sure who I was, at that moment. The cold ruthlessness of it all.

Was it possible that I was acting out based on Emil's own ruthless personality?

Was it possible that it wasn't really me who pulled the trigger?

I was under the influence of something—some *one*—dark and powerful, after all.

There was a slender, fragile part of me that hoped this was the truth. But there was a more open, raw part of me that was convinced it was a lie.

We need to get out of here, Jacob said.

"First, I have to destroy the video," I replied.

Emil's memories were cluing me in on all sorts of security measures in the apartment. Things that even Sol Rydell hadn't known about.

I went to the server closet on the other side of the penthouse suite and pulled the drives used to record video from the internal cameras. I smashed these using a marble statue in the living room, then microwaved the shattered bits of hard drive platter before dropping them down the garbage disposal.

There was no need to wipe anything down here. I wear gloves habitually. Nothing I could do about any stray DNA that may have drifted from me, but I thought it would be minimal. The important part was to wipe out all the digital records of me being here. There wasn't much I could do about the building's security footage, but I had worn a disguise the whole time. Maybe that would be enough.

I left the suite, re-engaging the alarm system as I left. A sort of smokescreen—I used Emil's own activation code for the system, which would confuse the hell out of anyone who checked these records. It would show that Emil had activated security after his time of death. I had effectively created a "locked door mystery" for police to solve.

There was one other thing working in my favor, concerning a police investigation. Emil was notorious for checking out and going off the radar for weeks. The board of directors and his assistants at Shallister Hoffman knew that he was leaving for China in a couple of days, and might assume he'd left early. No one would think to check the executive apartments for days.

Unless Sol told them to.

I wasn't sure what to do about Sol. I could lock him up

in here, leave him some food and water, put it down on the floor like I was feeding a dog. He could wet himself for all I cared—my concern for his well-being only extended so far. But eventually he would manage to get himself free, and he'd alert the police about Emil's murder, and point a pretty steady finger right at me.

Nothing to do for it, then. The best I could hope for was a head start.

But as it turned out, Sol was less of a concern than I had realized.

In the waiting area I found him slumped to the side, his head at an awkward angle. His complexion was blue, and he appeared to be very still. I refused to check for a pulse, since I couldn't be sure how long it had been since he died.

Asphyxiation, Henry said. *Guess you did more damage to his larynx than you thought.*

It was probably the gag, Jacob said. *He was already having trouble breathing, and you closed off the rest of his airway.*

Could we please just leave? Kristen said, her voice shaky. *This... this is horrible.*

I agreed with her. I hadn't intended to kill Sol. I hadn't really intended to kill Emil, when I'd come up here. It had just...

Well, it hadn't just *happened*. I had *done it*. I couldn't excuse myself, just because it hadn't been part of the original plan.

These two men were dead because of me. It didn't matter that they were a threat, to me and to Kristen and Henry. It didn't matter what kind of Dr. Evil plans Emil Lyon had for immortality, or for enslaving me. It only mattered that I had killed them, and I'd have to live with it.

Sol's death—another tick mark on my record. More red in my ledger, and on my hands.

It didn't bother me as much as Emil. Sol's memories had faded by now, his personality going with them. He was a complete outsider to me, now.

Emil would be with me forever, though.

And I planned to make his stay a living hell.

I TOOK Emil's personal elevator to the private garage in the basement of the building. The entire garage was reserved only for Emil and select executives. Privacy among the uber rich and powerful is a priority, which meant that security would be pretty light.

Emil depended on drivers to get him around the city, so any notion I might have had to steal a getaway car was out. But from the garage I *could* sneak onto the street without being noticed. I pulled my hoodie up, hiding my face and keeping my head down to avoid any more cameras.

Once on the street, I kept my face hidden until I could disappear into some blind spots. These days, there are cameras everywhere, and the police were getting pretty good at tracking people from one to another. With advances in artificial intelligence, facial recognition was getting faster and better. And less necessary—there were technologies now that could identify the gait of someone's walk.

Big Brother has been on the scene for a while now. But it's not a perfect system. It could be avoided.

For example—there wasn't an AI on Earth that could identify the gait of someone who had eight different personalities in his head, and could fall back on habits from any given one of them, or all of them at once.

Recognizing my face, of course, was still an issue.

Once I was deep into the streets, what followed was a couple of hours of dodging in and out of alleys and businesses, keeping to the dark as much as possible, and taking paths through the city that only someone like me would know. This being Manhattan, of course, there were plenty serendipitous close calls. At one point I walked by an open garage bay and thought I heard gunshots from somewhere inside the building. I kept my hoodie up and my head down, and managed to be a block away before the place was suddenly surrounded by FBI and police.

Close calls indeed.

As I walked, for the first half hour I used my phone to dictate and record everything I could from Emil's memories. I had Emil as a permanent hitchhiker now, but after the initial 30 minutes I'd lose my easy-pass to his memories. I'd have to fight him for anything I needed, after things faded. The dictated notes would have to be enough.

I copied everything into the cloud so I could reference it even if I had to ditch the burner phone.

Once I thought I was clear, I used the phone to get an Uber to my location, and the guy drive me to Teterboro Airport, about thirty minutes away. It would take me off the island, but Shallister Hoffman kept a couple of private jets on hold there.

Emil had planned to take one of them to China.

I was going to take it to Zelienople, PA. Or as close to it as I could get.

Zelie was where Kristen was living now. It was close to Pittsburgh, but a few hours from New York City. Close to family, but far from me.

Not a coincidence.

Zelie was a small town, and kind of quaint. I'd gone

there with Kristen a dozen times while we were dating, and even though I felt weird being out of the city, I had to admit there was something kind of nice about small town life. Quiet. Slower. Easier to move around. It kind of drove me nuts, but in the right light I could see the appeal. It was a safe place.

Usually.

Right now, it was just about the most dangerous place in the world for Kristen.

On the ride to the airport, I used the information I'd recorded from Emil's memories to log in to the airport's reservation system and request that the plane was fueled and standing by for a "guest." I specified that no one was to engage the man who arrived. No questions. No escorts. And no video surveillance.

Technically all of this was against TSA regulations. But it was a small relief airport, and I was entering through a private airline. Shallister Hoffman had a lot of pull. And so did Emil Lyon.

The car pulled into a covered drop off in front of the airport and I raced inside, still keeping my head down. I was greeted by a concierge who had been on the lookout for me. He ushered me through the doors and onto the plane. No questions. No check-ins. No security sweeps. I could be wearing a leisure suite made of $C4$, for all they knew.

God bless capitalism.

In less than fifteen minutes following my arrival, we were in the air.

The flight was fast. In just under an hour we touched down in a small, private airport in Pennsylvania, about thirty minutes from Zelie. While in the air, I used Emil's access and accounts to arrange for a car to be there, waiting. No driver necessary.

It was a shame that all the perks of having Emil in my head would disappear the minute someone discovered his body. A fugitive could get used to having a skeleton key to every door.

Once behind the wheel, I practically raced down the winding back roads toward Zelie, hurling along through snow-lined roads. There was no need to check GPS. I'd been here often enough that I knew where I was going.

I knew exactly where Kristen was living. But I wasn't going straight there.

Instead I pulled over about a block or so away, and got out of the car, keeping to the edge of the road, crunching my way through piles of snow in shoes meant for New York sidewalks. It was a cold, wet slog, but it couldn't be avoided. I had to keep moving. I had the target in my sights.

I was focused on the house across the street from Kristen.

The neighborhoods in Zelienople were very open. There weren't many fences around the yards, which for some reason I always found odd. There weren't even many trees. Instead, there were blocks of homes, loosely laid out in a grid, some of which were over a hundred years old. Many of them were beautiful—and *immense*, by New York City standards. But for all that, they didn't provide much privacy, or much cover.

I had the handgun in the pocket of my hoodie. The safety was off. I had my hands in my pockets, and my right hand was draped loosely over the gun, finger hovering near the trigger. I'd fire through the material if I had to.

I walked at what I hoped was a normal-seeming pace until I got closer to the house.

Quickly, I took a turn and cut through the yard next door, then sprinted to the back door of the house. Once I was there, I ducked low, and peeked into the window by the back door.

No one was there.

I was looking into a kitchen, and beyond that a living room. The house was a single story, so there was probably a bedroom up front, with a window facing Kristen's house, across the street. That's where they'd be.

There were two guys—well-trained, ex-military types, hired by Emil to keep an eye on Kristen, or to take her out, if Emil didn't check in on time. He hadn't been lying about that.

These guys were well-trained and they would definitely be on high alert. Getting to them wasn't going to be easy.

"That's it?" a voice said from inside as a man stepped into the living room. I crouched lower, peering through the bottom edge of the window. "Nothing else?"

"Coffee. Donuts. Smokes."

"This whole thing is being paid for by Daddy Warbucks. You can't think of a better grocery list? This sounds like you went to a gas station and grabbed stuff at random."

"Get in, get what we need, and get back," the other guy said.

The first man started walking toward the back door, and I ducked then crawled until I was hidden by the corner of the house. I realized, suddenly, that there was a car parked there. Which meant I was right in the path of the guy coming my way.

I made a run for it, heading straight for the neighbor's yard, and ducked behind the small wooden deck, just as I heard the back screen door creak open and then slam shut next door.

I peeked over the wood railing and saw the guy climb

into the driver's seat of the car, start the engine, and then pull away. Presumably on his way to find better fare than donuts and cigarettes.

Now was my chance.

I maybe had half an hour before the guy was back from his grocery run. According to my notes from Emil's memories, that meant there was just *one* highly trained, ex-military hitman in the house, with a silenced rifle trained on Kristen.

Lucky me.

Once again I sprinted, and this time I only made a quick peek through the window before opening the back door as quietly as possible and making my way inside.

The house was too quiet. No music or television to help mask my movements. And every move I made seemed to broadcast my presence like a car alarm.

I stepped as silently as possible, dreading every creak of the wood floor beneath my feet.

In the living room, there were two large lumps on the couch, covered in plastic. I was close enough to see some familiar and disturbing shapes.

Bodies.

I felt my guts twist, my chest tighten.

The couple that had lived here—regular people who had plans and dreams and maybe some family close by. People who visited neighbors, who shopped downtown, who took trips into Pittsburgh for special occasions. People who paid bills, had fights, made up, loved each other.

Two guys had snuffed them out for nothing more than a hiding place, so they could kill *another* innocent person if they were asked to. For money. For nothing.

The twist in my guts, the tightness in my chest, both turned into fire in my veins. My head throbbed. My jaw clenched. My fingers tightened around the gun in my pocket.

I suddenly felt a lot less troubled by what I was about to do.

Move like you mean it, Jacob said. *You have the element of surprise. Move, aim, fire. Don't hesitate.*

He was right.

I stopped trying to keep my movements subtle. I took the gun out of my pocket, held it like Jacob had taught me, and walked straight to the bedroom.

"You forget something?" the guy said, from his place at the window. He was kneeling beside a kitchen chair, turned so that he could use it to balance a rifle. He had his eye pressed to the scope. It was aimed at Kristen's house.

Before he could even look up, I put a bullet in the back of his head.

He slumped forward so hard, the rifle barrel broke through the glass of the window, sticking out through a small hole with jagged cracks radiating outward, like lightning streaking from a Van de Graaff machine.

I ran then, out the front door and straight to Kristen's house, around to the back where her car was parked. I jumped the steps and started pounding on her back door.

In moments, she opened it, confused.

I stared at her. It had been awhile since I'd seen her face. Her actual face.

"Jaylin? What... what are you doing here?"

I shook myself out of the spell I was in, stepping back slightly, holding out a gloved hand. "We have to leave! Right now!"

"What? I..."

"You're in danger! There are men with guns across the street. We have to leave now!"

She hesitated, then took my hand.

I reached inside the door and grabbed the keys to her car, from the hook where she always hung them.

She'd grown up in this house and had inherited it after her father died. It hadn't taken long for her to fall back into old habits. And I knew those habits, inside and out. I knew *her*.

We rushed to the car, and I climbed into the driver's seat. In moments we were on the street, heading in the opposite direction from the one the other guy had driven. There was a chance he would recognize her car and know something was up, and I wanted to avoid that.

I gunned it down the street, taking icy turns far too fast for Kristen's comfort.

"Jaylin, slow down! You're going to get us *killed!*"

She was right. This wasn't safe. It would also get us noticed.

I slowed. We were far enough away at this point that I figured we'd be ok.

Turn left up ahead, inner Kristen said, and I obeyed.

"Where are we going?" outer Kristen asked.

Steel mill, inner Kristen said.

"Steel mill," I repeated.

Outer Kristen said nothing.

A few minutes later we pulled onto a road that ran between a set of train tracks and the steel mill where Kristen's father had worked all of his life. I pulled to a stop behind a row of giant spools, coiled with a thick steel cable, and cut the engine.

"You promised me you'd never come here," Kristen said, staring off at the rows of rusted metal lining the gravel side road.

"I never wanted to break that promise, Kristen. But something has happened."

"Someone is after me because of you," she said, quietly.

"Yes."

Silence for a moment. Then, "Did *she* tell you to come here."

"No," I said. "Kristen... *inner* Kristen... is just along for the ride on this one. I wanted to leave you alone. I really did. We had no choice."

More silence. "So tell me what happened."

Over the next few minutes I explained about Henry and Emil Lyon, about Emil's plans and about Paradigm and the Chinese. At one point I turned the car back on to get the heat going, and the quiet hum of the engine seemed to help sooth things, even as it made it all feel that much more surreal.

I'd had a million conversations with Kristen since she left. But she hadn't heard from me in years. I kept having to backtrack, to catch her up.

"So what now?" she asked. "You're here. You saved me."

"Not entirely. There's another guy out there, with orders to kill you if Emil doesn't check in."

"Which he won't. Because you killed him." Her voice was quiet, and I could hear the fear in it.

"I did, Kristen. I had no choice."

"No choice?" she asked, looking at me sharply. "You had *no choice* but to kill an unarmed old man?"

I shook my head, looking away from her. "I had him in my head, Kristen. I have him now. He's not a good man. He had plans that went beyond all of this. And none of it was good. I couldn't let him hurt you, but I couldn't let him go, either."

"So this wasn't just about self preservation? You're

trying to tell me that you did this for the good of humanity or something?"

I shook my head. "Maybe I was trying to protect myself, and you. Is that so bad?"

"Henry really screwed you up," Kristen said, disgusted.

Hey! What'd I do? Henry complained.

You taught Jaylin to be a self preservationist, inner Kristen said.

I believe I taught him how to use his abilities, and how to survive. I think I'm owed some gratitude. Self-preservation isn't necessarily evil. Consider airplanes. "In the event of depressurization, put on your own mask before assisting others."

Typical, Kristen said. *Answers for everything.*

"They're talking to you now, aren't they? Henry and... and *her?*"

"Yes," I said. "Actually, they're talking to each other. Arguing."

"About whether Henry is an ass."

I smiled. "Something like that."

"It's not funny, Jaylin! My life is in danger because of you!"

I was quiet, then nodded. "Yes. I'm sorry. I'd change that if I could. Henry... outer Henry... He revealed who you were. He was tortured for it. He didn't have much choice."

"Is he alive?"

"Yes," I said.

"And he's in danger?"

"Yes. There are men watching him, too. They have the same orders. If they don't hear back from Emil Lyon at a certain time, they kill Henry."

"How much time does he have?

I checked the clock in the dash of the car. "Less than a day."

"Then we'd better get going," Kristen said.

"What? You want me to *save* him? You *hate* him."

"I'm not going to let a man die, just because I hate him," Kristen said.

And that's what makes her different from you, Henry, Jacob said.

Shut up, Henry replied.

But Jacob was wrong. Henry wouldn't let someone die just because he hated him, either. Not if he still found that person useful.

And Kristen was right. Henry had taught me well. If I had any skill outside of my ability, it was all about self preservation. Henry had drilled that into me over hundreds of uncomfortable days spent on the move. There was a time when I never slept in the same building twice, ever. We moved from spot to spot throughout the city, in an attempt to keep anyone from spotting any patterns, making any connections. Henry drilled me on keeping myself out of the wrong hands.

And Henry was right, too. Self preservation wasn't always an evil thing. It wasn't always selfish. Keeping myself free and alive was the only way to keep Kristen and Henry safe. It was the only way to keep Emil Lyon from using me to do some really bad stuff in the world.

I was starting to realize the truth.

I was putting on my own mask, so I could help others.

I put the car in drive and pulled away slowly, making my way onto the blacktop.

"Where are we going?" Kristen asked.

"You wanted to save Henry. It's a seven hour drive to Manhattan from here. If we're lucky, and if traffic is light.

Maybe 10 hours tops. I can't risk using the private jet again, with you in tow. So driving it is the only shot. We'll be cutting it close, but at least we have 10 hours of drive time to work out a plan."

Kristen said nothing, but stared out of the passenger side window as we drove.

It took half an hour to reach 80 by way of 79. We passed a sign reading "Grove City. Food, Restrooms, Gas."

"Can we stop?" Kristen asked. "I was about to make breakfast when you... when we had to leave," she said. "And... I really have to pee."

I nodded, and took the next exit, threading my way through back roads until we came to the small town. We stopped at a gas station across the street from a McDonald's.

"You really know how to pull out all the stops," Kristen said. "Whisking a girl away to fancy restaurants and exotic locales."

I smiled lightly. Things were still tense between us, but this was more like the Kristen I knew. A little edgy, kind of sarcastic, more than usual, but at least she didn't openly hate me.

"Nothing but the best," I said.

I pulled in to one of the pumps and used one of my pre-paid credit cards to fill the tank.

"I'm going to walk over," Kristen said.

"Don't," I said. "We'll go through the drive-thru. It's safer."

"There is nothing safe about what we're about to eat, and I have to *pee*."

I shook my head. "Just wait, ok?"

She gave me a hard look.

Uh-oh, inner Kristen said. *Here I go.*

Outer Kristen turned and started walking straight across the street, without another word.

"*Crap,*" I said, hurriedly finishing up with the fuel, recapping, and hopping in the driver's seat. I had the car started and was pulling out to cross the street when suddenly the world came to a jarring and painful halt.

A car came out of nowhere and slammed into the front wheel well of Kristen's car hard enough to slide the front end of the car into a hard right, and point me in a new direction. The impact caused me to slam my head against the driver's side window. Stars and an oozing darkness clouded my vision.

Jaylin! inner Kristen shouted.

Get up and get out, now! Jacob shouted. *It's the other guy. Get your gun.*

I was in a daze, and my head was pounding, but I managed to reach and unbuckle my seatbelt. I tried the door, but it wouldn't budge. The car—the same black sedan that had been parked across from Kristen's house—was pressed against the front wheel well and the edge of the door, keeping it in place. I saw the guy walk around to the front of the car and then raise a pistol with a silencer. He was aiming straight at me through the windshield.

Down down down! Jacob shouted.

I went down, just as pellets and shards of glass fell onto my back. There was no sound of gunfire, just the tink-tink-tink of bullets hitting the windshield.

The gun, Jaylin! Get the gun!

I had put the gun in the glove box, to keep it close but out of Kristen's sight. Now I fumbled to get the box open, and when I did the gun fell out onto the floor.

I wriggled down and grabbed it, sitting up quickly and taking aim.

The guy wasn't in front of the car anymore.

Across the street, I saw him rushing into the side door of the McDonald's.

He thinks he got you, Jacob said. *Didn't bother to check and make sure. Stupid move.*

"I'll take it," I said.

I climbed over the center console and out of the passenger side door, staggering a bit as I got my feet under me.

"Buddy, are you ok?" a man asked.

I looked up and saw his eyes go wide. I glanced down at the gun in my hand and then dropped it to my side.

"I... I don't want any trouble, guy," the man said, holding up his hands.

I ignored him and hobbled and limped across the street as quickly as I could. Suddenly I heard screaming, and a handful of people were making a quick exit from the restaurant. I saw an employee crawl out of the drive-thru window, with the help of a customer just outside. The two of them sped away.

I ducked low, keeping myself out of sight as I raced along the outside of the restaurant. I peeked through the glass door, but I could only see customers laying face down, covering their heads. A young mother was sitting against the counter, her toddler screaming and wailing in her arms as she tried to quiet him. She was a mess of tears and snot—but when she saw me her eyes went wide.

I held a finger to my lips, signaling her not to say anything. Then I mouthed, *Where is he?*

She understood and nodded with her head toward the short corridor to the right of the serving counter.

The restrooms.

I pulled the door open a bit and looked inside, leading

with my gun. I stayed low, crouching on the ground, but from this vantage point I could see the guy standing at the door of the ladies room.

"I know you're in there!" the guy shouted through the door. "Come out and no one here has to get hurt. Unlock the door, *now!*"

Don't, I said silently.

She won't, Kristen said.

Regardless, it would only be a matter of time before the guy managed to get inside, probably by shooting his way in. His orders were to kill Kristen, if things went wrong. This certainly qualified.

I raised the gun and took aim.

Breathe, Jacob said.

I breathed, steadying my arm, which was shaking more than normal.

You need a kill shot, Jacob said. *Can't risk him firing back.*

I nodded, and raised the sight, taking aim for the man's head.

In the movies, Head shots are easy. People make them all the time, even while running or leaning out of a moving vehicle. In reality, even from just a couple of feet away it can be like trying to throw a basketball into a hoop from half court. Not impossible, but more difficult than people think.

I aimed, took a breath, and squeezed the trigger.

My gun wasn't silenced, so the blast was loud, and people screamed. Mostly people who hadn't realized I was there.

And, unfortunately, I missed.

The guy ducked as the shot created a splintered hole in the door, just above his head. He turned and swept with the barrel of his gun, firing a couple of shots for cover.

I cringed and dropped lower, using my vantage point to keep me out of the line of fire, but I had to act quickly if I was going to keep that advantage. I raised up, firing two more rounds of my own. In the narrow hall leading to the restrooms, there was nowhere for the guy to hide. Both shots hit—one in the chest and one in the shoulder.

He fell back against the door and slumped to the floor, and I could see from where I was that he was dead.

I rose, cautiously, and moved toward him. I kept the gun pointed at him. When I reached him, I pressed it against his head while I grabbed his own gun, with the silencer. I also rifled through his pockets and took his wallet and every-thing else I could find.

I was extremely careful to avoid making skin-to-skin contact.

Five dead men in three days, inner Kristen said. *You're racking up quite a body count.*

I could hear the disgust in her voice. Or maybe it was my own sick feelings bleeding into what she was saying.

I wanted to throw up. I wanted to run, to hide some-where until the world forgot about me again. Until I could forget what I'd done.

It was never going to happen, and I knew it.

This was a part of me now. Just like my "hitchhikers," the memories I had of killing people—they were going to stick with me for the long ride.

This was who I was now. *What* I was now.

"Kristen!" I shouted through the door, as I tucked my gun in my jeans and held the other gun against my leg. "It's ok! He's down! You're safe to come out!"

After a long and frightening silence, I heard a click, and the door opened.

Kristen peered through, her face set in absolute fear.

She glanced down and saw the man lying dead at her feet. She sobbed.

I pushed the door open and took her shoulder, pulling her roughly out of the restroom and toward the exit.

People were still cowering and hiding. The woman with the toddler had moved away and was hiding behind the short wall that housed plastic trays of condiments. I glanced around the restaurant, taking note of the fear in everyone's eyes.

Fear of me.

I was the bad guy here.

Once out of the restaurant, we hurried across the street. I could already hear police sirens approaching from the distance.

Kristen's car was a wreck, and it wasn't going anywhere. The guy's car seemed only slightly damaged, though. I moved us toward it and was more than a little happy to find it still running.

"Climb in," I said.

"Shouldn't we just wait for the police?" she asked. "I can explain everything to them!"

I shook my head. "Henry dies, if I'm stuck here with the police," I said.

I was just going to mention that, Henry said.

"And I don't know how safe you'll be. Emil has... *had*... a lot of connections. I don't have direct access to his memories anymore, but I know he's usually got a Plan B. And a Plan C through Z. If you're in custody, they'll know where to find you."

She looked at me, hard, then shook her head and climbed into the car, settling into the passenger side.

I was about to climb in myself when I spotted something on the ground, near where the front bumper had impacted the wheel well of Kristen's car. A small, rectangular box with a tiny coil of antenna sticking out of it. The whole thing would have fit in the watch pocket of my jeans.

Tracker, Jacob said. *He followed us straight to this place. It was a mistake to take her car.*

I said nothing, just climbed into the guy's car, put it in reverse to pull away, then raced out of there as fast as I could. I took back roads and stayed away from heavy traffic until we were back on our route, and then I floored it.

I had no idea what would happen next, but I knew I had to get us as far away from here as possible. The sound of sirens were drowned out by the roar of the engine, and by the pounding of my heart.

CHAPTER THIRTEEN

We ditched the guy's car behind a restaurant on the frontage road. Next door was a consignment lot filled with old cars for sale. There was no one in the small building at the center of the lot. Just a sign that said, "See something you like? Call us today!"

I picked a small car close to the chain-link gate, wedged between a van and a large truck, which gave us plenty of cover to work.

That wire, Jacob said, directing me. *Twist it to the other one.*

I did as instructed, and the car sputtered a bit before starting.

"You hot wire cars now?" Kristen asked.

"Looks like it. Let's go," I said.

I had to press through the gate, snapping the chain against the car's bumper and gouging the paint on either side as we made it through, but in moments we were on the road and moving once again toward New York.

Kristen had been more or less silent since we'd escaped. I made no attempt to break that silence.

You should talk to her, inner Kristen said. *She's scared, and angry, and doesn't know what to do.*

I knew the feeling.

She's not going to make the first move, Kristen said. *She's waiting for you to say something.*

The trouble was, I had no clue what to say. Inner Kristen and I talked all the time, but outer Kristen would have no memory of those talks. So I would have to constantly check myself, to make sure I was saying something relatable. Otherwise I'd sound insane. Or annoying. Or both.

I decided to go with the only thing I could think of.

"So," I said. "Your hair is different."

Kristen gave me a sharp look, her hand involuntarily going to her hair. "That's what you want to talk about? My hair?"

"Just noticing," I said. "It was longer, when we were together. And red."

"Auburn," she said. "And it hasn't been that way for a long time." She looked out of the window at the passing landscape, and I thought the conversation may have ended before it had really started.

I was wrong.

"You killed him," she said. "How many does that make?"

I didn't want to answer. I didn't want to talk about it.

"Five," I said, and again I felt like throwing up.

"So this is what you are now? A serial killer?"

"I did it to protect you. Both of us, actually."

"I never asked you to do that! I didn't *want* that!"

I shook my head. What could I say? *I didn't want it either?*

I hadn't. But I'd do it again. I do it a million times, if it meant protecting her.

That, I knew, was something I could never say.

She was looking at me now, and her expression was hard. "But you're racing to save Henry now. Even though he tortured you."

"He was under duress," I said, though I wasn't entirely convinced he needed all that much persuasion. Emil Lyon was offering Henry something he wanted. It wasn't outside the bounds of imagination that Henry would put the screws to me to get what he wanted.

I would never torture you without good reason, Henry said.

That makes things all better, I replied.

Suddenly Kristen reached out a hand and put it on top of mine. There was a glove between us, but the gesture was still very intimate, considering. She knew exactly what physical contact with me meant. She knew why I avoided it.

I felt my heart race.

"Jaylin, this life... this isn't the life you wanted."

"It's the one I got," I shrugged, keeping my eyes glued to the road ahead. "Not much I can do about it."

"There is! We can find someone to help you! Maybe... maybe *cure* you."

I blinked. "Cure me? I'm not *sick*, Kristen. I can just *do* something. Like being a natural athlete, or being a genius."

Ha! Henry laughed. *Genius. Right.*

Silence, you, I grumbled.

"But your gift isn't like being able to throw a baseball or solve a math equation in your head. What you do, it isn't *natural*. It isn't *normal*."

"Actually, according to the President, there are other

people out there who can do some pretty abnormal things. I'm not so weird after all." I tried to smile at her.

Kristen shook her head.

"Look, let's say I turned myself over to someone," I said. "Maybe I walk into a lab somewhere and volunteer to be studied. I don't think a cure is going to be the first thing anyone works on. I think they'd strap me to a table and test me until they knew how this works. And I think I'd be dead by the end of it. Or wish I was." I shook my head. "I know that's what would happen, because it's exactly what Emil Lyon did to me."

She thought about this for a long while. "I know," she said, looking away. "But this... it can't go on like this."

I agreed. "When this is over, I'm going to make a new plan. I don't know what it will be yet. But you're right. It can't keep going like this. Too many people know about me now, for a start. And I've crossed some lines. People are going to want to find me, now more than ever. I have to get away, get a new start somewhere."

She looked back at me and squeezed my hand through the glove. "I'll help," she said.

I shook my head. "Thank you. But I don't think that's a good idea. When this is done, I think you need to distance yourself from me as much as possible. For good."

"We tried that, remember?" she said. "It ended up with me running for my life, with you showing up here anyway."

"We'll try again. This time we'll make it obvious that you and I have nothing to do with each other. Make it as public as possible. Maybe you go on the news and tell people I kidnapped you at gunpoint. There's plenty of evidence for that, now. Plenty of witnesses. It wouldn't take much to spin this story, so that I'm the bad guy."

"Jaylin, they'd *hunt* you! You'd be a *criminal*!"

"I'm already a criminal!" I said, bitterly. And then, quieter, "And a murderer."

She stared at me and pulled her hand away before looking out of her window again.

I've lost a lot in my life. I've felt emptiness and loneliness and despair in a way that no one else ever could. But that moment, as Kristen's hand left mine, was the worst of it.

Several hours later we were running on fumes, but the New York City skyline was looming on the horizon. After the incident in Grove City, I didn't want to stop until I could step out of the car and have concrete and subway tunnels under my feet. The car had other ideas, though.

We sputtered to a final stop, just as I pulled over in a suburban neighborhood. We were still a few miles from the city. The area was filled with houses with tiny yards, the occasional wooden picket fence. It might have been idyllic if not for the occasional presence of bars on some windows.

Despite the number of houses around us, and the small businesses that lined the streets a block up, everything felt low to the ground to me. It made me feel exposed somehow. It was better than the wide-open blankness of Zelienople, where one yard bled seamlessly into the next with no discernible break between the two. But it was in no way like being nestled into the concrete canyons of Manhattan, where the demand for anonymity was automatic among 1.6 million people.

This place was an alien landscape.

I felt vulnerable here.

We left the car and made our way down a few blocks until we were in a more rural-feeling area, though it still felt a bit "small town" to me.

I checked my phone, and saw to my relieve that we could get an Uber here, though it would take a little longer than I was used to. I set it up, and Kristen and I waited in a small diner until the car arrived nearly 20 minutes later.

Could we possibly speed things up? Henry asked. *The clock is ticking down for my outer self.*

You know, we can't be sure that whoever is watching outer Henry hasn't already put him down, Jacob said. *Tactically, that would be the right move. The mission may be FUBAR.*

Thanks for that, Henry said.

The car dropped us off a block from where my notes indicated they would be holding Henry. As we stepped out into the bustle of the city, buildings looming over us, traffic incessant in the streets surrounding us, it was like being able to breathe again. In fact, I inhaled deeply, and then coughed and cringed as I caught a whiff of urine and garbage and car exhaust.

"Home" *cough, cough* "sweet home," I said, wheezing.

"Lovely," Kristen said, crinkling her nose. "I see things haven't changed."

"Come on," I said, pulling her along. "I need to scope out the building."

We were across the street and hidden by scaffolding that framed the sidewalk. People were pushing by us, in a big hurry to be anywhere and nowhere in particular, and among the rush and press of it all I finally felt like I was "invisible" once again. All that open space had started to wear on my nerves, making me feel jumpy all the time. Here, at least, I could relax into my standard and comfortable paranoia.

How was I going to handle leaving this city, when this was all done?

Because it was starting to dawn on me that this was

exactly what I might have to do. Leave. Never come back. Never stop running.

"There," I said, pointing to an older building—a bit run down, and more or less shrouded in scaffolding. The ground floor was a retail space for a sushi restaurant and a hair salon. "One of Shallister Hoffman's holdings. The top floors are mostly empty, except for the lab and the area where they're holding Henry."

"So what do we do? How do we get in there?"

"Getting in isn't actually going to be a problem," I said. "Getting out with Henry, or without bullets in our bodies—that's going to be more of a challenge."

"I'm glad you're having a good time," Kristen said. "Because this scares the hell out of me."

"Which is exactly why you're going to wait here," I said.

"What? No way. I'm not standing out here in the open!"

"This is just about the safest place you can be right now," I said. "Other than one of my safe houses. And there's one of those a few blocks away. I don't think it's been compromised. It wasn't a very good safe house to begin with. Small. Dirty. But it will give you a place to escape to."

"Jaylin, I'm not leaving."

"You *will* leave, if things go wrong." I handed her the burner phone and a couple of pre-paid credit cards. "Use these. I put the address of the safe house on the phone. There's also a single contact in the contact list—a guy named Vic. You can trust him. If I'm not out of the building in 30 minutes, you go to the safe house and you lock yourself in. Use the computer there to get online and find out when it's safe to move out again, then call Vic. He'll help you get out of here. You can tell the police that I kidnapped you, and you escaped. Show them the safe house. Tell them that's where I kept you."

"Jaylin, I..."

"*Just do it!*" I said, my voice louder than I meant it to be. No one on the sidewalks bothered even looking our way. God bless New Yorkers.

Kristen seemed a little rattled, but she nodded. She took the phone and the credit cards, sliding them into her front pocket.

"Ok," I said, taking a deep breath and letting it out slowly. "I'm going in. Wait here for thirty minutes, then leave."

Again, Kristen nodded, and I left her standing under an awning, out of the way and, hopefully, safe.

At least that made one of us.

.

THE ALLEY REEKED of decaying fish, as well as other less identifiable smells. I pushed through, breathing from my mouth, though it didn't seem to help much.

I wasn't sure if it would be safe to go in through the back door of the building. Unlike the setup in Zelie, according to the information I'd recorded from Emil's memories, there were two guys watching Henry, and two guys who rotated in to relieve them. The rotation was set to happen right about now.

I stood by a reeking dumpster at the end of the alley, and watched as two men walked up to the back door, opening and entering.

I had to time this right. The last thing I needed was to face down four men instead of two.

I had the gun with its silencer, pressed against my leg.

My guts were twisted from fear and anxiety, and once again I felt like vomiting. I knew what I would have to do. I'd done it before. But despite all the "practice," it wasn't getting any easier. Just the opposite.

Keep it together, Jacob said. *This is war.*

I wanted him to be right. But it didn't *feel* like war. It felt like *murder.*

And worse.

It felt like I was losing something with each pull of the trigger.

When I absorb an engram, for the thirty minutes it's in my head it's *real.* The memories are mine. The skills and talents are mine. And then it just... leaves. It stops being a part of me so quickly and subtly that I sometimes don't notice until it's gone. Until I feel its absence.

That's what it felt like to take a life. Worse—unlike the fading engrams I absorbed, whatever I was losing with each kill was something I hadn't really felt was there. Losing an engram is like forgetting something you used to know. This felt more like losing something that defined me, shaped who I was.

Worse, as I lost more and more of whatever ineffable quality this was, I started to feel more and more numb to it.

I shook myself, trying to let all of this pass. I needed my head clear. I couldn't afford distractions from within. Distractions could get me and Henry killed, and put Kristen in worse danger.

You good? Jacob asked.

What was that tone? Concern? Jacob was usually tough as nails, never giving an inch. The consummate soldier. Also, I didn't think he liked me much.

But that tone—it almost sounded, almost *felt,* like caring.

"I'm good," I said, quiet. I wasn't sure it was true, but I was going to act as if, all the way through this.

The door opened again, and two more men exited. They moved out of the alley and were gone in moments.

Time to move, Jacob said.

I raced for the door. It wasn't locked, and I was able to get inside easily, then up the stairs to the third floor.

I was a little winded when I got there, but I could handle it. I held the gun with the barrel and silencer pointed up as I pressed back against a wall and peered around the corner, through the door of the stairwell and into a barely lit corridor.

There were three doors. One would be a restroom. Another was a maintenance closet. The third was where two men would be standing guard over Henry.

I had no idea what to expect on the other side of that door. Emil had never been here. Neither had Carter. Even if they had, they weren't going to willingly share any information with me. I'd have to fight for every scrap, and that would take time I didn't have.

I was on my own and going in blind.

You have this, Jacob said. *We're here to help.*

Unless you happen to have a few of those Chinese clones I can use, I replied, *I don't think you'll be able to help much.*

Don't be glib, Henry said. *There are ways we can help. You know that.*

I thought for a moment. *When I faced Sol, suddenly I could use all your skills. The adrenaline activated them automatically, I think.*

Seems to be the case, Henry said. *Are you proposing we try that again? It's an untested hypothesis.*

But you have to admit, it would be handy to have some martial arts skills right now, I replied.

Just focus on thinking your way in and out, Jacob said. *Force has its place, but it's not the answer to every challenge.*

It was odd hearing it from one of the seasoned warriors of the group, but I knew he was right. The problem was that I was on the edge of not being able to think clearly. All of this stress was stacking up—too many close calls, too many lethal choices. I was barely holding it together.

You are not doing this alone, Kristen said.

Her voice was softer than usual. Kinder. It was the voice I remembered, when I dreamed. The loving voice, the *discovering* voice that was at first very glad to be a part of me, inside my head, even if only for thirty minutes at a time.

It was the voice she had used before things went wrong between us.

It was the voice I needed to hear the most.

I moved down the hallway and stopped just in front of the door.

We have the element of surprise on our side, Jacob said. *The guards are just getting here, just settling in. They have no reason to expect us to attack.*

Is that what we're going to do, then? Henry asked. *Burst through the door, guns blazing?*

You got a better plan? We're listening, Jacob replied.

Actually, another voice said, *I do have a better plan.*

It took a moment for me to realize who had spoken, because until now he'd remained completely silent. His voice was strange and new, which made it a little startling.

Emil Lyon.

Great, Jacob said. *The new guy.*

The guy who wants us dead, Henry said.

Oh, Henry, that was before. Now I very much want us all to stay alive. For better or worse, this is where I live now.

Keeping Evergreen alive is now my top priority, for my own survival.

Great, Kristen said. *Another one.*

Don't knock self preservation, sweetheart, Jacob said. *We're literally all in this together. If Jaylin goes, we all go.*

My head was buzzing with all the chatter, and meanwhile my heart was pounding its way out of my chest. Adrenaline was flowing. Fight or flight was kicking in. I knew that if I didn't stop and think things through, logic and reason might go right out of the window.

This wasn't the time for automatic responses. This was the time for a plan.

Ok, Emil, I thought. *You know more about what we should expect than any of us. You're in. Welcome to the team. Now... what do we do?*

You're just going to trust him? Henry asked.

He's right, I said. *He's in this now. He's a part of me. The last living bit of him is in my head. If I die, he dies. He's hoping he can find a way out. Actually, I'm good with that plan, too. So there's more reason to trust him than not. For now, at least.*

And so we have a deal, Emil said. *I will help you rescue Henry...* outer *Henry. In exchange, you will help me to transfer my engram from your mind to the ERD, and from there to one of the clones.*

Kristen, of all people, asked, *And why shouldn't we just play along until we can destroy the ERD with you in it?*

That is one danger I face, Emil said. *A risk. But I've learned to measure risk, and to play the highest odds that are in my favor. If I am to choose a life in which I am locked away in the back of someone else's mind, unable to have any impact on the world, or risk everything for the chance of a new body and a new life, I will choose the risk.*

Good, I said. *Then it's a deal.*

You can't be serious! Henry said.

He's our best shot at rescuing outer Henry and getting out of this alive, I said. *So yeah, I'm serious.*

None of them responded to that, which Emil took as consent. *Excellent. Now, put your weapon away, Evergreen. We won't be needing it.*

Call me Jaylin, I said, tucking the gun into the back of my waistband and covering it with the tail of my hoodie. *We're all friends now, right?*

Quite, Emil said. *Now, friend, do exactly as I say.*

CHAPTER FOURTEEN

THE DOOR OPENED SLIGHTLY, AT MY KNOCK, AND IN AN instant there was a gun pointed directly at my head.

No dodging that, Joesph said, grumbling.

He won't have to, Emil replied. *Now Jaylin, say the word.*

"*Aperi*," I said, calmly.

The Latin word for "open." As passwords go, I suppose it was a good one. But for a second or two, there was no response, and I was starting to wonder if Emil had pulled a fast one.

The gun lowered, finally, and the guy opened the door wider. Though I still wasn't yet allowed to enter. "Who are you?" the gunman asked.

"Mr. Lyon sent me. I'm supposed to talk to our guest. A last interview."

"Last interview?" the guy asked.

"There won't be a check in," I said in a low tone, hoping I sounded ominous.

The guy looked me over, apparently taking in my jeans

and hoodie. Street clothes, sent on an errand given by a bespoke suit. It probably didn't look right.

Then again, these guys were street themselves, in their way. Hired muscle. Suits off the rack.

The guy finished looking me up and down, then nodded. "Right. Ok." He opened the door, gesturing, and I walked inside.

The password would do more than just get me in. It gave me a bit of authority with these mooks for hire. That was good. It would come in handy. But it only went so far.

Nothing short of an order from Emil Lyon himself could get me out of this place with Henry in tow. And the man wasn't in any shape to make a phone call or do a drop-by.

But Emil had a plan for that as well.

"He's through that door," the guy said, nodding.

"He has an escort?" I asked.

"Hal's in there with him."

"You wait here," I said, putting some nonchalant authority in my tone.

I walked to the door and knocked.

"Who is it?" a voice asked.

"*Aperi,*" I said again.

In a repeat of the scene from moments ago, the door opened, and a gun was pointed at my head. Hal, the guard watching Henry, looked past me to his buddy, who gave him a nod.

Hal opened the door, and I stepped inside.

Henry was sitting at a long table that was covered in papers and bits of equipment. He was working at a soldering station, and a tendril of faint white smoke curled upward as he tinkered with whatever device was in front of him. Looking closer, I could see that it was another ERD. Or the guts of one. The casing was set to the side.

"My time is up, I assume," Henry said, without looking up from his work.

"It's getting closer," I said.

Henry stopped, and looked up, seeing me for the first time. His eyes went wide, and I gave a slight shake of the head, willing him to keep quiet. He got the message.

"So now what?" he asked.

"Now you wrap up what you're doing. Mr. Lyon wants to have everything ready for the transfer."

"So he's honoring his deal?" Henry asked.

Yes, Emil said. *Though there are some modifications.*

"Yes," I said.

Henry eyed, me, and then his gaze flicked over to the ERD on the table. He turned and quickly reassembled it, pressing the circuitry into the metal casing. He handed it to me.

"This is *it*," Henry said.

I blinked, turning the ERD over in my hand, glancing up at Henry.

The way he'd emphasized *it*. There was something in his voice. A message.

He's saying it's important to you specifically, inner Henry said.

I nodded and put the ERD in the inner pocket of my hoodie.

Now, Emil said, *things are going to get complicated.*

I listened to his instructions and kept my features still as I turned back to face Hal. "You know the protocol?"

Hal nodded. "It's almost time."

"He wants it done in the white room," I said, repeating what Emil was telling me.

Hal looked confused. "The white room? Why the..."

"Look, Hal, I don't question Mr. Lyon. It's just bad policy. Do *you* question Mr. Lyon, Hal?"

Hal stopped and shook his head.

"He wants one of you to stay here and keep an eye on the street. There was an... *incident*. Something that could derail Mr. Lyon's plans. His man, Sol Rydell, got himself killed right in Mr. Lyon's apartment. Mr. Lyon isn't happy about it. And the guy who did it is still out there, and maybe knows too much about this place. So we need all of this locked down. No one in or out. Clear?"

Hal nodded. "I'll tell Jack."

Hal left the room, and Henry and I were alone for a moment.

"They're planning to kill me," Henry said. "They think I don't know, but I'm hardly an idiot."

"There's supposed to be a call from Emil. It's not going to happen."

"Your work? Did you really kill Sol Rydell?"

I nodded.

"Interesting."

"And for some reason, here I am," I said, holding my hands out and turning slightly. "And given that this is all your doing, I'm wondering why I shouldn't just let them pop you."

Henry shook his head and smiled. "We go too far back for that. But also, there's more to this than you think. Before, at the apartment, I was trying to tell you. But *he* got in the way."

"Who?" I asked. "What are you..."

Before I could finish, the door opened, and Hal stood in the doorway. He nodded to me and gestured that we should follow.

I gave Henry a similar gesture, standing aside and motioning him to proceed. "After you."

Henry stood, leaning a bit on the cane, and hobbled from the room.

Well this seems a strange turn of events, inner Henry said. *I'm apparently much more clever than I realized.*

Self adulation is an unattractive quality, Henry, Emil said.

As is baseless arrogance, Henry replied.

Will both of you shut up? Kristen said. *Dear God, it was bad enough having* one *pompous ass in here.*

I was glad for Kristen to step in. Most of the time, I can cope with the noise in my head. In fact, most of the time, the voices tend to keep quiet, and keep to themselves. It's not often that they actually interact with each other. But high stress can bring them to the surface, and this situation certainly qualified.

Lately, though, it seemed as if I was hearing from all of them at once, and more frequently. Caleb was still on the quiet side, as usual. Carter, thankfully, hadn't yet managed to work his way out of the "cell." And Julia—thank God she just listened and went back to whatever hole she occupied in the back of my mind. Having her voice—her *voices*—in my head was a little like standing next to the speakers at a heavy metal concert.

Henry and I followed Hal through the room to the corridor where we mounted a set of stairs to the next floor. The other guard stayed behind, as "ordered."

So far, so good.

One flight up from where Henry had been kept was the White Room—a lab that was static-guarded, grounded through the walls of the building to thick iron rods buried in the pavement below, and hidden in the alleys on either side. This room was also self-contained and completely off the grid—running from a series of generators and backup generators in the basement, all connected to a large backup uninterrupted power supply that would keep power going even as the generators switched from one to another. The whole space was in a Farraday cage, shielded against any radio waves of every kind. There was a hardline connection for internet and communications, and that could only be accessed through a heavily secured computer system in the room. Henry didn't have the biometrics to even turn it on.

Nothing could get in or out unless it was meant to.

Almost nothing.

The wooden door leading into the room was pure camouflage. Once open, I could see that it was nearly three inches thick, with a steel core. It revealed a sort of airlock where you'd have to step in, close the door behind you, wait for a scan, and then step through the second door once it opened.

Nothing got in or out of the white room unless the security system allowed it. And the doors were completely bullet proof.

Hal stood in the hall, holding the wood door open as I punched in the security code. The thick glass and steel door to the airlock slid open, and I nudged Henry in first.

"Wait," I said to Hal, holding up a hand. "The ERD... did you grab it?"

"What? That metal donut thing? No. I thought *you* had it."

I swore. "He must have left it downstairs." I eyed Henry, as if I were pissed at him. "He's pulling something," I said. I pulled the gun with the silencer out from under my coat and pushed it against Henry's head. "Are you pulling something, old man?" I put as much menace in my voice as I could, to really sell it.

"N-no! I swear!" Henry said in a convincing stutter. "I... I just forgot it. I left it on the table. It's just sitting there!"

I looked over my shoulder at Hal. "Get it," I said.

"I don't leave his side," Hal said. "Those are my orders."

"And these are you *new* orders!" I said loudly. "Mr. Lyon wants that device in place before this happens, to make sure this piece of crap hasn't *sabotaged* it." I pushed Henry's head with the silencer, to emphasize my point. "He's not going anywhere. I'll lock him in here and close the airlock door. See?"

I stepped in and hit the button to close the airlock.

The door slid closed, and the room became eerily quiet. The space was so well sound insulated that all I could see was Hal shouting from outside. He had his own gun out now, alert and ready. I pointed to the stairs and then made a circle with my thumb and forefinger.

Hal, hesitating but realizing he had few choices, shook his head and then turned and jogged down the stairs.

The wood door closed as he left, giving us cover. As soon as we were out of sight I punched the code for the door on the other side, and we were in the white room. I closed the door, then shot the keypad, compromising the housing and causing the security system to deadlock both doors in place.

"Wait!" Henry said. "That's our only way out of this room! We should have run for the stairs!"

"It's the only way out that you knew about," I said, and I grabbed his arm, forcing him to hobble quickly to the other side of the room.

Against the far wall was a case of metal shelves, lined with equipment. An old oscilloscope was on one shelf, pushed into the corner. I turned three of the knobs on its front in a specific pattern, dictated to me by Emil, and there was a click as the display popped outward. I pulled this open to reveal another security keypad inside. I hit the code for this and stepped back.

The book case moved upward, revealing a very modern elevator bank. The doors to the elevator slid open, and I pushed Henry inside.

"Wait here," I said.

I heard a series of soft thuds, and looked up to see Hal and Jack, guns out, firing into the glass on the outside of the air lock. Their bullets had made very small divots in the glass. At that rate, it would take a month and about two-hundred-thousand rounds of ammunition to shoot their way through the first door alone. We were pretty safe in here.

Which gave me time to start wrecking everything in the lab.

I started with the computer hard drives, putting bullets through the casings, shattering the platters inside. I yanked the cables from all the ethernet ports and put more bullets through the hard drives in the server tower. There was a backup, offsite, but I already had a plan for dealing with that. Thanks to Emil.

His vested interest in giving me a leg up might run out at some point, but for the moment I felt I could depend on his intel.

Next I started soaking everything in the room with an accelerant from a metal cabinet in one corner. Oddly enough, this was the very purpose of the accelerant—to burn this place to the ground if it were ever compromised.

And just to ensure his survival, if he happened to be here when things went south, Emil had ordered this escape hatch installed. The elevator led directly to a tunnel below the building, which led to a private garage across the street. There would be a car there, with a proximity key hidden inside. I had the door code for the car door as well. We could be out of here in a few minutes.

Looking around, ensuring everything was thoroughly soaked, I stepped into the elevator and raised the gun, aiming for one of the metal cans that had held the highly flammable liquid. I punched the button to close the elevator doors, and in the next instant I fired into the can. The shot ignited the fuel inside, and the canister exploded, catching the rest of the white room on fire.

The elevators closed on a hellish scene, with Hal and Jack on the far side of it, stepping away and running for the stairs.

And that was it.

We were out. Or on our way out, at least.

No one died.

We were making our escape, and no one had to be killed.

I was really hoping it would stay that way for a while.

"MOVE!" I shouted, as Henry hobbled as fast as he could. The tunnel was long, but well-lit. The lights were LED and on motion sensors—they only activated as we entered a new segment.

We were moving a lot slower than I would have liked.

"Emil, do the guards know about the garage?"

Of course, Emil said.

"So they're on their way?"

Yes. But it will be difficult for them to get inside. If you shoot Henry, we can make it.

What? Hey, don't! inner Henry said.

"I'm not going to shoot Henry," I said.

"Good to know," outer Henry huffed as he struggled to pick up speed. "Those guys probably know where we're headed."

"Emil says they do," I said.

Henry gawked at me. "Did you... is he *permanent?*"

I said nothing, but took Henry's arm and practically dragged him through the tunnel.

We came to yet another door locked with a keypad. I entered the code, and there was a click. I opened the door slowly and took a quick look while making a sweep with the gun in front of me. Once I saw that the place was clear I moved and pulled Henry along.

The garage was pristine. And *vast*.

I've lived in New York all my life. Parking here is... well, it's *expensive*. There are people who pay more for their parking space than for their apartments. Having a private garage is practically unheard of. Having one that looks like a highly polished show-room floor was more than I would think even Emil Lyon could afford.

Don't underestimate my wealth, Emil said.

"I don't think it's your wealth anymore," I replied. "Dead guys don't need money, much."

I'm hardly dead, though, am I? And true wealth is calculated in resources, not money. Even now, in this state, I have more resources than most of humanity. Something you may want to bear in mind.

I didn't have time for a philosophical discussion about the nature of wealth. I'd save it for another day. With Emil onboard full-time, there would be plenty of opportunities.

As long as I lived through this.

I pulled Henry along, and we were nearly to the car when a door opened on the far side of the garage.

Shots were fired immediately, and I pulled Henry down as we used the car for cover.

I glanced over the hood of the car and saw that Hal and Jack had been joined by a couple of other guys.

"More guards," I said.

There were two here in the garage, but I thought we'd have time, Emil said.

"You should have told me!" I shouted.

Let's yell at him later, Kristen said, her voice tense. *What do we do now?*

We get in the vehicle, Jacob said. *I assume it's armored?*

Of course, Emil replied.

I punched the code into the keypad on the door handle and the LEDs blinked to tell me it was unlocked, I opened it, and turned to Henry to tell him to get inside.

He was leaning against the car, hand against his chest. Blood was streaming from a gunshot wound I hadn't noticed that he'd taken.

His face was already ashen and pale. He was soaked in blood. I could see him fading.

"Henry!"

"I think I am... in need of medical attention," Henry said, his voice low.

I peeked over the hood again. The guards were trying to spread out from the door, to get to cover and surround me. I fired a couple of rounds, letting the whizzing ricochet of the bullets tell them to stand where they were. The vast, hollow space of the garage made each shot and whining ricochet echo from everywhere.

I tugged at Henry, trying to get him to his feet, but he was dead weight.

"I'm... sorry, Jaylin," He said, quietly.

"No," I said, shaking my head. "Don't be. It's fine. I understand."

"What? That... that I betrayed you?" He chuckled. "I did, you know. I can't make up for that."

I looked again, and again fired shots over the hood to keep the guards from moving.

There was an eerie sort of calmness settling over me. Maybe it was a side effect of my ability. Maybe it was the adrenaline numbing my emotions. Maybe it was shock.

I'm dying, inner Henry said.

It was quiet. Not so much shock as fascination.

I'm watching myself die.

Outer Henry winced and groaned. "There's more... you need to know," he said. He reached to grab my sleeve, pulling at it, but his grip went weak. His hand flexed, one last time, and then it slackened and fell away.

Henry—the man who had trained me, and the man who had betrayed me.

Henry—my friend, my mentor, my enemy.

Henry was dead.

I looked again, and the guards had the door closed almost completely. They were coordinating, making a plan. I had to act now, or I was done.

Touch him, inner Henry said.

"What?" I asked.

He had more he needed to tell you. There's something else going on. Touch him. Find out what you need to know.

He was right. And, given that I already had a permanent engram of Henry in my head, there wasn't much to worry about. The two engrams should merge with only a few bumps.

In theory. I hadn't exactly done this before. Not *this*.

Absorbing an engram from someone recently dead usually had some negative consequences. What would happen if I absorbed someone that already had a permanent copy in my head? Would I go catatonic? Go into a seizure? Have some kind of blinding, debilitating backlash?

There was only one way to find out, and I was running out of time either way.

I took off one of my gloves and swept my hand over Henry's face, closing his eyes like I was giving him last rites.

In an instant I absorbed all of his memories.

There was a clash in my head—a doubling of memories, with minor conflicts smoothing themselves out as a few years of new information was suddenly integrated with an "old backup."

Oh my, Henry said. *This is an odd experience. I'm learning and remembering all at once.*

Marvel over it later, Jacob said. *We need to get out of here right now! Jaylin, kid... you good to go?*

I blinked, shook my head, took some deep breaths. "I... think so," I said, shaking it off.

There was a lot happening. My mind and heart were both racing. But Jacob was right. There would be time to sort this all out later. Right now, we had to move.

I rolled Henry to the floor of the garage, saying my goodbyes, though I hadn't really lost him at all. As a last nod, or maybe out of some habit I'd just absorbed from Henry, I grabbed his cane as I climbed into the car. I locked the doors and found the proximity key in the center console. I hit the start button in the dash, and the car roared. Seconds later I was racing through the garage, thuds of gunfire hitting the trunk and back glass as tires squealed on the concrete.

As I approached the bay doors of the garage, the proximity sensors opened them, and in seconds I was out on the street, with the rolling doors closing behind me.

I gunned it, dodging through traffic, and making a circle around the block.

Where are we going? Emil asked. *We should get as far from here as possible!*

"Kristen!" I said.

And, as if I'd conjured her with her name, I saw her. She was standing under the awning, just as I'd told her to. She looked terrified.

I slammed the brakes, and the car screeched to a stop. Kristen backed away, hugging the wall, clearly afraid, ready to run. The tinted windows prevented her from seeing me.

I reached over and opened the passenger side door. "Kristen! It's me! Get in now! We have to *run*!"

Kristen hesitated only for a second and looked down the street. I followed her gaze, and saw men running from one of the doorways, guns drawn.

"*Now!*" I shouted.

Kristen ran for the car, even as bullets thudded against the windshield, leaving small pockmarks from their impact.

Kristen was inside, the door closed, and the locks engaged. I slammed on the gas and we sped away, squeals and smoke rising from the tires, leaving a hazy wake between us and our pursuers.

The guards were in the street, firing at us as we barreled toward them, then leaping aside once they realized we weren't stopping. I heard a thump and a scream as I clipped one guard. I was pretty sure I ran over his leg.

Poor bastard. May he rot in hell.

"Are you ok?" I said, patting at Kristen's arm and shoulder. "Were you hit?"

"No! I'm fine!" she shouted. "What happened?"

"Someone left out some key information," I said, scowling.

I do apologize, Emil said. *I was certain we would have more time.*

I shook my head, not wanting to comment.

"Where's Henry?" Kristen asked.

I huffed. Emotion rose in my throat and I swallowed it down, reminding myself that things were complicated on that score.

"Dead," I said, and despite myself there was a catch in my throat.

"Oh... Jaylin..."

I shook my head. "But not gone," I said. "He's in here." I tapped my forehead. "Merged with inner Henry."

I guess we're both inner Henry now, Henry said. There was a tone in his voice that wasn't quite right. Something new. He was acting nonchalant, but this had affected him.

"What do we do now?" Kristen asked, glancing at the side mirror.

"You still have my phone?" I asked.

She held it up.

"Text Vic," I said. "Tell him we should grab a cup of coffee at Rudyard's next Tuesday."

"You're making a coffee date?" Kristen asked, incredulous.

"It's a code," I said. "He'll know when and where to meet us."

Kristen nodded and sent the text.

I concentrated on getting us deeper into the grid of the city, slowing the car to a legal speed, and finding a spot where we could ditch it and take to foot so we could get lost in the crowds.

I needed to get Kristen to some place safe. And the safest place would be as far from me as possible.

CHAPTER FIFTEEN

I WAS GRIPPING HENRY'S CANE, STUDYING THE intricate silver of the handle. It had a comforting heft. And since I couldn't very well walk around with one of the guns out, it would have to do as a quick weapon, if I needed it.

I loathe that cane, Henry said. *If Emil were still alive, I'd shove it straight up his—*

"Cool it," I said.

Yes, Henry. Cool it. Emil taunted. *You know that you would never get within five feet of me.*

"You, too," I said.

"Inner voices acting up?" Kristen said.

I nodded.

She reached out and took my gloved hand, which did wonders to comfort me.

We'd worked out long ago that the activity in my head was more or less triggered by my emotional state. Kristen even had a theory that with training and mental discipline, I might be able to keep from absorbing engrams entirely. She believed it was a matter of focus, control, and calm. Which was why she had learned as much as she could about Zen practice, yoga, and even Tai Chi. She taught me a few things. They helped. A little. But she'd left before we could really get into anything advanced.

We walked into the cafe where Vic would arrive at a pre-set time.

"Want anything?" I asked Kristen. "Hungry?"

She nodded. It had been almost a full day since we'd high-tailed it from Zelie, and we hadn't been able to grab lunch thanks to unforeseen attempted murder. I had to admit, I was pretty hungry, too.

The meeting spot was a mid-Eastern cafe called Gaza-las, near Central Park. It was a quiet place, with a good atmosphere, and the food was terrific. We ordered Kafta Tahini, and when that was devoured we lingered over Baklava and Turkish coffee. It was the most peaceful moment I'd had in the past several days, and I had to fight to keep my paranoia from lapsing.

It was nice to be able to just enjoy a space for a little while. Being here, with Kristen, made everything feel less dangerous. Which was the biggest danger of all.

Complacency could lead to trouble. Better to keep the shields up at all times than to let them down and get yourself and everyone around you killed.

That was the hard lesson of my life, to date.

I continued to enjoy the coffee and the soft conversation with Kristen, but I kept my guard up.

Right on schedule, Vic entered the cafe, glancing around until he spotted me. I dropped some cash on the table, and as Kristen and I walked toward the exit, I pulled off a glove and made a small show of recognizing my "old friend."

"Vic! Great to see you!"

Vic smiled, and took my hand, playing along with the show. "You too! Leaving so soon?"

I shook my head, regretfully. "We're meeting friends in a bit. But we should definitely catch up!"

So far so good. Vic's memories showed all was clear. He hadn't been approached by anyone and had been extra careful about his route here.

This is it, though, inner Vic said. *This is the last time. I always wondered how you did it. I thought you were some kind of Sherlock or something. But this is even cooler! You're like a super hero!*

No, I said. *Not a superhero. Nothing like that.*

We left Gazalas and made a block before taking the stairs down to the subway.

"So, that was strange," Kristen said. "I thought we were meeting him to chat."

"It was a check in. Gives me a chance to get a read, to make sure he hadn't ratted me out to the Feds or the mafia or something. He'll meet us at another spot. He picked a place at random, and he had the address in his head."

"Does he... does he know what you can do?"

I shook my head. "He thinks I'm just really good at figuring things out. That was the last skin-to-skin contact I can make with him, though. I'll have to recruit a new... helper." I really needed a better word to describe the guys I used for this stuff.

"I see," Kristen said, mulling all of it over.

We took a set of stairs down and boarded the subway, then bumped along quietly. Kristen seemed contemplative, and I was happy enough for the two of us to sit in silence. It was good enough just to have her there with me. It had been a long time since we'd been together like this—riding along on the subway, sitting close enough to each other that I could feel the warmth of her even through our coats. It was the kind of "normal" I'd been missing. I hadn't even realized I'd been missing it.

Three stops later we left the train and made our way to a small coffee shop on the street, above, a couple of blocks from the subway exit. We circled the block and came at it from the back entrance after ducking through a clothing store and exiting into the shared alley.

"This is all very cloak and dagger," Kristen said. "Does it really help?"

"It keeps me from moving in straight lines. Keeps me from being predictable. That's the point."

"It keeps you from ever feeling normal," Kristen said.

"It's the most normal thing about me," I replied.

We took seats in the coffee shop, in a booth at the back, near the exit. Kristen stayed seated while I ordered three Americanos. I brought the coffees, along with cream and sugar for Kristen, back to the table.

Vic had taken a car to get here, which helped him move a bit faster than we had, so he'd been able to linger at Gazalas for a while to throw off anyone who might be watching. Soon he wandered in through the front door, and once he spotted me he came straight to our table, sitting in front of his cup of coffee. He sipped it and smiled. "Thanks, boss," he said.

"I'm not your boss, Vic. From now on, you're a free agent again."

Vic studied me and nodded. "Last one," he said. "I knew it was coming. Thought it would be different."

"Something came up, thanks to the previous gig."

"Are we in trouble?" Vic asked, going stiff.

"I am. You're not. I have one last job for you, though, and it's easy. When it's done you can go on and forget you ever knew me."

Vic laughed, "Fat chance of that, boss."

I smiled and nodded. I knew what he meant. His memories had faded by now, on the long subway ride over, but I'd seen into his head. I knew him pretty well by this point. He liked this work. He liked the mystique of it all. I actually regretted closing this particular loop, because people like Vic are rare. It was going to be tough to find someone to replace him.

"I need a few things, and it would be safer for you to get them than for me to spend too much time out in the open."

"Whatever you need," Vic said.

I nodded. "Also, I need to make an adjustment to your commission from the last job."

Vic looked worried. "He didn't pay?"

"They always pay up front," I said. "Part of my conditions of employment. This time, though, he paid a lot more than we had originally agreed. The money has bounced around a bit, so I think it's safe to transfer your cut."

Vic's eyes widened. "How much?" he asked.

"You got the 20K already?"

He nodded.

"I'm moving 180 into your account today."

Vic actually stopped breathing, long enough that I started to worry about him.

"That's... my cut is 200K? That's the whole thing!"

I smiled. "I did a bit of upselling," I said. "Don't worry, I'm all set. And you're still getting the bonus, just as we agreed."

Vic settled back, his hands forming a circle around the

base of his coffee cup. "I can go full time," he said quietly, staring at his coffee as if it might reveal some secret.

"Go where?" Kristen asked, glancing from Vic to me.

"College," I said. "Vic's going to college. A good one, too. He's been working for me to help pay for some classes, but he couldn't afford full-time tuition. Until now."

"I'll be done in just a couple of semesters now," Vic said, looking up at us. "Boss... I can't tell you... I'm just..."

"You more than earned it, Vic. I appreciate your help. I'm sad to see things come to an end."

Vic stared and nodded. "Right. Me too. So, what do you need? Since this is my last gig, let's do it right."

I smiled. "For starters, I need two new burner phones and a new laptop. Use the petty cash account."

He nodded. "What else?"

"Passports."

"The guy?" Vic asked.

"He still owes me."

"What guy?" Kristen asked.

"One of the freebies," Vic said.

"Sometimes I do favors for people who don't have a lot of cash, but might have other resources I can use."

"Criminals," Kristen said, and I heard the tone in her voice. I knew that tone very well. I heard it in my head pretty often.

"I'll set it up. He'll need photos."

"He already has them," I said.

Vic glanced from me to Kristen.

"Her, too. I... well, it's an old arrangement."

"You have a passport photo of me on file with a criminal?" Kristen said.

"You know, when you put it that way, it sounds more like a *bad* idea."

"Ya think?" Kristen said.

"Vic, I'll text you with a code for the drop point. But this will be the last time you and I talk face to face."

Vic nodded, his expression somber. "Boss... I just realized, I don't even know your real name."

"You don't need to," I said. "You don't want to. Trust me."

Again he nodded, sipped his coffee, sighed. "Thank you," he said, and there was real emotion in his voice. "This has been amazing. And it's giving me a chance I didn't have before. Thank you."

I nodded, and we shook hands, though this time my glove was on, and I was careful not to make skin-to-skin contact.

Vic left through the front door, coffee cup in hand. I took Kristen by the elbow, and we made our way out of the back door.

"He likes you," Kristen said as we ducked through the alley.

"He's a good guy. I'll miss him."

"You don't have to, you know," she said. "It's ok to have good people in your life."

"It's not," I said grimly. "It never will be."

"Why? Because of what you can do?" she asked.

I shook my head. "Because of everything I've *done*," I said.

She was quiet then, remembering a lot of what I'd done just in the past 24 hours.

She's right, though, inner Kristen said. *You don't have to be alone.*

I say I do, I replied.

We left the alley and kept our heads down as we moved to the next location.

THE THING about being on the run is it becomes a habit.

For the past few years I've lived by that habit. I was used to it. I had routines and plans and backup plans. I was used to the pace.

Kristen wasn't.

"Can we... can we just *stop* for a second? Catch our breath somewhere?"

"When we get there," I said, keeping my pace.

"Where, Jaylin? Where are we going?"

I stopped then, looking back at her. "I... actually I don't know."

I slumped a little, leaning against the wall of the building next to us. I felt very heavy, all of a sudden.

Kristen looked at me, concerned. She reached up, about to test my forehead, to get my temperature.

I jerked away.

Kristen pulled her hand back, as if she'd nearly been bitten by a snake. "Oh, I'm sorry... it was... reflex."

I nodded.

"You look tired," she said. "When was the last time you slept?"

"It's been a while," I said. "I'm running on coffee and adrenaline right now. And mostly coffee."

"Even more reason to get to someplace where you can rest."

I nodded. "There will be plenty of time to sleep on the plane," I said.

"Plane? That's why you needed the passports? Where are we flying?"

"China," I said.

Kristen shook her head. "I'm not flying to China, Jaylin."

I looked at her, gauging. She was serious, of course. "I don't know if it's safe here yet," I said.

"You don't know if China will be safe, either. And I can't think of a worse idea than using a fake passport to fly into a country known to be pretty rough on Americans they think might be up to something illegal."

She was right. China could be a little unforgiving, under those circumstances. But it was the only lead I had, the only direction I knew. Henry had died for whatever was going on there. Emil had sacrificed everything for the technology they were developing. And speaking of Emil...

"I made a promise. Emil helped me to rescue Henry, and in exchange I agreed to help him get to the technology in China." I decided to keep the cloning part quiet for the time being.

Kristen watched me for a while, then shook her head. "I can't go, Jaylin. I just... I have a life, and I'd like to get back to it. In fact... I'd like you to come with me. Somehow, we can make it work. A quiet life, Jaylin. Away from... well, all of this. We'll find a way to manage your... condition."

"We've had this conversation before," I said.

She nodded. "I remember. And I remember how it ended."

"This thing I can do... it's part of me. Maybe there's a way I can manage it better, control it. My best shot at that was always Henry."

"The man who betrayed you and nearly got you killed."

"I'm starting to wonder about that," I said.

"He's in there? In your head right now?" she asked.

I nodded.

"Then ask him. What does he have to lose now? He should tell you everything. No more secrets. What was it he had planned, and why did he do it?"

I stared at her face. She was right. Henry owed me.

Well? I asked.

It's complicated, Henry said. *But I never wanted to betray you, Jaylin. Not like you think. I used you, that's true. I had plans, for what you can do. But things just got out of control very quickly. And now...*

Now you're dead, I said. *Now it's too late for whatever you had in mind.*

No, Henry said, his tone sounding somber. *It isn't.*

I was about to ask him what he meant when suddenly things started to click.

I thought about everything that had happened, since I'd met Henry. The training to use my abilities. The testing to see how things worked, to establish the rules. The experiments to how far things could be pushed, what my limits might be.

And then there was the tech. The ERD wasn't an idea Henry whipped up in prison. It was something he'd been working on while we were together. Something he'd been building as part of a plan. Something he'd needed more resources for—more equipment, more facilities, more money.

In all the time we'd worked together, Henry had been out of a job. He'd lost his tenure and his position. He'd lost access to his facility and labs. He'd lost everything.

We'd funded some of what he was doing with my... "consulting." The work I did with the criminal underworld brought in enough cash to keep us going.

Or, had it?

I thought about this, then cursed aloud.

"What is it?" Kristen asked. "What did he tell you?"

"He didn't tell me anything," I said. "Which tells me everything."

"What is it?" she asked.

"I just realized," I said, shaking my head. "I'm an idiot." I looked at her, saw the concern on her face. I sighed. "He knew about the Chinese tech. He knew about the cloning. All of it. He may have been working for Emil under duress, but he would have done the work anyway. He had plans of his own for that tech. The same plans as Emil Lyon."

"What plans?" Kristen asked.

I looked at her, thought about everything she'd had to go through, because of me. Because of my abilities. Because of the plans of evil men. "He wants to live forever," I said.

Evergreen, Emil's voice said in my mind.

"Evergreen," I said aloud. And suddenly it clicked.

"That ridiculous code name?" Kristen said.

I shook my head, my breathing a little rapid now. "I believed Henry's story about that, about the EEG and the printouts. Green ink," I said, scornfully. I pressed my gloved palms to my eyes. "God, I just *swallowed* it, never doubted it, because at least Henry was someone who *knew*. He was someone I could ask questions, someone who might have answers. I believed him. I was an idiot."

"What does it really mean?" Kristen asked.

"Immortality," I said. "That was what he was after all along. I'm a bridge, to get his consciousness into a new body. Just like Emil wanted—*wants*. They both played me for the same game. Henry was working for Emil so he could get closer to the Chinese. He must have known they'd have access to his ERD technology once they acquired Paradigm. He's known what the Chinese were up to all along."

Isn't it brilliant? Emil said, and I could hear the mental Cheshire grin in his voice. *I knew, of course. Henry is quite bright, but not nearly as devious as he pretends to be. It was transparent from the beginning. He was too easy to turn. Too eager to engage in corporate espionage. It was his research and designs, largely, that made Paradigm's technology work. His name is on all the patents. He could have just let them bring a product to market and he would have reaped millions. But I saw right away that his goals went beyond money. They were the same as mine. Immortality. Eternal youth. To be evergreen!*

Henry stayed silent during all of this.

"So now you're going to China to, what, give Henry and Emil exactly what they wanted?"

"He said there was more I needed to know," I said. "Outer Henry. When he died, those were his last words. I absorbed him, and his pattern integrated with the one I had in my head. I was in such a rush at the time, I didn't really have a chance to explore his memories. I don't know what it was he was thinking. And I don't know if I can trust him if I ask now."

"Ask anyway," Kristen said.

I looked at her, then nodded. "But not here. We have time, before Vic gets back to us. I have a place close by. A safe house. We can rest, take a moment to breathe. Then... I can arrange a way for you to get back to your life. There will be some chaos, but I think there's enough evidence out there for you to make the case that you were kidnapped. In a few weeks, things should blow over."

She nodded and followed me as I made my way to the safe house—another vacationer's apartment that would be clear for the next week or so. I'd been holding it in reserve, as a place to crash for a night or two. When all the heat started, I had decided not to risk it. But now, I couldn't think of any place that would be any safer.

I snagged the key from where it hung in the small plant next to the door.

"Who's place is this?" Kristen asked.

"Jillian and Carter Riggs," I said. "They're a nice couple. He's a user experience consultant. She's a web developer. They travel a lot."

"And... you're friends with them?" she asked.

I shook my head. "Only met Jillian last week, for a few seconds as she and Carter used the subway to get to the airport."

"So you 'acquired' this place," Kristen said, disapproving.

"It's safe. And comfortable," I said, locking the door and moving to the fridge without hesitation, opening it to pilfer whatever I could find there.

Kristen shook her head, but slumped onto the sofa without another word.

I snagged two bottles of water from the fridge, handing her one.

"I pay," I said. "I don't steal."

"Just borrow," she said.

"Something like that."

"That's new. When I left, you had no problem stealing."

"I had a problem with it," I replied. "I just believed Henry at the time. That it was somehow my due. Or that it was necessary."

"And now? Why the change of heart? What convinced you that you're not due someone else's property?"

"You," I said. I didn't need to say more. She understood what I meant.

You changed me. You made me better. I carry you in my

head, like a mental Jiminy Cricket. And I'm so ashamed of the life I live, I can't stand to hear what you think of me.

I dropped to the couch beside her, feeling the weight of the day press me down into the cushions. It was a soft, comfortable sofa. The place was quiet and warm. Kristen was so close I could feel the press of her next to me. I was nearly asleep.

My phone chirped to let me know I had a new email. It was from Vic.

"Mmph?" Kristen roused a bit, hearing the phone. She must have drifted off. I didn't say anything, and instead looked at the message, then thumbed a response. Everything was in our pre-arranged code, and I was able to confirm a meeting for later tonight. Vic would bring both passports, but I wasn't sure if Kristen would need hers after all. In fact, as I sank back into the sofa cushions, I started questioning the whole plan that I'd been operating from.

Why did I want her to go with me? It wouldn't do much more than put her in danger. Again. She'd be safer once she was away from me. I knew that. But still.

You love her, a voice said.

Kristen's voice.

I love you, I replied.

Me. Her. We're pretty much the same, right? She's just out there. She has no idea who you really are. But I do.

That stung a bit, but I was used to that from Kristen. She was honest. She never held back. Unless someone was taking from her, without her permission. That's how she saw my "gift." Taking, without consent.

I tried to ignore inner Kristen, and I let outer Kristen sleep. I slipped off of the sofa and made my way to the ancient desktop computer that Jillian and Carter Riggs used mostly for surfing the web and keeping their books. I had all the passwords to get in and get online. I used a VPN to log into a few accounts Emil had on the side—mostly as part of various backup and contingency plans.

There were a couple of bank accounts that were off the books, filled with more money than I'd ever had access to in one place. No one but Emil had ever known about them. That could come in handy.

What I was after now, though, was transportation.

There was no way I was getting into China without going through some sort of security, but I could at least minimize that by leaving from a private airport, aboard one of the planes Emil kept in reserve. These were also "off the books." Shallister Hoffman had no record of them, in case Shallister Hoffman was the reason Emil needed to fly away.

"You were a sneaky man, Emil."

I prefer the term "cautious." And perhaps that's a good thing, considering. You will certainly benefit from my precautions.

"Maybe," I said. "If the police haven't managed to lock down everything to do with you."

Are you looking for sympathy from the man you murdered? Emil asked.

"It's in your best interest to help me get to China safely. So no, not sympathy. Help, though. I expect that."

Very well, Emil said. *Since you are honoring our agreement, I am inclined to ensure you reach your destination.*

"And self preservation clearly has nothing to do with it."

For the next few minutes, Emil helped me create a profile that made me—or at least, the name on my fake passport—an official employee of Shallister Hoffman, according to all public records. Vic had included my new name in his email, slipping it in as a quick mention of a friend he'd bumped into, along with his girlfriend.

Craig Herbert, Emil said, a note of distaste in his voice. *Dreary sounding name.*

"I like Craig. It sounds solid to me."

Craig Herbert was now a consultant for Shallister Hoffman, with carte blanche to move around using their network of resources. This flight was off the books, but if the police (or anyone else) somehow connected the dots to get to this sideline charter flight, I'd stand a better chance of passing scrutiny now.

Flight arrangements made, I checked online for news about Emil's death.

Nothing yet.

Emil came and went so frequently, it was possible his body was currently rotting in silence in his penthouse apartment, undiscovered. The same would be true of Sol. It could be awhile before anyone found them and started investigating, which worked to my advantage.

Or, they could both be in a morgue right now, and the police were keeping things quiet while they investigated and circled in to snag me.

Life was full of questions.

I switched gears then and looked for news on the two guys who had tried to kill Kristen. Police were pursuing leads, but as yet had not identified either the gunman in the McDonalds or the man found dead in the home of Kristen's neighbors. Judging from the murder of the neighbors and the nature of both gunman deaths, the police suspected mafia ties. The current theory was that Kristen was a collateral hostage who had blundered into the middle of a mafia war.

That was good. It would lend some credibility to Kristen's story, that she was kidnapped and wasn't a willing participant. I could feed her some details, coach a little, and the story she'd give the police and the press would probably be taken at face value.

The next bit of news I checked on was Henry.

His body had been found in a dumpster several blocks from where I'd last seen him. They made it look like a robbery gone wrong, stripping him of any cash, but leaving his wallet so that he'd be easy to identify. The reports talked about his recent release from prison and hinted that he may have simply fallen in with the wrong crowd.

A man should never have to read his own obituary, Henry said. *It's morbid.*

"I'll keep that in mind," I said.

I shut off the computer and stood, looking at Kristen, who was stretched out now on the sofa.

I went to her and knelt beside her, studying her face as she slept.

There was nothing I wanted more than to kiss her right then. Her lips were in a sweet and soft pucker, and they were the most inviting thing I'd ever seen. But that kiss would be the worst kind of betrayal, in her mind. It would rip a copy of everything she knew and burn it directly into my brain. The two engrams would blend, and I'd actually know more about Kristen than she knew about herself.

That kiss would deepen everything I knew about her, join her to me in a way that no couple in history had ever been joined. And then I'd lose her forever.

That kiss was forbidden.

Instead, I reached out with a gloved hand, and brushed the hair from her cheek. "Kristen," I said, quietly. "Kristen, wake up."

She opened her eyes and just stared at me for a moment, silent.

There was a depth to that stare. God, so much.

Emotion, questioning, wondering. It had been a long time since I'd seen those eyes. It had been a long time since I'd had to wonder what she was thinking. What she thought of *me*.

"Time to go," I said, standing and turning more to break that stare than for any other reason.

CHAPTER SIXTEEN

I GAVE ONE OF THE BURNER PHONES TO KRISTEN, BUT kept her passport in the envelope Vic had given me.

"Once I step out of the car, the driver will take you to the closest police station. Just walk in and tell them you escaped. They'll ask you a lot of questions, and the best policy is to tell them as much of the truth as you can."

"What if they ask me about you?" she asked.

"Tell them whatever you need to," I said. "Tell them whatever it takes to keep you free and get you back to your life. Don't worry about me."

She stared at me. "You don't think you're coming back," she said.

"I don't know if I am," I replied. "This is risky."

"Then why do it!" she said, louder, tears in her eyes.

I thought about that for a moment. "I can't say for sure," I said. "I think it's because I'm tired."

"Then stay! Rest! Don't *go*, Jaylin. Don't do this!"

"I could stay, but I'd never rest. They'll never let me, if I don't follow through."

"The voices," she said.

"Henry. Emil. You."

"My voice is telling you to go?" she asked, shocked.

"In a way. She's not telling me to stay. Which, for her, is the equivalent of saying I should go."

"But why?" she asked.

I shook my head.

Kristen watched me. "I wish I could do what you do. I wish I could know what's in your head. It would help."

I smiled. "It doesn't help. Not really. It complicates everything. It takes things from you, to know how someone else thinks and feels."

"What things?" she asked.

"Everything," I replied.

Suddenly, without warning, Kristen bent forward and grabbed the back of my head, then kissed me, hard.

At once a rush of memories filled me. Everything this Kristen knew was suddenly blended with everything inner Kristen knew. The collisions came and resolved themselves quickly. The conflicts settled. The engrams were integrated and updated.

And I didn't care about any of that.

All I really cared about was the feeling of Kristen's lips on mine, the smell of her skin, the taste of her mouth. I put a hand behind her neck, holding her to me. All this time, I had avoided this very touch, and now I felt like I could *devour* her. I couldn't be close enough to her. There was too much *us* between us.

The kiss ended, lingering in small pecks and nips. We sat in the back seat of the car, our foreheads touching. It was unbelievable and indescribable, and everything I had ever wanted.

"You have it all now," she said.

I did, too. All of it. I remembered every long night of Kristen alone in her house in Zelie, wondering where I was and what I was doing. I remembered her teaching and instructing, helping locals learn to be present, to practice Zen and yoga, and thinking the entire time that she knew these things only because of me. I remembered her aching for me.

"I don't have it all," I said. "I don't have you."

"You have the parts of me that matter," she said.

I forgive you, inner Kristen said.

And I cried.

Outer Kristen wiped my tears and made me sit up. "Time to go," she said. "I can't pretend to understand what it is you're doing. But I know you have to do it."

"I don't understand it either," I said. "But it's true. I do. I have to do it."

"Be careful. Come back to me."

"I will," I said.

I got out then, looking back one last time. Kristen was looking up at me from the car, and all I really wanted to do was climb back in and have the driver take us somewhere else—somewhere that we could live together and escape this all forever.

But it couldn't happen. No such place existed. Not yet. Not until this was all over. If it was ever over.

"I love you," she said.

"I love you," I replied.

And then I shut the door and watched the car pull away.

I had work to do.

Inside the small private airport's main office I met with a man who offered to act as my valet for the trip. "No thank you," I responded. "What I have to do won't require much. I'm hoping this is a very quick trip."

"As you like," the man said. He settled on carrying my small bag onto the plane and seeing that I had a drink in my hand before he exited.

The plane was larger than the one I had used to fly to Zelie. It was comfortable and clean. "You certainly travel in style," I said.

This is nothing, Emil replied. *Richard Branson has a seat reserved for me on his extra-atmospheric flights.*

"Maybe we should have used that. I could be in China in a couple of hours."

Too high profile, Emil said. *Take the time to rest and recuperate. When we land, I will do all I can to advise you on staying alive and out of a Chinese prison.*

"Swell," I said.

But his invitation to rest was a good one, and welcome. I settled into the large, comfortable seat, leaning it back and closing my eyes. In moments I was sound asleep, for the first time in days.

It was nearly eighteen hours later when I awoke. I'd been a little more exhausted than I'd realized, apparently.

An attendant was gently nudging my arm. "Mr. Herbert, we will be landing soon. Would you care for anything before we lock up the galley?"

"No," I said, feeling a bit groggy. Had I really just slept through an eighteen-hour flight? I sat up, slapping my cheeks and rubbing sleep from my eyes. At that point, I wished I had asked for coffee.

The plane made its descent without incident and touched down gently. I rose, and the attendant brought my bag.

In the outside pocket was my new passport, along with

the burner phone. Inside the bag was my laptop, and not much else. I hadn't brought a change of clothes. I was hoping I wouldn't need them.

Now, time for the hard part. Airport security.

Do exactly as I say, Emil said.

As we approached a man behind a security checkpoint window, I handed him my passport.

"Your reason for visiting China?" he asked, with no hint of a Chinese accent.

"Business," I said.

"Duration of your stay?"

"I'm hoping to leave tomorrow," I said.

The man looked at me, and I felt my heart thud.

"A very quick trip," he said.

"Necessary," I said. "My employer insists that I make face-to-face contact with our investors, but the work I do for them must take place in the States."

Emil was coaching me through this entire exchange, and for that I was grateful.

"Your Chinese is excellent. No hint of an accent," the man said.

I blinked. *Chinese?*

You didn't realize? Emil said. *I'm translating and directing your speech. Now say...*

"Yes. Thank you. I studied abroad, in my youth."

The man nodded and handed back my passport. I was ushered through security, where I was scanned and my things were searched before I was released into the small airport. Another car waited for me outside.

I had no idea that could happen, I said.

Henry was aware of it, Emil said.

I postulated a theory, Henry said. *I had no idea it would actually work.*

What worked? What's the theory? I asked.

When you communicate with the engrams in your head, you're not just listening to a voice, saying things that you can translate. The information is in your brain. Everything we knew is here, floating around in your head. The thoughts you're "hearing" aren't necessarily in English. Emil was telling you what to say by placing the words directly in your thoughts. You said them, fully understanding what they were, without even realizing that you were speaking one of the Chinese dialects. And Emil was translating instantly, letting you know exactly what was being said, in real time.

I thought about this during the ride to the Paradigm China offices. It opened a lot of possibilities. It also meant that Henry had hidden yet more information from me. How much more could there be? What else did Henry know about me that I didn't know myself?

Eventually, I'd have to pin Henry down for some real answers. But for the moment, I didn't have time to worry about it. We had arrived.

The offices for Paradigm China were largely nondescript. No large sign advertising their presence. Nothing special on the street-facing side of the structure. For all intents and purposes it was just like any building I might pass in New York.

The Chinese certainly wouldn't advertise what this company does, Emil said.

The company is public, isn't it? I asked.

Yes. But there are many ways to hide in full view of stockholders and the public at large.

I was ushered into the building and escorted by two security guards wearing dark suits. They had very slight builds, which I found surprising.

Don't be fooled, Jacob said. *Look at the way they hold*

themselves. They're ready for anything. They wouldn't even need guns or knives to take out everyone in this room.

Noted. I kept my eyes straight ahead as we moved to the front desk.

I showed my passport as identification, and spoke to the man behind the desk with Emil's prompting, saying just the right things to pass the scrutiny of security. In the end I was issued a security badge with my photo on it, which gave me access to some of the midlevel floors of the facility. Mostly the labs.

Their system will indicate that you are an expert on engrammatic research and technology, Emil said. *They're expecting my arrival tomorrow—which will, unfortunately, be quite delayed. But my pending arrival means I have an interest, possibly as an investor. They would not be surprised by me sending an expert ahead, to verify their reports.*

I was extremely nervous about all of this. *I'm not sure if I can pass myself off as an expert,* I said.

Nonsense, Henry replied. *There's hardly anyone on the planet who understands engrammatic transfer better than you, from a practical perspective. And you have me to prompt you on the science.*

True. Though it wasn't making me feel much better.

In fact, I was becoming increasingly nervous about every bit of this. I was depending on the two men who had recently kidnapped and tortured me in an effort to get me to this very spot. It was possible I hadn't completely thought this through.

Bad life decision or not, though, here I was. No turning back now. Time to make the brain-sucking metal donuts.

I was escorted to one of the labs, where I was left in the hands of Wu Cheng Wen, one of the researchers heading the Engrammatic Technology Development Division of Paradigm China.

Wen was excited for me to be there, presumably because it meant that Emil Lyon still had a strong interest in all of this. But there may have been some pride involved. As Wen led me on a tour of the lab, he was beaming at every piece of equipment, like a father pointing out his kid winning a spelling bee.

"You can see that we have made great progress in developing the recording technology," Wen said, slowly fanning a hand over the lab. "A recent breakthrough has improved our capabilities in implanting engrams in a new host, but it is still in early development."

"How are you testing it?" I asked.

"Volunteers. There are many who wish to experience what it must feel like to know the thoughts of others."

It ain't all it's cracked up to be, Jacob said.

Agreed, Henry replied.

I'm rather enjoying it, Emil said.

Trying to concentrate here, I projected.

Hearing from Henry and Emil wasn't that surprising. Both were pompous and self-important tool bags. The presence of Jacob was the sign of something else, though. It meant I was feeling threatened. My subconscious drags certain personalities and traits to front and center sometimes.

Feeling threatened was understandable, given everything I'd been through recently. But what I needed right now, whether I liked it or not, were the men in my head whom I disliked the most—the scientist and the billionaire business man.

I used some breathing techniques Kristen had taught me to calm myself and bring my pulse down.

"Are you distressed?" Wen asked.

"I'm sorry?"

Wen nodded to my badge, which had an indicator under my photo. I hadn't paid much attention to it before, but now I saw that it was a dark black.

Jacob spoke, disgusted. *You gotta be kidding me.* Mood *badges?*

A bit more sophisticated, Henry said. *But essentially, yes. Jaylin, you'll need to keep your emotions in check.*

How do I do that? I asked, feeling my heart thump in my chest.

For starters, Emil said, *stop panicking. Relax.*

Easy for you to say. I took another breath, which didn't seem to be working at the moment.

Jaylin, Kristen's voice said. *Listen to my voice. You are in control. You have nothing to fear. You are with people who care about you. You are loved. You are safe. You are protected. We are here for you.*

She went on like that for a while, repeating it like a mantra. It sank into the background of my thoughts, a rhythm that soothed me as the forward part of my mind thought and directed my actions. I calmed and smiled.

"I get a bit stressed when I travel," I said to Wen. "Fatigue. But my girlfriend taught me some techniques. Zen breathing, that sort of thing. It helps."

Wen nodded. "Do you require anything?"

"No, thank you." Emil started prompting me with things to say. "Actually, if you don't mind, I'd like to have access to the original data sent to Mr. Lyon, and any updates that have been entered into the record."

"Very well," Wen said, nodding, and he then led me to a small room that contained only a desk and a laptop computer.

I sat in front of it, putting my bag and my own laptop on the floor next to me.

Wen left me there alone, which was a relief.

You won't learn anything new here, Emil said. *We need access to the cloning lab.*

Do you know where that is? I asked.

No. But I believe you have a means of discovery.

He was right. I knew it would come down to this eventually, but I had hoped it could be avoided. But here, in what Jacob would term "hostile territory," my abilities were an advantage I couldn't ignore.

I left my laptop bag in the room and made my way out into the larger lab space.

Who should you make contact with? Kristen asked.

Good question, I replied.

What about Wen? Jacob asked. *He's head of this lab, right?*

It was as good a lead as any.

I spotted Wen talking with a few other researchers and went directly to him. I had taken my glove off as I left the office, keeping my hands in my pockets to prevent accidental contact. Now I extended it to Wen. "I apologize. In my weariness, I neglected to thank you for your hospitality."

Wen took my hand after only a brief pause, bowing slightly. "It is my duty," Wen said.

And in that instant, Wen was in my head, staring back at himself.

I nodded in return, releasing outer Wen's hand.

Remarkable, Wen said. *You have initiated a spontaneous engrammatic transfer through tactile engagement.*

He touched you, and now you're part of his mind menagerie, Jacob said.

I believe that is more or less what he was saying, Henry replied.

"Where may I find the restroom?" I asked.

Wen gave me directions, and I left the lab. Though once I was in the corridor, I turned in the opposite direction and made straight for the elevator.

The labs I needed access to were downstairs, not up. Below the lobby was a basement floor that was used primarily for housing equipment used in the building's day-to-day operations. General power, plumbing, main climate control, that sort of thing. Below that, accessible only by a secure elevator and a set of equally secure stairs, were three floors that housed the genetics research and technology division of Paradigm.

The cloning labs were down there.

Wen had access, but only via his security badge and a retinal scan. I might have his memories, but I lacked his retinas. I'd have to find another way.

The best I could do, for now, was ride down to the basement.

I EXITED the elevator and quickly made my way deep into the maze of large machinery, including backup generators and climate control systems. These were redundant—meant to kick in during an outage or emergency. The full-time equipment and machinery were locked behind a series of doors on the far end of the basement.

I had full access to Wen's memories, and I was scanning them now to see if there was anything I could use to get into the floors below.

Nothing, I said, dismayed. *Wen has never needed to visit those floors without his security clearance. He's never even thought about it.*

There has to be a way in, Kristen said.

A facility like this is tight, Jacob replied. *They consider every angle. It's possible that security is already on its way, ready to take us down.*

I hadn't considered that and wished that Jacob had either spoken up sooner or hadn't said anything at all.

Suddenly, I felt an odd sensation come over me.

It was like standing in a room when the lights are slowly dimmed. You're still aware of what you're seeing, but the tone and volume of the light changes. A sort of eeriness tickles the back of your neck, like sensing that someone has entered the room, from an unseen door.

The strangeness rises.

Julia was there.

I know a way in, Julia's voice said.

I shivered.

This wasn't good. Julia hardly ever came up from the darker corners of my mind. When she did, it was almost *always* bad. Because Julia might not actually *be* Julia.

In some ways, she was the engram that was most like me.

Julia, Henry said carefully. *Which one are you, right now?*

I'm me right now, Julia said. *Or I think I am.*

Great, Jacob said. *Exactly what we need. A schizophrenic spy.*

I know a way into those lower levels. Julia said. *You can trust me, or not.*

I considered this.

Having Julia in my head was one of the mistakes that had led to me parting ways with Henry. She was one of his experiments—trying to press the boundaries of what I could do. "Let's see what happens" was a fairly benign expression, most of the time, but with Henry it became a blunt instrument. And for some reason, I always went along.

In those early days, when I didn't know what the hell was happening to me, when I was desperate to find *anyone* who could teach me what I was, and how to control what I could do—well, you could say I was vulnerable. When you think you have no options, you're a lot more willing to overlook red flags. When it came to Henry, I had overlooked an entire United Nations of red flags.

With Julia, things had started benign enough. Henry had wanted to know if I could separate the personalities. Could I absorb only the primary engram? Could I sift through the fractured personas of a deeply troubled psyche, and rescue the single, original personality?

That seemed like a noble enough cause to me. If I could somehow use my ability to help someone suffering like that —suffering in a way I could relate to better than most— wouldn't that be a worthy effort? Wouldn't that be worth any risks? Besides, it wasn't like I was in any physical danger. And by this time, I'd done hundreds of transfers in the name of science, many of whom were coma patients, just like Julia.

What Henry had failed to tell me was that Julia wasn't in a coma.

Minutes before I arrived at the hospital, Julia had died. And this was where we learned that there's a difference between being alive and being *kept* alive.

The machines were keeping Julia's heart and lungs moving and working, but they had been forced to start them from a dead stop. Literally. Julia's heart, her lungs, her brain activity had all stopped, down to zero, and it was only through the valiant effort of her well-meaning doctors that she was revived.

Henry hadn't deceived me on purpose, exactly. At least, I had chosen to believe he hadn't. He had just made a bad assumption.

If the heart was beating and the lungs were pumping, then the subject was still *alive*, right? By any technical definition, that was true.

But when it comes to humans, technical definitions of life aren't always the reality. Life starts and stops on its own timeline. Any technical definition we use is irrelevant.

At that moment, though, Henry believed she was still technically alive. And I believed Henry.

And so, my abilities should only have the usual, temporary effect. 30 minutes.

But the instant I touched her, I knew the truth. She was gone. The damage she'd done to herself was too much. She'd wanted out, and she'd gotten her wish. Despite the wires, the tubes, the medications, the surgeries, she'd gotten what she wanted. She'd finally shed the mortal coil.

And then she was cheated of it, by Henry.

By me.

For months afterward, I was a wreck. In part because of what I'd learned—about Julia and her life, and about the tragedy and horror she faced every day, locked in her own mind. I'd also learned about Henry's deception, and it dawned on me finally, that this was not a one-time thing. Henry had a drive to learn more about what I could do, and he was willing to take huge risks—to make *me* take huge risk —to test his theories.

Julia was a casualty of Henry's avarice. So was I.

I walked out on him shortly after that. And I may have done some vengeful, get-him-arrested things as I left.

I didn't care what happened to Henry from that point out. I didn't care that he was going to rot in prison. Just like he didn't care that I was now a walking prison cell for a woman who was tortured non-stop by her own mind, driven to schizophrenia and madness, fragmented personalities now free to torture her for years more. She had wanted an escape and had gotten it. Henry had robbed her of that, and used me to do it.

And now, here we were. Dependent on the most unstable, tortured engram in my head.

For now, at least, she seemed lucid. And that was good. Because Julia had skills we could use.

She had been a deep cover special agent, in her former life, before exposure to a psychotropic drug fractured her personality and drove her insane. But if she could keep it together, she might actually come in handy, here in this high security facility.

"Ok, Julia," I said. "What do we do?"

These backup climate control systems connect to the main ductwork, but they're gated with metal slats. If the main system goes down, the slats open automatically, letting air pass through. It's the only time that there's direct, unsecured access to the ventilation system.

Emil asked, *How do you know that?*

This building was used for a eugenics project that I infiltrated five years ago, Julia said.

A real infiltration, or one you think you had? Jacob asked.

Julia ignored him. *If we interrupt power to the main climate control system, we'll have a ten minute window to get into a shaft leading to the next floor down.*

What then? Henry asked.

There was no hesitation as Julia replied, *Jaylin, does*

Wen have a memory of the layout? Does he know where the cloning facility is?

"Yes," I said, then checked the time on my burner phone. "But I'm only going to have his memories for another twenty-two minutes."

Can we note the layout somehow? Kristen asked.

Why can't you just remember it? Emil asked.

The memory is tied to the engram, Henry said. *Once the engram fades, the memories go with it. Jaylin hasn't yet found a way to transition engrammatic memory to his own long-term memory without some sort of go-between. Notes, recordings, etc.*

So make a note, Jacob said.

We're wasting time, Henry said. *If Jaylin stops to note everything, we risk missing our window. Someone could come through here any moment. We have to act now.*

I was listening to all of this even as I was moving to the secured door of the room where the main climate control system was housed.

"Julia... what do I do?"

See the vent, on the side of that large piece of equipment? That's an access vent, for maintenance. It's held on by thumb screws.

I ran to it and started turning the screws until the vent was loose. I pulled it free and climbed inside, pulling the grating back into place as I entered.

Take off your coat, Julia said.

I did so, snaking the phone out of the coat pocket and putting it in the front pocket of my pants.

Climb, fast. You don't have much time.

I climbed up into a T-shaped section of the ventilation system, and at Julia's urging I wriggled down a path until I came to a junction. To my right, a couple of large, metal flaps were open, pressed against the top and bottom of the duct. To my left, two identical flaps were closed, forming a seal in the middle, blocking airflow.

Pull those two flaps together, and jam your coat between them as they close.

I did this, though it took some effort. Soon, though, The two flaps formed only a narrow gap, and with my coat tangled among them the flaps stayed locked in place.

An alarm sounded.

That sound means hurry, Henry supplied.

The two flaps to my left opened, exposing the ductwork behind them. I scrambled through this, squeezing between the flaps and wriggling along until I came to another T-shaped intersection. The path continued on ahead, but there was a drop just in front of me.

Bridge that gap, Julia said. *The one you want is coming up next.*

I made my way carefully over the drop and kept moving.

How are we on time? Jacob asked.

I can't get to my phone right now, I said, focusing on crawling.

I estimate we have twelve minutes remaining, Julia said.

I came to the end of the duct, at the edge of a drop that seemed to go down forever.

Next stop, sub-basement, Julia said.

I poked my head over the edge, then turned to look upward. The shaft continued up to the next floor from here. I wormed into that section so I could get my feet under me, and then pressed against the walls of the vertical duct, letting myself slide bit by bit, making progress downward.

I silently thanked God for my gloves—there were definitely spots where exposed edges in the metal shaft would have cheese-grated my hands to shreds.

Several minutes later, and an indeterminable distance down, Julia finally said, *This is it. There's a vent down that way. You'll come out from the ceiling, over a hallway.*

Won't we be spotted? Henry asked.

You thought you'd just sneak in and out without being seen? Jacob asked.

I quickly made my way to the vent, pressed down hard until it popped open, and then dropped to the floor of the hallway.

I was filthy. No way would I be able to "blend in" the way I'd hoped I would. My shirt was filthy, my pants were ripped, and my gloves were tattered along the palms—an alarming bit of flesh visible through the tears. I'd have to be careful.

Adding insult to injury, the alarm I'd heard was sure to bring security, which meant everyone would be on high alert. The whole building might be in lockdown.

Tell me again why we're doing this? Jacob asked. *Emil gets a new body. What do the rest of us get? Life in a Chinese prison?*

I assure you, I will ensure your freedom, Emil said.

Pardon me if I don't find you trustworthy, Jacob said.

Jaylin gets something he's after, Henry said, and suddenly everyone was quiet.

And what's that? Jacob asked. *What does he get?*

Jaylin, Kristen asked. *Do you know something? Are you hiding something from us?*

I didn't respond. Instead, I asked, "Julia, are you still with me?"

Puppets. Ropes and strings, she said. *The* secrets. *They* all *have secrets. They all had lives. No more. No lives. No more. I'm here, I'm here, I'm always HERE.*

Great, Jacob said. *She's cracking up. She's going to be very helpful.*

"Julia, you can do this. Pull it together. I need you."

I'm here, she said, sounding haggard. *I'm here. I... I don't know for how much longer.*

I accessed Wen's memories, which were on the verge of fading. "If we get to the main lab on this floor, we can lock it from the inside."

What does that do for us? Emil asked.

"For starters, it keeps security off of us while we figure out what to do next. But it also happens to be where we most want to go. Better than nothing."

I raced for the lab and, using a keypad to the side of the door, I punched in Wen's access code. The door opened, and I stepped inside, locking it behind me. I leaned back against the door just as Wen's memories faded.

"Wen has left the building," I said. "We are now on our own."

I turned and looked into the lab, which was a long room lit intermittently with wall sconces rather than overheads. There were work surfaces with desk lamps, most of which were turned off. No one seemed to be here, at the moment.

Where is everybody? Jacob asked.

Alarms, Julia said. *They followed protocol. They're all gathered in the lobby. There will be guards moving from floor to floor and room to room.*

Which means we have some time, Emil said. *My body awaits.*

I moved past the tables and into an area lined with numerous metal cylinders. It was a scene from a sci-fi movie—dozens of pods standing erect, tubes and wires coiling in and out of them, blinking lights on access panels.

Unlike the movies, though, these were opaque, not transparent. We couldn't see the cloned bodies inside.

Find 1138, Emil said. *That was the identifier on the body designated for me.*

You already had this prearranged? Kristen asked. *You were coming here to get a new body?*

Not quite. I was coming to verify their success, and to pass on the data that Henry had gathered. It was a partnership, of sorts. And, obviously, I wanted them to have the latest version of my memories, before attempting the engrammatic transfer. No gaps.

Replication, Henry corrected. *Not transfer. Your mind would still be in your actual body. You'd just be redundant.*

"So they'd have to kill the original before the copy could assert himself," I said.

The conundrum of cloning and teleportation alike, Henry replied. *So far, there's no way to separate the engram from the original host and literally* move *it. The best we've managed is to make a copy of it in a secondary host.*

"So this is all just make believe," I said. "The life you'll have, Emil—it's not *real.* It's a copy. A knockoff."

I'll take it, Emil said. *Especially since the alternative seems to be oblivion. And do not forget, I am not currently in my old, living body. I'm a ghost, for all intents and purposes. I have already outlived my old body. Success.*

When you put it that way, Jacob said, *it's downright poetic. Now, can we get on with this and then work on getting out of this place alive? I'm not all that convinced that Julia is going to be helpful for much longer.*

I'm still here, Julia said, though she didn't sound entirely certain.

I moved quickly, checking the metal identification tags riveted to each of the tubes. It took a moment, but I found 1138, and I stood before it, looking at it from top to bottom. "Here it is," I said.

Now what? Kristen asked.

Now Jaylin uses the ERD, Henry replied.

I reached into my pocket and brought out the small, metal donut that Henry had been tinkering with just before I rescued him. There was a duplicate of this back in my safe house in New York. They were virtually identical, at least in design.

The programming, though, was slightly different.

I took a deep breath and then touched the ERD to my forehead.

There was a jolt, and the muscles in my neck and shoulders tightened even as my knees buckled. I went to the floor, hard. The transfer had momentarily disrupted the connection between my thoughts and my body, kind of unplugging me for a second. But I barely felt anything.

I was too busy with the world *inside* my head.

Images of places I'd never been rose around me, forming crystal walls that stretched in every direction. It was like a maze of memories, rising from the floor, encircling and trapping me. I could see...

Well, I wasn't entirely sure what I was seeing. Shadows. Glimmers. Reflections.

It was like I was seeing layers of reality. And, just like before, I could see threads—slender strings made of light, twisting into knotwork patterns that were thing folded into even more threads and knots and patterns.

As my consciousness pulled away, those patterns overlapped, tangled together, blended until they started to look more and more solid.

And now I was back, looking at the world through my natural eyes.

I forced myself to stand and to focus on unit 1138, keeping my attention riveted to where Emil's new body was being stored. I needed something to use as an anchor, to get myself rooted back to the here and now, and to use a phrase Jacob was fond of, "The objective is the directive."

I still had a job to do.

On the panel, next to a small display, was a port shaped perfectly for the ERD, built to exacting specifications sent ahead of Henry's arrival.

I pulled the ERD from my forehead, forcing my arms to work again through sheer willpower, and slowly but deliberately pressed the small, metal circle into the port. There was a *click* as the magnets embedded in the port locked onto the device, holding it in place and aligning it for precise contact.

The display lit up, and I watched the display mounted to the pod as data was transferred in a familiar jagged green waveform. Multiple waves, cascading from right to left, creating a forest of data, the personality of a human being wriggling from a piece of technology into a flesh and blood body.

The transfer of a soul.

Because, I realized, that's what we were really dealing with.

The memory maze had begun to fade once I removed the ERD from my forehead, but in the last shadowy remnants of it I saw them...

Henry, Kristen, Julia, Caleb, Jacob.

Emil was gone, of course. He had his own body again. And...

"Wait," I said, "What happened to Carter?"

You have him siloed, don't you? Henry said.

"I did, but..."

Alarms sounded from the panel in front of me, and I looked to see it flashing alternately between green and red.

Data collisions! Henry said. *The waveform is collapsing! Carter must have hitched a ride!*

The screen was going crazy, and I stepped back, uncertain. "Henry, what do I do?"

I don't know! I could sense Henry shaking his head. *Lean closer, get a better view of the data panel.*

I did as I was told, and maybe it was an echo of Henry's thoughts, but it seemed like I was able to understand and interpret what I was seeing. I was just starting to click to it, to understand it, when Julia spoke up.

You need to leave, she said. *Now. They'll be here, very soon.*

I'm with Schizo, Jacob said. *Never thought I'd say that.*

Can we go? Caleb said. He was always so silent, always hiding in the back of my mind, it was almost shocking to hear him. But now his voice was louder, filled with fear.

"Yeah," I said, looking one last time at the display and the cylinder.

The almost-got-it feeling was gone. The data was back to looking like gibberish to me. But I filed the whole thing away. I needed to understand what had just happened.

Later. Right then, I needed to get the hell out of there.

I turned and sprinted, but not back toward the door where we had entered.

Where are we going? Kristen asked.

There is no exit here, Julia said.

No, Henry said. *There isn't.*

I raced between cylinders until finally I came to the door at the far end of the room. There was nothing to prevent me from opening this door—no security codes or retina scans. It was just a door. But everything was on the other side.

I opened it and went through, entering a small control room. "This is it, Henry?"

Yes, Henry said.

What? What is this? Kristen asked.

Junior, what are you up to? Jacob asked.

"Which one?"

To your right, middle display. The large one. Password is "Evergreen."

"Of course it is," I said, rolling my eyes.

Could you maybe tell me what's happening right now? Kristen said.

"Kristen, I wanted to tell you, but with Emil in my head I couldn't risk it. I had to get him out, and I had to gain access to these systems."

Why? Kristen asked.

Jacob interjected, *What's happening, Jaylin?*

"I can't let this technology exist," I said. "Henry gave me a way to shut it down for good."

I entered "Evergreen" at the password prompt, and the screen came alive with a complex interface, with small windows of data streaming and updating in real time.

Do exactly as I tell you, Jaylin, Henry said.

Are you really going to trust this guy? Jacob asked.

He will, Julia said. *He has to. This is the mission.*

I'm scared, Caleb said. *Hey, I'm scared, ok? Can we just... can we leave? Can we just go home?*

It's ok, Caleb, Kristen said, soothingly, a calming presence in the midst of all the fear and uncertainty and anxiety floating around in my head.

She was with me. She didn't know what I was doing, but she trusted me.

That was new. That was a step forward from where we'd been for so long. Touching outer Kristen, updating inner Kristen, had done something. Changed something.

If I lived through this, I'd have to think about what that meant.

If I lived through this. Which seemed less and less likely by the minute.

Henry read off a sequence of keystrokes and commands, and I input each of them quickly. After several moments, the data on the screens changed. Many of the data streams flat lined. Some of the streaming data stopped rolling down the screen. And one window, the one Henry had told me to watch, was showing a percentage counting down.

When it reached zero, I stood and stepped away.

It was done.

"That's all of it?" I asked. "What about backups?"

"These were *the backups,* Henry said. *The primary data was deleted when you used the ERD on Emil's tube, along with a virus that is currently causing every ERD port in this facility to start shorting out and overheating. Sort of a failsafe I built in back when Emil was blackmailing me.*

So you built some kind of Trojan Horse? Jacob asked. *Why?*

Can we maybe work out the rest of this story later? Kristen asked. *Maybe back in a safe house in New York?*

The Chinese are going to make it very difficult to get out of this country, Julia said.

Impossible? Jacob asked.

Nothing's impossible, Julia said. *Just very, very difficult.*

I left the control room and raced through the lab and through the door. It was locked tight from the outside, and only a code could open it. But it was designed to let people exit, unless a system lockdown was in place.

That should have been a clue that something was wrong.

I was just stepping into the hall when I was hit square in the chest, and thrown back, stumbling to the floor. I gasped, the wind knocked out of me, and my ribs felt bruised as I struggled to catch a breath.

The two wiry guards from downstairs walked into the room and eyed me.

They didn't have their guns drawn.

They wouldn't need them.

CHAPTER SEVENTEEN

MY TURN, JULIA SAID.

Suddenly I felt a sort of numbness overtake me, even as my muscles seemed to tighten. It was as if I'd had a shot of Novocain. I could feel my body, but it was like feeling it from a distance.

I sprang to my feet in a move I'd only seen in Kung Fu films. The two guards lunged then, making strikes with their fists, their legs, even their heads.

Or, actually, they *tried* to make strikes.

Every time they came close to connecting, I was suddenly somewhere else.

And then I returned fire.

My hands moved with more speed than I thought possible, making impact with soft tissue—eyes, throats, groins. Some of the blows were blocked, but enough made contact that they were having an effect.

I was thrilled to see I was winning this fight. It was just that I wasn't the one fighting.

Julia.

She was good at this. She'd been trained in a variety of

martial arts, but tended to favor *Krav Maga*—a singularly brutal Israeli combat style that really wasn't for people with weak stomachs.

The name literally translates to "contact combat." And the contact wasn't gentle.

There was blood. And lots of it. And plenty of broken bones.

The two guards were no slouches themselves, though. They were clearly highly trained in hand-to-hand combat, and had a higher pain threshold than average. That more or less made this a fair fight—if you ignored the fact that it was two against one, and the one was not actually in "fighting shape."

I was going to feel all these blows in the morning. If I lived that long.

One of the guards did a sweeping kick that connected and brought me crashing to the ground. Even through the remote control haze I felt that one. The wind was knocked out of me, and the lights dimmed in a quick pulse. I had nearly blacked out.

Despite this, however, I was up almost instantly, stooped in a crouching position. The first guard lunged then, going for a strike to the back of my head. I rolled forward, and then sprang upward in an explosive leap, my arms shooting upward, my hands forming stiff, driving blades.

I made contact with the throat of the other guard, who had tried to deflect the blow with no success. He dropped back, and I instantly leapt at him again, ramming the palm of my right hand into his nose with enough force to cause a sickening, audible crunch. The guard screamed and stumbled back again, assisted by a quick push from me as I dropped into a sweeping kick on the floor.

The first guard was back now, landing a solid kick into my side and sending me sprawling. Again I rolled with it, getting to my knees and facing him like a wolf about to pounce. He took up a defensive stance, changing his approach.

I quickly pulled my feet up and under me, and sprang upward into a sprint toward him, trying to punch him in the throat, the bridge of the nose, the sternum.

He deflected these blows with ease, and I dropped back.

I was panting heavily now, and even through the mental distance I could feel that my body was getting tired. Everything Julia was doing, using my body, required an explosive use of energy and momentum. It couldn't last indefinitely.

I wasn't in quite the shape that a special agent would be in. I was fit, but not Olympic athlete fit. I could only sustain this kind of activity for so long.

Willpower might see it through, but even with six wills to draw from, there was only so much to go around.

I made a feint, lunging forward and leaning in, as if I were overstepping. The guard easily deflected the blow and then tried to seize the opportunity brought on by my seemingly overzealous attack.

Julia was ready for that.

She allowed him to make the strike—a solid punch to the temple that rung my bell a little. Thank God the guards were wearing gloves—there would have been enough skin-to-skin contact to make a transfer with that punch alone.

As it was, though, I suddenly rolled a bit, my back now facing the floor, and I literally *fell* to the floor in a back-flop before doing some sort of scissor kick that resulted in a hard contact with the guard's groin and then his face, as he doubled over from the pain.

His head snapped back, and I was up and making a final

strike in an instant, using the palm of my hand to hit him *hard* in the nose and then the throat.

He went down.

Both men were slumped to the ground, groaning, and I sprang on top of the first guard, raising a knife-like hand for a killing blow.

"No!" I shouted

And I froze.

Suddenly the numbness wore off. My body was under my control again. The remote control faded, and it was just me making the decisions about what my now sore and aching body would do.

I huffed, completely out of breath. I was going to have a lot of bruises, and possibly some broken ribs. And a few injuries I couldn't fully catalog yet.

I was going to need a very long nap and about twelve hours in an Epsom salt bath.

But I was alive. We all were.

"Julia," I said, huffing.

How did you do *that?* Jacob asked.

You were able to seize control of Jaylin's body, Henry said, astounded. *I didn't think that was possible.*

"Neither did I," I said, bracing myself against the wall of the corridor.

Search them. Get their guns and their security cards, Julia said.

I did, along with their wallets and mobile phones. The phones I would ditch. The wallets I searched, liberating cash and credit cards that might come in handy later.

I also took one of their suit jackets, pulling it on over my filthy shirt. It was a little snug. I was a pretty trim guy, but the guard was slimmer and leaner.

Still, it would help. It wouldn't pass close inspection,

but it might prevent anyone from paying too much attention to me.

For good measure, I touched the first guard, taking in his memories so I could plot the best and fastest way out of here.

I made my way into the hall, punched in the lock code for the door, and shot it for good measure.

Will that even work? Kristen asked.

Probably not, Henry said. *This isn't the movies.*

"It worked last time," I said. "Now what do I do, Julia?"

Everything I tell you, she said.

For the next several minutes I played robot, doing anything and everything Julia told me to do, assisting with some inside information from the guard when it was needed.

When I came to a door leading to the stairwell, I took the stairs to the ground floor. The doors opened without trouble from this side, allowing people to use them as emergency exits.

In seconds, then, I was out of the stairwell and moving quickly through the lobby.

There were official-looking people milling about, so on Julia's directive I stayed close to the wall, moving at the edge, slowly but deliberately.

Eventually I came to a door that had a security pad beside it. It wasn't being watched as closely as the other exits, since it was secured.

I punched the code, grateful that I'd grabbed the guard's memories. I slipped through without being noticed and found myself in a corridor that led to a service elevator on one side and a set of metal doors leading outside on the other.

Don't stop moving, Julia said. *Get into the guts of the city. Blend in.*

I actually started to relax then. This part—dodging though thousands of strangers amid skyscrapers and honking cars, ducking into alleys and keeping a low profile —this was familiar territory for me. Different city, same strategy.

Maybe there was some hope for leaving Manhattan after all.

SEVERAL BLOCKS AWAY, I slipped into the lobby of a Marriott and used my ability to get some inside information from the manager. When no one was looking, I booked a room, paid for with my prepaid credit card, and slipped upstairs.

I couldn't stay here for long, I knew. I needed to put as much distance between me and China as possible, and as quickly as I could.

But it was good to have a moment of peace—some time to catch my breath and figure out what to do next.

In my room, I stripped off my shirt and stuffed it into the bathroom sink as I filled it with water. I used the little bottle of shampoo and a bar of soap to clean it up as best I could. It wasn't too bad, when I was finished. Still a bit stained, but it would do. I used the hair dryer to blow it dry, and pulled it back on, along with the guard's suit jacket.

I looked presentable enough. Now I just needed some place to go.

We still have access to the plane, Henry said. *We could use that to get back to the states.*

We won't make it past airport security, Julia said.

They'll have us in a room with a bag over our head before we even know what hit us.

Have I mentioned that I'm really glad Julia's hanging out with us now? Jacob said. *Feels festive.*

We need to get to a boat, Julia said, ignoring him.

About an hour later, after making a lunch of chocolates and canned nuts from the minibar, and washing it down with a can of ginger ale, I left the room and took the stairs to the ground floor. I had the concierge call a taxi, and I rode in a state of abject paranoia and barely contained panic all the way to the docks.

His name is Wei Qing, Julia said. *He won't know you, so he'll be very cautious. He'll play dumb, like he has no idea why you'd ever think he could give you a ride.*

"So how do I convince him?" I asked.

Isn't that why you took the cash from the guards?

I patted my coat pocket. There was quite a bit of cash there, all local currency.

I found Wei Qing exactly where Julia said he would be. I shook his hand, absorbing his engram, and in perfect Chinese I talked to him about a ride to coordinates supplied by Julia. As predicted, he pretended to have no idea what I was talking about. But I had the advantage of both Julia's knowledge and Wei Qing's own. It only took a couple of minutes to give him enough inside information to build some trust, so that he was willing to help me. The cash was a bonus.

I boarded Wei Qing's small boat, shucking the suit jacket and rolling up my shirt sleeves, settling in for the long ride.

It took nearly an hour to come to a small island off the coast, surrounded by choppy seas and not much else. I was feeling a bit sea sick by the time we got there.

Keep your eyes on the horizon, Jacob offered.

"I'm just focusing on keeping my lunch in my stomach," I replied.

There was a mental chuckle from Jacob. *You did good, kid. This whole thing... there were some fumbles, but it came off. You'd make a hell of an operative.*

"No thanks," I replied, scoffing. "I can't wait for this to be over and for things to get back to normal."

Again, I felt Jacob's laugh. *Normal? When was anything about you normal? Look, kid, sometimes you get to choose the life you want, and sometimes the life chooses you. If you want anything good to come of it, you have to be willing to roll with whatever comes your way. You may not want to be an "operative," but you're not getting much of a choice in it. You'll do better, and be happier, when you can accept that. Own it, or it will own you.*

I didn't respond. How could I? I understood what he was saying, but I didn't want it to be true. And when you come to a point where you can't agree with the voices in your head, psychologists call that *cognitive dissonance.*

I call it life.

We docked, and I was no sooner standing with both feet firmly on the pier than Wei Qing had gunned his boat back to full speed, racing away from the island without looking back.

I watched with some regret as he receded to a dot in the distance. His memories had already faded, and I was suddenly feeling very alone and very vulnerable, in a strange and dangerous place.

It's not far from here, Julia said.

What's not far? Kristen asked.

The airstrip, Julia said.

I left the pier, picking my way through jungle growth

for the better part of an hour until it suddenly opened up, revealing a small airstrip. There was a jet parked there—a tiny, private aircraft covered by a camouflaged net.

Julia directed me in pulling the netting free, opening the door to get inside, and doing a preflight check.

"I may not have mentioned this," I said, as I worked switches and pulled knobs and levers and tapped on screens all at Julia's best, "but I don't know how to fly a jet."

It's ok, Julia said. *Jacob does.*

Yeah, Jacob said. *I do. Now do what I say, and we should be fine. Next stop, New York. With maybe a few hundred layovers along the way.*

EPILOGUE

THERE WAS A COLD WIND BLOWING OFF OF THE Hudson—what locals used to refer to as a "Hudson Hawk," before Bruce Willis and Danny Aiello made a movie with that title—and I pulled my coat tight to protect against it.

It had been three days since I'd managed to get back to New York, and two weeks since we'd left the airstrip. Jacob had talked me through the flight, and Julia had directed me to a series of CIA-backed landing strips where I could refuel and regroup, making the fight home in clandestine little hops. The final leg had been aboard a boat, smuggled inside a shipping container that had been decked out like a small apartment—part of a smuggling operation for getting high profile individuals into the US.

Scary stuff to know about, right?

Everything was paid for using bank transfers—partly from Julia's old network and partly from some touch-and-grab tricks of my own. I don't like to steal, but I don't like being in prison or dead, either. Some "moral flexibility" is occasionally required, when you're me. I was learning that, anyway.

Now that I was back home, I was still feeling kind of frazzled and run down. I needed a vacation. Some solid time avoiding all humans, maybe binge watching something on Netflix for ten hours a day.

That might come later. For now, at least, I was safe. Or as safe as I ever was.

Kristen—outer Kristen—had done exactly what we planned. She told the police and the press that she'd been kidnapped, held against her will as two different mafia families fought it out on either side of her. She claimed to have no idea what they were after, and police had settled on keeping a detail on her for the time being, watching her closely as they continued to investigate in the background.

She hadn't given them my name, or any details about me. And, I was happily surprised to learn, there were no clear photos or video of my face. Most shots had me wearing my hoodie. Bless it.

Kristen's calls were being monitored, but the police hadn't known about the burner phone. I made contact as soon as I was back on US soil.

"You're back," she said. I could hear the relief in her voice. And the worry.

"I'm back," I replied. "Sorry I was out of touch for so long. I didn't know how safe it would be to reach out. If the police had the burner, they might be able to track where I was."

"I understand," she said. "Jaylin... Are you ok?"

I sighed, looking out over the Hudson, feeling the bracing cold of the wind. "I've been warmer," I smiled. "But yeah, I'm ok. I'm going to take a break. Find a place to bunker for a while. Eat bad food and watch crappy TV."

She laughed. "Saturdays," she said.

I smiled again. "Miss them?"

There was a pause, a brief hesitation, and I almost regretted everything I'd said up to now.

"I miss *you*," she said, finally.

My eyes felt warm, even in the cold breeze. I felt a tear streak down my chin, dried instantly by the wind.

"I miss you, too," I said quietly. "But... you know it's safer, right? For me to stay away?"

"Is it?" she asked.

Now it was my turn to hesitate. And I wasn't sure what to say. Was it safer? Was I just being paranoid? Could I just get a car and drive to Zelie, pick her up for a night out in Pittsburgh? Could we start a normal life, together?

Police. Feds. Foreign governments. Maniacal billionaires. Mad scientists.

There were a thousand reasons why we'd always have to keep our eyes open. We'd never be able to rest. There would always be danger closing in on us.

I promised I would get in touch again, when the heat died down. I was planning to visit her in person in a few weeks, if it seemed safe.

It was going to be a very long few weeks.

It might not happen, I warned her. It might never be safe.

She agreed. She understood. She cried.

When I hung up with her, I was crying too. Not something I did often, and now I'd done it twice in the space of forty minutes.

I threw the burner phone into the Hudson and burrowed my gloved hands into my coat pockets as I walked away.

DURING MY MULTI-STEPPED jaunt between China and New York, a day after the Paradigm China incident, Emil Lyon and Sol Rydell were found dead in the penthouse of the Shallister Hoffman building. The suspect was Craig Herbert—a consultant who had, apparently, used Emil's credentials to get a flight to China, where he was also wanted for corporate espionage and intellectual property theft, plus some pretty impressive destruction of property and multiple assault charges.

It was nearly an international incident, especially once it was discovered that Craig Herbert wasn't a real person, and was traveling with a fake passport. Airport security footage showed my face pretty clearly, which was alarming, but there was nothing I could really do about that at the moment.

I'd be on FBI and CIA watch lists forever now. Facial recognition software would always be a worry.

I'd have to keep a low profile until I could figure out a way to fix that.

Luckily, keeping a low profile was already a skill I possessed.

The technology developed by Paradigm was still a problem. Their data might be gone, but it wouldn't take much to reconstruct it, under the right conditions. Henry's ERD technology would be the key to that. One of the keys, anyway.

I had managed to snag the only two working prototypes in existence—at least, the only two that really did work. Paradigm had versions of their own, though they hadn't yet worked out the engrammatic replication. Not well enough to make it viable. Keeping the real thing out of their hands was slowing things down.

This would buy some time, but there was no way to

know how much. Without Henry and his research, or at the very least one of the prototypes, Paradigm only knew that it was *possible* to replicate and transfer an engram, but they wouldn't know exactly *how*.

They likely didn't even know I existed.

I hoped.

All in all, things were far from completely settled. There was still a lot of danger out in the world. For me. For Kristen.

Actually, from what I could tell there was a lot of danger just for the average Joe, if the ERD tech ever was perfected.

The nature of what it would mean to just be *human* was in serious jeopardy.

That would have to be a problem for another day. And, hopefully, a problem for someone else to deal with.

So what will you do now? Kristen asked.

"There's a lot I need to think about," I said. "I've learned a lot, over the past few weeks. A lot about me, as much as anything. One thing I've learned is that there's more to what I can do than what I thought. I need to start looking a little closer, pushing to see what my limits are."

Just like the old days, Henry said.

Not quite, Kristen said. *This time, he won't be manipulated by the one person who was supposed to help him.*

I did what I had to do, Henry said. *I have no regrets.*

That's exactly why you can't be trusted, Kristen replied.

I let the conversation end there. Because they were both right. Henry *couldn't* be trusted, but it was true that he'd done what he had to do. I could see that now. Even if I might not fully agree with it.

And even though it would never *really* be "just like the old days," it would be good to have Henry on my side again.

Even as a voice in my head. He knew too much about all of this to just ignore him. He could be useful.

Later. For now, I had an appointment to keep.

I made my way to a cafe where I had arranged to meet an old friend one last time.

I sat with my coffee and smiled as Vic walked in. He started to fall into the old pattern, the routine we had pre-established, but I waved him over instead. I should have been more paranoid. Direct contact, without being able to check and see if Vic had been compromised, was a big risk. But over the past few weeks I'd become more comfortable with risk. I'd learned I could be careful even while taking those risks.

Vic approached, cautious and curious.

"I thought I'd never see you again," he said. "It's been weeks. I thought we were done."

"Not just yet," I smiled. "How's college?"

Vic grinned. "Great, man. Really great. I can't thank you enough."

"You would have gotten there, one way or another. The money wouldn't have stopped you."

He shook his head. "I don't know about that."

"I do. But listen, I have one last job for you after all. It's an easy one. I usually take care of this myself, but I thought you might be able to help. I need someone to take your place, to help me vet clients."

Vic nodded. "I know some guys who might be good candidates. One of them is my brother."

"Your brother? I thought he lived in Boston now?"

"He's back," Vic shrugged. "He needs a job. Things didn't work out at his old one. He's staying with me right now, sleeping on my sofa."

I nodded. "Ok. Him, then."

Vic blinked. "Just like that? You've never met him, how do you know you can trust him?"

I smiled. "You trust him. That's all I need for now. I can vet him when I meet him."

Vic studied me for a moment, then nodded.

We wrapped up, and as Vic left through the front, I left through the back. Vic's brother, Danny, would be in touch in a couple of days, using the prearranged channels Vic would show him. I knew Danny would be a good choice. According to Vic's memories, he shared a lot of his brother's values. They were good kids. And this would help him out, which I was happy to do.

So you're just going right back to the way you did things before? Kristen asked. She sounded mildly disappointed. *Just going to be Evergreen again?*

I took a deep breath. "Yes and no. I have plenty of money, thanks to Emil's offshore accounts. So I don't need to do this to make a living anymore. But now I have a new reason. A mission."

What's that? Kristen asked.

"I haven't completely worked it out yet, but I think I want to use what I can do to actually *help* people. Or, at least, I want to stop people like Emil Lyon and companies like Paradigm from *hurting* people. I want to do something that helps to make the world safe."

Altruistic, Henry said. *And dangerous.*

Stupid, Jacob replied. *You'll get yourself killed. Or captured. And us with you. Count me in.*

Kind of like a superhero! Caleb said.

We will help you, Julia replied.

I smiled.

I was on the move, and I took a few turns and worked my way through a few shops, mixing up my route until I finally entered the hotel where I would spend the night before moving on in the morning.

I knew that Julia was right. They would all help.

They were my team.

My secret weapon.

And together, we were Evergreen.

A NOTE AT THE END (FOR THE SECOND EDITION)

This book was written in a single day.

Ok... I know that sounds nuts. It *is* nuts. But it's true. Here's the story:

I wrote *Evergreen* while I was traveling with my wife's family, spending the US Thanksgiving holiday in Manhattan. Which is, you have to admit, a pretty amazing time to be in Manhattan.

Parades. Ice skating. The Rockettes and Radio City Music Hall. The Macy's Thanksgiving Day Parade and a giant balloon shaped like Spider-man—the whole works!

Plus, you know, family and turkey and togetherness. The whole point of Thanksgiving is to spend it with family.

Except for this one day...

At the time this book was written I had already written and published four or five other titles, mostly sci-fi and fantasy stories. I hadn't yet written any of my *Dan Kotler Archaeological Thrillers*, which would ultimately create my biggest success as an author (basically starting my career as the author I am today).

The idea of Kotler was there, more or less, but other

than the few scraps and pieces that I would eventually cobble together into the prologue of *The Coelho Medallion*, I hadn't written a word.

But I *had* already had the chat with my friend and fellow author, Nick Thacker.

We were live on a podcast when he dared me to write a thriller. And while I don't remember the exact conversation, word for word (and, tragically, it seems to be lost to history), I do recall that he *insisted* I would love the genre, and that it was a perfect fit for me.

I was intrigued. And a little excited about the idea. I just couldn't decide the best way to get started.

So I wrote *Evergreen*.

At least, I had the idea for *Evergreen*, which I figured would be a nice hybrid between the scifi and fantasy work I'd been writing and this new genre I was attempting.

From my perspective, I was following in the footsteps of authors like Dean Koontz, who was frequently referred to as a "paranormal thriller writer." In fact, years ago I read his book *Cold Fire*, which in many ways has a similar protagonist to Jaylin Rowlin.

So I figured I was safely in "thriller" territory.

Except Nick told me, after the book released, that he didn't consider it a thriller. And at the time, I believed him.

I disagree *now*, but at the time I figured he'd know better than I would. After all, he was already making a solid living from writing thrillers. And he'd definitely read more thrillers than I had. He, of all people would know, I figured.

So I quietly removed the "thriller" label from *Evergreen* and lumped it in with my sci-fi work. I couldn't really think of a better genre for it, at the time.

Time to move on.

And move on I did. The next book to leave my fingertips was something completely at odds with everything I'd written before. Something new.

If *Evergreen* wasn't a thriller, then I had to come up with a working definition for what a thriller actually was. I needed some rules. Guidelines. Benchmarks.

When you can't quite define what something *is*, sometimes you have to start with what it *is not*.

Evergreen had a protagonist with a paranormal ability. Regardless of any political intrigue, corporate espionage, and international action and adventure the book might contain, regardless of being set in a recognizable contemporary world, regardless of technology grounded in current reality, the fact that this kid had super powers was knocking it off course.

So the rule seemed obvious to me: Thriller heroes do not have paranormal abilities.

I extrapolated from there, taking it further, deciding that thriller novels *themselves* do not have paranormal activity of any kind. Everything in a thriller story has to be grounded in the mundane, contemporary world in which we live. Even the technology has to be a logical next step for modern tech, at the very least.

So basically, no super powers. No futuristic technology. No magic. Nothing that cannot be explained by current science.

Sounded kind of boring, but I figured I could swing it.

So even though Evergreen became one of my most popular books, at the time, and even though I'd told people I was planning to write a sequel, I scrapped all of that.

Instead, I took a look at my "stalled starts," the stories I've started writing but never finished, and picked a few that I thought had some mundane promise.

I cobbled these together, polished them, wove a plot around them, and *voila!*

The Coelho Medallion, and a thriller-writing career, was born!

And for the next four years, I would go on to write eleven full-length novels, three novellas, and one full-length crossover in that series. And they would be the most successful work of my career! I was, by even Nick's stringent guidelines, a bonafide thriller writer.

And. I. Loved it.

But let's back up...

It was 2015, and I was in Manhattan, where Kara and I had been for a couple of weeks.

I was with family, and we'd done a ton of touristy stuff. Empire State Building—check. Central Park—check. Ghostbusters fire house—check. I'd even gotten the opportunity to drink a Sonic Screwdriver and take a leak in a life-sized TARDIS at the Way Station bar in Brooklyn.

It was a good trip.

And then, on one rainy, cold, nasty day, Kara and her family were getting together to do something—what, exactly, none of us can remember—and I planned to stay behind.

Actually, I had originally planned to find a bar or a cafe or a coffee shop, and to spend the day getting a decent start on this book I'd been inspired to write—the thriller that wasn't a thriller, by Nick's standards. I figured I'd get a good chunk started, and I could finish up when we got back to Texas. And besides, I was in *Manhattan*. What writer doesn't work on a book while in Manhattan?

Not this writer. There are rules.

But on this day, with Kara and her family off site, I got up at my usual 4 AM (at the time... I've softened since then) and made my way down to the hotel restaurant. I got a cup of coffee, told the girl working there that I was probably going to be in for the day, keep it comin', and... I started.

And then I had a brief moment of insanity.

I have this thing about first-person stories. For most of my career, I've avoided writing them. I've had some books come out in first person—I even have an entire trilogy written in that POV—but for the most part I've always written in third person. And my reasons are kind of weird.

Writing in first person feels like *cheating*.

I don't know when or why I started thinking like this, but for most of my writing career I've considered first-person stories to be a cheat. Or a kind of shortcut.

It was like I was able to skip characterization and all that other jazz, when I wrote first person. It was like I was just putting on a costume and letting the story flow out of me—the Adventures of Character X, played by Kevin Tumlinson.

So I have no idea why I started writing *Evergreen* in first person. Maybe it was because I'd just finished up the second *Sawyer Jackson* book, and I was still in that headspace.

But I think that may be, in part, one of the reasons why what happened next... well... happened next.

I've always been a fast writer. Putting down 5,000 words in an hour is not uncommon for me. And when I'm really in the zone, I can chunk out around 8,000. Sometimes more.

There can be a little bit of sweat and tears involved, but it can happen.

On this day, starting at 4 AM, writing in first person, and having the inspiration of Manhattan and coffee to fuel me, I hit the zone.

There have been many times in my career when I've pushed myself to see how much I could produce, in as short a time as possible. When I first started writing and publishing, it took two years to finish my first book. The second and third took just as much time. Then I figured out a formula (some call it "discipline"), and I got to where I could produce a book in 30 days.

Then I went for 15.

Then I wrote a book in a week.

It became a game. How much could I push myself? How fast can I go?

I was, on average, aiming for 50-60,000 words per book, back then. I still sort of aim for 60K, to be honest, because that feels like a solid length to tell a story, to me. Not a lot of fluff, just pure, energy-driven story. It makes the books feel much more fast-paced. Because they *are* fast-paced.

So it was with *Evergreen*. I was aiming for 60,000 words. And, at 5,000 to 8,000 words per hour...

I have a background in Engineering, but I'm not a math whiz. I use a calculator for everything, and sometimes I have to Google something to figure it out. But even I can do the kind of math that tells me that if I'm writing at least 5,000 words per hour, I can write 60,000 words in 12 hours.

If I write 8,000 words per hour, it's more like 8 hours.

So... why not? It's coffee and carpal tunnel syndrome all the way down.

Having decided to do it, I dove in with both feet.

Starting at 4 AM, I wrote through the day. Rain and cold kept me from wanting to go outside, anyway. Friendly waitresses and bartenders bringing me coffee and food kept me from leaving my seat for long. At one point, I begged a couple next to me to watch my laptop as I ran for the men's room. I probably should have done that more than once, thinking back.

But, after about 12 hours, give or take thirty minutes here or there for "breaks," I... well...

I was finished.

Now, before anyone get's too excited (or incredulous), let me make something clear: I did *not* have a letter-perfect, completed book, written in one day.

What I had was the *first draft* of a book, written in one day.

All 60,000-ish words of it.

It wasn't ready for prime time, but it was there. Something to work with. And I would spend the next month editing that book, doing rewrites, and getting it ready to publish.

So in reality, I guess I can't honestly say I actually wrote a whole book in 30 days. I wrote a pretty rough draft of one, though. And I'd still defy John Grisham to do *that*.

I'm kidding... I love you, John! Please answer my letters.

Basically, though, I don't think any author in their right mind would bother trying to write a book in a day, anyway. Nor should they. It's a grueling, painful, teeth-gnashing process I wouldn't wish on anyone.

But damn, I'm proud of it.

So the book you've just read is a testament to a philosophy I've long held, as an author: Your limits are mostly set by *you*.

True, there are certain *physical* limitations. I couldn't write 60K words in an hour, for example (not that I haven't tried). I still needed that entire long, empty day to do the work. And there was a cost: I stayed focused, but afterward I was a worthless wreck. I didn't write another word for months, honestly.

So it's not something I'd want to try again.

But I wouldn't trade that experience, or this book, for anything.

Since then, I've switched genres. I've written dozens of books in my Dan Kotler series, and a couple in my *Quake Runner: Alex Kayne* thrillers. Plus novellas. Plus about four non-fiction books, aimed at the author market. And I'm guessing maybe a few million words in blog posts and articles, etc.

That's a lot of output. The old adage, "The first million words are practice," turns out to be true. And I've practiced a lot.

Evergreen was written in November 2015, and it was in the front end of 2016 that I started writing thrillers. Or, I started writing books that fit my new, personal definition of thrillers—a definition that seemed to satisfy Nick and everyone else.

Of course, since then Nick has changed his *own* definition of a thriller. These days he sees "thriller" as more of a "storytelling style" than a genre.

And I agree with him.

Which is why I decided I needed to loop back around, give this book a dust-off, and christen it as a second edition, bringing it back into the thriller fold.

That, though, is just the start.

Over the years I've thought about writing a sequel to *Evergreen*. In fact, I'm starting to think I might like to write more than one.

I'm starting to think this could be one hell of a series.

I've spent some time daydreaming about what might have been: What if I'd stuck with *Evergreen* as my main series? What if I'd written 11 books in *that* series? What if

I'd kept at it for the past four years, building it up, talking about it, sharing it with readers and would-be readers?

I have no way to answer these questions, other than to roll up my sleeves and write some more of these books.

I am not writing each book in a day, though.

So the question is, would you like to see more *Evergreen* books? If so, go to https://kevintumlinson.com/contact and send me a note to say so. I'm thinking of possible plots, and I'd love to hear what you thought of this book.

And for those of you coming in from my Dan Kotler or Alex Kayne books, don't worry. I'm writing more of those, too. They may be a little more spaced out than what you're used to, but they're coming. I love those characters too much to abandon them!

Besides... I have plans. Plans I can't discuss. Delicious plans that will fill you with joy and delight! Mwahaha.

I hope you enjoyed this book as much as I enjoyed writing it. I hope you take some of it home with you. I hope it settles into you, becoming part of you, like one of Jaylin's engrams.

That's kind of what characters from good books are anyway, right? Some other personality that takes up space in your head, whispering stories to you, giving you insight and wisdom and entertainment all at once.

We readers are all a little Evergreen.

Thank you for reading. And I hope we see each other again very soon.

Good health and God bless,
Kevin Tumlinson
Hot Springs, South Dakota (#VanLife!)
04 October 2020

HERE'S HOW TO HELP ME REACH MORE READERS

If you loved this book, you can help me reach more readers with just a few easy acts of kindness.

(1) REVIEW THIS BOOK

Leaving a review for this book is a great way to help other readers find it. Just go to the site where you bought the book, search for the title, and leave a review. It really helps, and I really appreciate it.

(2) SUBSCRIBE TO MY EMAIL LIST

I regularly write a special email to the people on my list, just keeping everyone up to date on what I'm working on. When I announce new book releases, giveaways, or anything else, the people on my list hear about it first. Sometimes, there are special deals I'll *only* give to my list, so it's worth being a part of the crowd.

Join the conversation and get a free ebook, just for signing up! Visit https://www.kevintumlinson.com/joinme.

(3) TELL YOUR FRIENDS

Word of mouth is still the best marketing there is, so I would greatly appreciate it if you'd tell your friends and family about this book, and the others I've written.

You can find a comprehensive list of all of my books at http://kevintumlinson.com/books.

Thanks so much for your help. And thanks for reading.

ABOUT THE AUTHOR

J. Kevin Tumlinson, award-winning and bestselling author of fast-paced, hopeful fiction and inspiring nonfiction. He and his wife Kara live in Texas, and she insists they travel the world to find new perspectives, new stories, and new tantalizing bits of history and thought to share with his readers.

Kevin grew up in Wild Peach, Texas, where he started learning the craft of storytelling at a young age. He began writing the moment he knew how, and never stopped. And, God willing, never will.

Kevin's love of history, archaeology, science, and philosophy has fueled every word of what he's written, and gives him all the excuse he needs to look closer at anything he finds interesting.

Connect with J. Kevin Tumlinson
jkevintumlinson.com
kevintumlinson.substack.com

www.ingramcontent.com/pod-product-compliance
Lightning Source LLC
Chambersburg PA
CBHW020614260626
47157CB00003B/1010